T0131798

San Juan Sunrise

EDWARD J. LEHNER

BALBOA.
PRESS
A DIVISION OF HAY HOUSE

Balboa Press books may be ordered through booksellers or by contacting:

Balboa Press
A Division of Hay House
1663 Liberty Drive
Bloomington, IN 47403
www.balboapress.com
1 (877) 407-4847

Print information available on the last page.

ISBN: 978-1-5043-8379-0 (sc)
ISBN: 978-1-5043-8380-6 (hc)
ISBN: 978-1-5043-8381-3 (e)

Library of Congress Control Number: 2017910119

Balboa Press rev. date: 07/11/2017

I wish to dedicate this book to my wife, Julianne Ward, who was very patient as a cheerleader, critic, and helper.

I want to recognize Pauline Tarn (a.k.a. Renée Vivien, 1877–1909), a great poet and writer, who was an inspiration and muse.

Also I want to thank Ellen Wernick for her editing work as well as the editorial staff at Balboa Press who were extremely helpful in the final editing process.

And a big thank you to Judi Jones, Susan Lander, Eileen Music, and Rini Twait for reading the early stages of my manuscript and giving me helpful, supportive, and critical feedback.

Ours is essentially a tragic age, so we refuse to take it tragically. The cataclysm has happened, we are among the ruins, we start to build up new little habitats, to have new little hopes. It is rather hard work: there is now no smooth road into the future: but we go round, or scramble over the obstacles. We've got to live, no matter how many skies have fallen.

—D. H. Lawrence, *Lady Chatterley's Lover*

Sometimes, one has to face his or her fear of the unknown and venture forth into the abyss. So it was for the young woman looking out over the vast, shimmering mountain landscape, arms wrapped around herself, trying to stay warm, under a cold, bright sunrise unfolding over the San Juan Mountains. She inhaled deeply, filling her lungs with the sharp, thin mountain air.

She had stood at the edge of this ridge, at eleven thousand feet, high above the valley below, many times over the past years, never tiring of the expansiveness that seemed to let her heart sail free. She was comforted that there was no one else around, that she was completely alone. But it was only for the moment; her memories were still there—all of it was still there, haunting her, following her, surrounding her, like a pack of hungry wolves, waiting their time to attack and devour her very soul.

Chapter 1

Jennifer Kathryn Morse was twenty-five years old, five foot ten, and lean and fit from a summer of backpacking and living in the San Juan Mountains in southwestern Colorado. She had cold, gray eyes and dirty-blond, shaggy, dreadlocked hair from cutting it herself with her knife and bathing all summer in cold mountain streams and waterfalls.

Jenny had spent another summer living in the high country. She loved being alone up in the mountains, which seemed to console her, like a mother she had not ever known. But it was getting late in the season and getting very cold at night, the chill barely leaving during the day. She was not at all equipped for cold, her gear being barely adequate for summer. She chastised herself for prolonging her trip down to the cabin where she had spent last winter. It was time to head down, which was a long two days of hiking through rough terrain.

Nobody knew where she was. If she died up here, nobody would ever know. Nobody would even miss her, except maybe her brother and her grandparents, the only people who know she even still existed. And they probably wondered if she still did since she had barely been in touch the past two years. Jenny dreaded going back to civilization after the last four months of solitude other than brief trips down to get supplies. She had to leave now.

Jenny went back to her camp, had a quick breakfast of a PowerBar, and packed up her small, secluded camp, which was about half a mile off any trail at around nine thousand feet in elevation. She shouldered her backpack and headed out. There wouldn't be any trace that anyone had ever been there.

Two long days later, she hiked into the north end of the Animas River Valley, a glacial plain that extends from Durango, a small mountain town in southwestern Colorado, up about fifteen miles to where the river narrows into a rocky canyon. Jenny arrived at the spot where the cabin should have stood. But the cabin wasn't there. All she saw was a pile of burnt rubble, the old cast-iron wood stove, and the stone foundation. The old outhouse was all that was left standing.

Shit, shit, shit! What should I do now? She could camp by the burned-down cabin for the night, but she decided she wanted to be inside someplace warm and cozy. *Why not? I can certainly afford it.* She turned and headed back out to the road toward Durango, hoping to hitch a ride. She was thinking about a nice hotel room, a hot shower, and a dinner with wine.

After two miles of hiking down the road, there were no cars and no ride. The sun had set over the mountains thirty minutes ago, clouds had been moving in, and the temperature was dropping.

God, I'm totally exhausted. I need to stop. It's all private land here. No place to legally set up camp. Just gotta keep going.

After another mile of hiking, she saw what looked like a ranch house on her right. There were lights on. The house sat a few hundred yards down a gravel drive in some pine trees. There was a three-car garage, an open outbuilding with an old pickup inside, and what looked like a cabin off to the left. She really didn't want to, but she felt she had no choice other than to ask permission to camp there. She reluctantly walked down the drive, went up on the porch, and knocked timidly on a solid-looking door that looked to be made of old, weathered boards. The large brass lockset clicked with the sound of a precision mechanism as it opened.

A tall, nice-looking man, with soft, dark eyes and graying hair and a well-trimmed beard, stood facing her.

"Yes, how may I help you?" he said, frowning.

"Hi. So very sorry to bother you. I'm Jenny. I was trying to hitch a ride to town. No luck, and it's getting late. I'm totally exhausted. Been hiking down from the mountains the last two days. Would you mind if I pitched my tent somewhere in your yard for the night? Please? I promise not to disturb you or make any mess, and I'll be gone in the morning. Promise." She was close to tears, her voice starting to tremble.

The man stared at her for a long moment. She hadn't had the advantage of a hot shower for four months. Her clothes, secondhand when she had bought them, were now frayed and torn. She looked pretty rough.

"Are you homeless or what?" he asked. "I really don't want to start having any homeless people around here. Maybe you should just move on."

She smiled a sad smile, "Please, mister, I've been on an extended backpack trip for a few months in the mountains, and I'm headed back down to town for the winter. I've been gathering material for a new book I'm writing. I'm not homeless. I just don't think I can make it to my condo in town tonight. I couldn't catch a ride. I'm really exhausted and just need a place to camp for the night. I'll be seriously gone in the morning, and you won't even know I was here. Promise."

The man looked at her for another few moments, contemplating her words and appearance. "I suppose you can camp out in my yard as long as you are out of here in the morning. I don't want to start letting folks think that they can start camping here. My name is William, by the way. Make yourself at home out there."

"Sure, William. No problem. Thanks so much. You're so great. I really appreciate your kindness and understanding. Would over by that grove of pines be okay?" she asked as she started to back away.

"Yes, sure, that would be fine. Have a good night," he said as he turned and quietly closed the door.

Not very friendly, but I know I must look pretty awful. Can't really blame him.

She turned and headed to a grove of pines about one hundred yards from the house to pitch her tent, eat the remaining trail mix, and thankfully sleep.

When she awoke the next morning, she was shivering. The temperature had gotten much colder than normal for early October. She checked her watch. It was eight o'clock, but it still looked to be almost dark. Then she noticed that the tent was sagging. *No, no, no!* She sat bolt upright, unzipping the door flap.

A pile of wet snow tumbled into her tent. Looking out, she saw there was at least a foot of new, wet snow, and it was still coming down heavily. She had known from seeing the clouds building in the west at sunset that bad weather was coming in, but she'd never expected snow at this lower elevation this early. Rain she could handle but not this.

Dammit! This is not good. I am so screwed. I am freezing, and I don't have any warm clothes for this kind of weather. I know better!

The temperature had dropped along with the snow. It had still been warm when she crawled into her sleeping bag wearing only shorts and a T-shirt. Now she was cold; her teeth were chattering. The weather wouldn't warm up until the sun came out.

Dammit, I hate to bother that guy again.

She pulled on her light leggings, a light fleece rain jacket, and boots; and waded through the snow up to the house. With hesitation, she knocked. She waited for what seemed like an hour, shivering, teeth chattering. It took about two minutes for the door to swing open, and there stood William, staring at her.

"What do you want now? You said you would be gone. I really like my privacy and don't like being bothered."

"I am so sorry, William, but ... have you seen how much snow there is out here? I hadn't expected this. I'm so cold. I was totally unprepared. I should've come down two weeks ago. I know better ... I screwed up. I'm really scared. Please. I just need to warm up. Just for a little while. I'm so very sorry to bother you, but I'm really scared that I might be close to hypothermia."

He stared at her for a few moments, noticing that she was shivering, and then looked out at the snow. "Oh my! I hadn't really paid attention. I saw there was snow but didn't realize there was this much.

"Okay, come on in and get warm. I have some fresh coffee, and I'll make some toast if you want. Eggs? I have some ham. I sure don't want you freezing to death in my yard. And I doubt there will be anybody along on this road now until after this quits. There's never this much snow this early."

"Thank you, thank you, thank you." She brushed the snow off herself, kicked off her boots, and unknowingly entered a new part of her life.

Chapter 2

There was a blazing fire in the fireplace. William told her to go over and warm herself, which she gladly did. The fire felt so warm. There was the aroma from the burning pine logs mixed in with the smell of freshly brewed coffee. He brought her a large cup of the steaming brew and two slices of toast slathered with butter, along with a jar of peanut butter and a knife. She smelled eggs and ham frying. Jenny thought this man was truly an angel in disguise.

Jenny hardly trusted anyone, especially men; she was extremely wary of being alone in this house with a man whom she knew nothing about. Even if she did know him, she would have been wary. She fingered her six-inch sheath knife she wore on her belt.

"Oh my God, this is so kind of you. Thank you so much. You're a life saver."

"Get yourself warm. Have a seat here by the fire. Please. You don't have to stand."

"I'm just going to get warm and get out of your way, try to hitch a ride to town."

William gave her a sarcastic smile. "As I just said, there won't be anybody out on the roads now. Wait until it quits snowing. Just relax. I am really not as bad as I sometimes seem to be. I'm just used to not being bothered by anyone. It's okay. So, I truly want you to stay in here where it's warm."

Jenny eyed him, suddenly realizing her predicament. She was trapped in here for the duration of this storm. If she decided to bolt, she might freeze to death.

Maybe I could find someplace else down the road. But shit, I can't get through this heavy snow. I'd be soaked and get hypothermia for sure. Dammit, how could I be so stupid?

She looked around the house, seeking ways to escape if she needed to. She then noticed walls lined with bookshelves completely filled with books. There were soft chairs in which to read them. She could see that the house was old but updated. It had a great room consisting of a modern kitchen, a large dining table with twelve chairs, along with a very cozy sitting area, all with darkened pine woodwork and off-white walls. She heard classical music coming from somewhere. Where there weren't bookshelves, there was nice, modernist art on walls. The place felt so warm and inviting, like a small, intimate library. It was a place she could feel comfortable being in … under different circumstances.

She considered her options, but there really weren't any. *So try to be safe.* Maybe she could try to show some sort of the social grace her grandparents had taught her.

"You have a wonderful house, William. I'm admiring all your books. Wow!"

"These are only a small part of those I have read over the years. I am a prolific reader with a bad habit of buying books until I am out of space and then finally do some trading with the used bookstores in town or simply donate to our library. But it seems my collection never gets any smaller. These are ones I don't want to part with. They are like old friends, all the great authors who I want to believe wrote their great literary genius just for me.

"I am an author myself and have a number of books published. Probably not anything you may have read unless you read trashy novels that are airport books or vacation throwaways. I inadvertently entered into that genre early on and never was able to get out of it. They have made me wealthy, but I am not very proud of them. You said that you are a writer?"

"Oh my god, you're a writer. Do you have any of your books here? I'd love to read something you wrote. What's your last name? Maybe I've already read something you wrote. I've bought a lot of books from the used bookstores in town when I used to hitch from my cabin to town for supplies in the winter."

William motioned her to one particular shelf. "Everything I wrote is over there on the shelf, all in chronological order. Have a look, but unless you like books with the covers showing busty women with torn bodices and hunky guys, well, let it be said that's the genre: easily read, schmaltzy romances that are cheap entertainment for desperate women. As I said, they are all formulated stories my publisher wanted, that would sell, but they're a far cry from being literary masterpieces."

Jenny went over to see all his books. He was apparently prolific, since there were a few dozen. She pulled a few from the shelf and looked at the covers. He was right about the torn bodices and hunks. And there was his name emblazoned on every one: William Brighton. She had never heard of him.

As she was looking through one, she said, "I'm so embarrassed that I told you I was a writer last night. Let's just say that, ah, I *want* to be a writer. I've written poems and short stories in college and some since I graduated, but I thought they were all pretty lame. My college professors all liked my work, though, and thought I had great potential, potential I certainly haven't realized for sure. I entered some short stories and poems into some contests when I was in college but nothing much since then.

"I hang out in the mountains during the summer and winter in an old cabin a few miles north of you, writing in my Moleskine notebooks, hoping something might click, but nothing ever does. I keep thinking that if I just keep writing, the muse might shine her light on me someday. I try not to get discouraged. I just try to keep going, hoping I might be able to write something decent, some good story." She trailed off into silence, looking down at the floor, then adding, "I just can't seem to get a good focus on anything that I think might be interesting."

William brought her a plate off ham, scrambled eggs, toast, and butter, setting it on the breakfast counter. "Here is some food for you. Sorry for not asking you how you like your eggs prepared."

"Thanks, William. I haven't eaten a feast like this in months."

William asked her about her family, where she grew up, and her education.

Jenny was warming up; hot food and coffee helped. She loved being in this beautiful, warm house, comfort she hadn't allowed herself in several years. She was slowly warming to this man, starting to feel a little bit more at ease, but, remembering her past, she still kept her guard up. It would be very, very unusual for her to be completely relaxed.

"Well," she began, in between mouthfuls of food, "I grew up in a commune everyone just called 'the Farm' in northern California with my twin brother, Michael. I was homeschooled by my hippie parents and the rest of the folks who lived there. I got out of there about seven years ago, went to a junior college up in Denver for two years, and got my GED. Then I got into CU-Boulder, where I graduated with a degree in English literature and rhetoric in three years—with honors, I might add. My parents never knew where I was or what I was doing. I was never in contact with them once I left. I just left early one morning." She stopped for a minute, her voice quivering.

"My grandparents somehow found me and sent me money for my birthday when I turned eighteen. They supported me through college, and they still do. I haven't seen them since I graduated and moved down here two years ago. I try to write them now and then.

"The last two winters I stayed in that old cabin, but it burned down since I left last spring. And yeah, I lied to you last night about having a condo in town. Sorry, but it was the only credible thing I could come up with at the time that might convince you I was solvent and not homeless."

"I know that cabin," William said. "I knew that someone was staying up there in the winter. That was you? It burned down last July. Everyone thinks someone torched it, but I guess no one really knows or cares."

Jenny continued, "That sucks about the cabin. I asked around before I ever moved in, and no one seemed to know who it belonged to. Everyone said to just move in for as long as I wanted or until someone kicked me out. It was pretty rustic, but it had a good wood-burning stove, a decent roof, and it was pretty comfy—after I got rid of all the critters, that is. I bought a saw and axe, and used deadfall for heat, hitching to and from town for provisions. It was good."

She stopped for a chance to keep eating her food before it got cold. *Maybe if I keep talking, he'll be too occupied to try anything.*

"And the truth is, I'm okay financially, thanks to my grandparents, who seem to have more money than most small countries. They gave up hope on their wayward son, my father, their only offspring, and set up a trust fund for my brother, Michael, and me, putting their hopes on their grandkids to be more successful with their lives, I guess. My grandparents wrote to me that Michael is studying to be a doctor. He's in premed in Colorado Springs. Me, they probably wonder about.

"I don't spend much money and live as simply as I can. Guess that comes from living in a commune where there was really never any sort of luxury or any friends for that matter."

She took a bite of food and hesitated. *What am I doing? I'm telling some complete stranger my life story. Be careful.* She continued, deciding to tell just a little more about her life to William. "We lived in a yurt with no privacy, no personal space, no real kid things. I liked being alone, losing myself in whatever books I could scrounge.

"The only thing I really have is a storage locker in town where I keep a few things: my books, notebooks, and a few other things—not much, not much at all.

"As I said, I haven't been in touch with my parents since I left seven years ago. I was tired of their lifestyle, a bunch of stoned hippies living out some 1960s dream that never was. I think my dad was a drug dealer. I think he's in prison now, according to my brother's last letter from over a year ago. I think they were probably happy to be rid of me. I worked so hard getting my college degree. I've done everything on my own since I left, as has my brother. I think maybe he's in contact, lets them know I'm still alive. Other than that, I don't think they could care less. I know I don't really give a shit. Sorry for the language.

"And I guess that's the short version. I'm just a wanderer, wanting some solitude from the world, trying to figure out who the hell I am, wanting to be a writer.

"So ... what about you, William?"

"Me? Well, like you, I am sort of a recluse, looking for the muse to strike and give me an idea for a truly meaningful novel, not the crap I made my living on. I sold a zillion of these schmaltzy reads and had several turned into mildly successful movies. They made me some money, but I feel far from successful. I really want to be known for at least one decent piece of what might be thought of as actual literature.

"I bought this old house and ten acres, part of an old ranch, around twenty-five years ago. I remodeled and modernized it, and have lived here off and on through several wives. I have been here permanently for the last six years, still writing but getting nowhere."

The snow started to slow; now there were only intermittent snow showers, with the sun starting to break through.

William said, "The way the weather is starting to break, the roads should be okay in a few hours. I need to go into town and will give you a ride, save you from trying to hitchhike."

She responded quickly. "That would be great." *I can be out of here and away from this guy. He seems nice, but I can't trust that he's not just like all the rest.*

William cleaned up the dishes and excused himself to go to his office.

"I can trust you won't riffle through my house for my valuables?" he said half in jest but half serious.

"You can trust me. There's nothing here I need or want. All I need is in my backpack. If you don't mind, I'll just browse through some of your books. I will certainly return them to their rightful places," she said, finishing with an edge to her voice.

Fuck him. Thinks I'm going to steal from him. What an asshole!

He gave her a warning look, turned, and disappeared into his office. The house went completely silent. She could hear him make a phone call, then heard a printer.

Jenny pulled one of his books down and started to read. She read the first few chapters, then skipped through some later chapters. She thought the writing was sophomoric at best, but he had indicated he wrote junk. Bored, she put the book away and went to the window.

The sun was fully out now, and snow was melting off the porch roof. She found her fleece top and jacket, and went out. The sun was warm and now making the day pleasant to be outdoors. She waded through the snow to her camp, gathered and packed her things, and took down her tent, carrying it and her pack to the porch. She spread the tent over the railing in the sun to dry.

It felt good to be out of the house and free, not feeling trapped.

By two thirty, her tent had dried, and she had everything packed. But no William. She went to his office and knocked quietly on the door. "William, sorry to bother you, but the sun is out. If you're still planning on going to town, I'm packed and ready to go whenever."

She heard a rustling from inside. Then: "Thanks for reminding me. I wasn't paying attention to the time or what was going on outside. Looks good. Give me a minute."

I haven't a clue where I'll stay tonight. A motel? But I look like shit—I'm filthy and ragged. Come on, William. Let's go! Maybe I could get to a thrift store for some better clothes if you would just hurry up.

"Okay," he said, pulling on a jacket, "I'm ready."

She followed him to the garage and put her pack in the back of his Subaru hatchback. The four-wheel drive car got them out to the paved county road, which had been plowed, and he headed south toward Durango. There wasn't any snow by the time they got to the north city limits, but it looked like it had rained instead. Such was Colorado weather.

He asked her where she wanted to be dropped off. She hadn't any idea but, seeing a cheesy motel, said, "Right here's good." He pulled in. She retrieved her pack and closed the hatch.

"Are you sure this is where you want to go?"

"It's fine, William. Thanks."

"Well, I'll be off then. Good luck and nice to meet you."

"Yeah, thanks for everything. See ya."

* * *

The sign read, "Rooms: $39.00 and up." She checked to see how much cash she had. *Shit, only fourteen dollars. Why didn't I have him take me downtown by the bank? I was in such a rush to get out of there … dumb, dumb, dumb! Dammit, it's at least twenty blocks to the bank. It's late. It'll be closed by the time I walk there. Maybe the trolley? Maybe I should have asked to stay another night. Dammit, I know better.*

She found a trolley stop. *Crap, just missed it. Another half hour to wait. The fucking bank will be closed. Shit. Why the hell didn't I get that ATM card I was offered when I opened my account? I'm going to end up sleeping out with the homeless people tonight. Why not? That's what I am, I'm homeless.*

The more she thought, the more she felt like a complete waste, a derelict. She could live better if she chose. *But this is what I choose, so suffer through it.*

Where's the fucking trolley? Maybe broke down? Dammit. I'm screwed!

Out of desperation, she began walking toward downtown. After five blocks, a car pulled into a driveway right in front of her and stopped. She saw it was William. "Hey, you okay? I thought you were getting a room, but then I saw you walking."

She explained her dilemma. By the time she had finished, she was on the verge of crying. William said, "Hey, why don't you jump in and come back to my place for the night? You can use the guestroom. Things will be better in the morning. I can bring you back here then. What do you say?"

Jenny felt panic form in her gut, felt her knife, and reluctantly accepted, wanting to accept his offer more than the alternative of sleeping out with who knows what.

Back at the house, William showed her the guestroom. "The guest bath is right over here; there are clean towels.

Please make yourself at home. Anything in the fridge is yours for whatever you want or need for your dinner. Be comfortable, and please call me Will. All my friends do."

She went in and immediately let out a little scream. "William, there's a fucking cat sleeping on the bed. I hate cats, William. I'm really afraid of them, William. I really am. I can't stay in here with a fucking cat, William."

"That's just Cat, Jenny. She is harmless and really loves people. Not to worry."

"That's not the point. I just don't like them, or dogs for that matter ... I just don't like them. Please get this cat out of here," she implored.

"Hey, all right. I will get her, but she's really a sweet cat."

"I don't care. Please, please get it out of here. They scare me ... and you named your cat 'Cat'?"

William came in and picked up Cat, who yowled mildly in protest.

"I named her after Holly Golightly's cat in *Breakfast at Tiffany's*. Cat was a stray that moved in with me several years ago. She is really a nice cat. I am guessing someone just put her out and abandoned her. It happens too frequently around here. People want a pet and then discover having a pet is something that takes time and effort, so they just abandon them rather than taking them to the animal shelter. Sad, really."

He was petting her while he talked; Cat purred contentedly. He took her away, put her in his bedroom, and closed the door. He came back, wanting to talk with her, and sat on the bed.

"I need to be alone now, William or Will. Thank you. You're a kind man. But please stay off my bed and out of this bedroom—no funny business. I sleep with this under my pillow every night." She brandished her knife.

William held up both hands. "Hey, no need for that. I am not that kind of guy. Seriously, please trust me on that. You are perfectly safe. Promise."

With that, he got up and left her to her thoughts.

She looked around the room; it was the same woodwork as the great room, but the walls were painted in a restful, soft gray green, and there was some nice artwork, an iron-framed queen bed, two pine end tables with matching lamps, a small matching dresser, and a closet. She liked it; it felt comfortable, like the rest of the house. The place was so clean; it smelled so fresh.

She took a really hot shower that she wanted to last forever. She washed her hair twice and then rinsed out her clothes and hung them on the shower rail to dry. She found a soft terry cloth robe in the closet. It was early evening now, and she was hungry, so she raided the fridge for a cold dinner of salami, crackers, cheese, and an orange. She also helped herself to some iced tea.

William had disappeared back in his office. She thought about him. What struck her was how kind and gentle he was with the cat. Then she remembered the commune, recalling Annie and her two cats and how kind and gentle she'd been with them. Annie had been the only person she felt okay to be around there, the only one who'd elicited any trust. Annie always asked her in for tea and cookies whenever she saw her, always talked with her, and treated her so kindly. Annie grew herbs, and her cabin always smelled so wonderful from her drying them inside. Jenny wistfully wondered how Annie was, her one ray of sunshine.

Then her mind drifted to the ugliness and sadness she'd experienced, thinking back to one time when she was twelve, when she'd been out at her favorite place in her little world on the top of a secluded cliff that overlooked a beautiful valley below. She was reading a book she'd scrounged, enjoying her solace, when Old George, one of the Farm's founders, interrupted her.

Jenny thought about her annoyance when he sat down beside her, wanting to talk and interrupting her privacy. She recalled that she'd pretended to ignore him and continued to read. He'd been quiet for a while, and she glanced over. Saw that he had his pants down and was masturbating. He noticed her looking at him and asked her to do it for him. He wanted her to pull down her pants, too, but her blood turned to ice. She ran away from him as fast as she could, back to her yurt, and told her mother about what had happened.

Her mother looked at her with a blank expression and told her that all men wanted to do was have you suck their cock, fuck you, or beat you. And if she wasn't careful, she would end up with two kids like her and her brother. She was becoming old enough now with her little titties. Her father would like that she was getting some attention. He might be able to pawn her off to some of the young studs and make a few bucks.

It was then and there that she knew she would never get any support from her mother or father; it really wasn't a surprise since she had never trusted her mother. She truly didn't even like her most of the time. Her father was hardly ever around. She knew for certain she would always be on her own. There was no one she could trust.

She finally came back to the present, having finished eating some time ago. She cleaned up and went to check out William's books, finding *Nightwood* by Djuna Barnes. She read the first page. It looked interesting, so she snuggled into a nice, big armchair.

What have I gotten myself into? Why did I end up here with this guy? He seems nice enough and has taken me, a complete ragged-looking stranger, into his house. I don't do this stuff. Why should he be any different? Right now I don't have a choice until I get out of here tomorrow. Where will I go? Where will I go?

She read until her eyelids started dropping. She got up and went into the guestroom, locked the door, and fell instantly asleep—her knife lying out of reach on the dresser.

* * *

The next morning she awoke to find Cat snuggled in next to her. She jumped out of bed to the side of the room and looked at the animal. Cat, now stirred awake, yawned, calmly did some morning cat stretches, had a little bath, and then began purring and moving toward Jenny. She put her hand up and said, "Stay!" like she had seen people with dogs do. Cat stopped, sat, cocked her head, and looked at her. Jenny cocked her head and looked back, not sure what to do. The cat then turned and found the warm place where Jenny had been sleeping, curled up, and went back to sleep. She considered the creature for a moment.

Interesting. Seems harmless enough ... Must have sneaked back in when I was eating dinner. Still don't like them.

She had no idea what else to do and didn't want to have a fit like she had last night, so she got dressed and went out to inviting smells of fresh coffee, bacon, eggs, and toast. Cat jumped up off the bed and accompanied her, going to her food bowl.

"Good morning," William said. "See you have a new friend. Wondered what happened to her. I was just about going to come wake you up for breakfast. Have a seat. There's some fresh juice poured for you. Sorry I left you on your own for dinner last night. I had a ton of important e-mails I had to answer and two phone calls to the west coast. Hope you found something to eat."

"I had a wonderful night. Thanks, William—I mean, Will. Cat was in bed with me when I woke up. I thought you took her out."

"I did and put her in my bedroom, but cats can be sneaky when they want to be. Are you okay?"

"Yeah, I'm fine. I sort of overreacted last night. Just afraid of them. Wow, another wonderful breakfast. I haven't eaten like this since I was at my grandparents' place. Susan, my grandmother, pampered me to death. It's a wonder I don't weigh seven hundred pounds. Thank you so much."

"Sleep okay? That knife didn't jab you, did it?" he said with a laugh.

"I slept great, and no, I didn't stab myself," she said sarcastically. "I appreciate it and everything. When are you going to town?"

"Ah, Jenny, I was thinking. I might have an offer for you. The old bunkhouse out back is in pretty decent shape. It has indoor plumbing, is furnished, and has central heating, plus a good wood stove. If you would like to stay there for the winter, it is yours … if you want.

"And another thing. I would love to help you with your writing, if you want. Maybe I could help you to focus in on an idea, help you develop it. Maybe a few short stories."

"William, you don't know anything about me other than that I'm a homeless drifter who knocked on your door. Why? Just why would you do this? You said you like your privacy. Now you want me living here? I'm not at all sure I understand, but thanks for the offer."

"Listen, Jenny, I see an opportunity to help a young writer. Maybe give you some support I never had when I was starting out. I would love to be your coach and critic. I would just like for you to be comfortable and able to spend time writing. I would want to see how and what you write. Think it over. Other than that, you would be on your own.

And that bunkhouse will be way, way more comfortable than that old cabin ever was."

She looked at him, her head cocked to one side, expressionless.

"Want to go and have a look after we eat?"

"Sure," she said, a little giddy with excitement. *He wants to help me write. Even though he writes trash, he's published. Oh my God, this is amazing! I'm happy now that I didn't tell him what I thought of the book I looked at.*

He led her out to the little bunkhouse, explaining on the way that at one time, it had been an actual bunkhouse for the hired hands or cowboys.

William said, "I had this updated a bit as a guesthouse for my kids when they came to visit. As it turns out, they never do, except for Peter, who's in law school in Denver. He usually stays in the guest room, so this remains vacant. Probably needs a lot of work to make it decent."

He opened the door for her, and she went in and looked around with amazement. It had a great room, finished and furnished like the main house with a fully furnished modern kitchen, all on a smaller scale. It had one bedroom with a queen bed, dresser, and closet along with a nice bath and tiled shower. It was like stepping into a dream for her; she loved it. As for "a lot of work," it could use a minor cleaning, maybe, and it would be perfect.

William said, "You will have to furnish linens, blankets, towels, and such. There are dishes, silverware, pots and pans, some cooking spoons and spatulas. You are welcome to use my washer and dryer in the main house whenever you want. Other than that, make yourself at home."

"Oh my God, Will. This is so wonderful. I wasn't expecting anything like this. Oh, thank you."

Not knowing how else to respond, she turned and reached out to shake his hand. He gently returned her handshake.

"I'm happy you like it. Please enjoy."

William told Jenny he would be happy to take her to town to get what she needed, to which she replied, "Well, yeah, is there a Walmart or something so I can get bed clothes? I really need to get some decent clothes too and burn these old rags I'm wearing. I really must, now that the road's open. I don't want to bother you."

He smiled and said, "Tell you what. Why don't you take my car and go in? You have a lot to do, and I have some more business to handle here." He reached into his pocket and handed her the keys to his Subaru.

She looked at him incredulously. "Really? You'd trust me with your car? You don't know me or if I can even drive or if I even have a driver's license ... which I actually do."

He laughed. "You will be fine. Just bring yourself and the car back in one piece. Please?"

I could just abandon his car and get what I need to go down into the desert, maybe, into New Mexico.

Off she went to town. First stop, she went to the post office and checked whether she had any mail. There was nothing. *Not surprising.* Then she walked to her bank, where she withdrew $300 and reluctantly applied for a bank card. She went to the sports exchange store, where she found some warm things for winter, then went to Walmart for some underwear, since going commando for the last few months had gotten old. She also got what she needed for sheets, blankets, and towels. She was beginning to feel a little extravagant but was careful not to get carried away. Her total expenditures came to $175.39.

She stopped on her way out of town for some groceries and bought William a nice bottle of wine.

Chapter 3

Jenny relished the freedom of driving a car. She had only ever driven a little at the Farm. She'd taken a driver's education course when she was working toward her GED in Denver and gotten her license. She had then driven only a few times since, with her grandparents' car. The sun was out, the roads were melting and wet, and driving was fun. She returned safe, sound, and smiling.

"Thank you so much, William. I bought you a bottle of wine as a thank-you present. You're smiling at me. Want to see what else I bought?"

"By all means. Will you be modeling?" he teased.

"Only the outerwear," she said with a smile.

She was beginning to feel a little more comfortable around him, even though she had known him only for the last two days and had stayed alone with him in his house. While he had seemed so cold when she first met, he was really very kind, kinder than anyone she had ever known, other than her grandparents. He left her alone, didn't bother her, and didn't seem threatening ... so far, anyway. He treated her like an adult; she felt that maybe he even respected her. She enjoyed talking with him. He seemed to actually be interested in her, care about her. His interest seemed genuine. He'd given her a place to stay, food, and warmth; and he'd joked around with her. But somewhere down in her deepest place, a little voice kept telling her not to trust him; he would turn out like all the rest; he would want to get into her bed at some point. He would try to take advantage of her.

If it was too good to be true, it wasn't for her. Be wary, don't let your guard down, and don't get too close. You'll get hurt.

"I also got what I need for the bunkhouse and some groceries," Jenny said. "Can I go over and get it set up?"

"Sure," William replied. "There are some cleaning supplies already there under the kitchen sink. Want some help?"

"Nah, don't think so. You've got stuff to do, and I can take care of whatever needs to be done, but thanks." With that, she went out and unloaded her purchases into her new, little house. It felt warm and cozy.

That night, William invited her over for some homemade pizza and salad, and she accepted. He opened the wine she'd brought. She ate his delicious pizza but avoided the wine, afraid that if she drank it, she might let her guard down.

Great food, another hot, steamy shower, books, a wonderful bed. I'm in paradise. I could get used to this way of living. But not too used to it. I'm sure something will happen. Just be careful, Jenny, very careful.

"No wine?" he asked.

"Not tonight but thanks. Just water."

After they ate and she cleaned up the kitchen, he asked her to sit down to talk.

"What do you like to read, Jenny?"

"Well, I pulled down *Nightwood* that first night. Read 'til I couldn't keep my eyes open anymore. Loved it. Finished it yesterday. Poetic, sweetly written ... like I'd like to be able to write someday."

"Then do it. Read her, study her style, read her poetry. She was mainly a poet, you know. There were a number of great women writers in her era. Check out Gertrude Stein, Alice B. Toklas, Natalie Barney, Reneé Vivien. They are not as well known or popular as the men: Joyce, Hemingway, D.

H. Lawrence, F. Scott Fitzgerald, and other male writers of that period. But, nonetheless, these women were great. Read and study those you are drawn to. Study their styles. Then write your own stories, your own poems."

Jenny sat quietly for a moment. "I've read Hemingway, Lawrence, Fitzgerald. I can't write like they did. They were so really good. They had great stories. They lived in a time of great stories. I have no stories, no stories like they had."

"No, you don't have *their* stories. That was their time. This is *your* time; you have your own stories, so just let your heroes guide you. You have the stories and the skills. Check out these women. They had their demons, but they tried to conquer them with their words. The night you first came here, you told me a lot about your early life. I cannot help but believe that there is much more that you haven't told me, which is fine. We can become whole by telling our stories. Let your words come out unhindered and try to conquer your own demons."

They sat and talked for another hour about writing and said good night around ten o'clock at night. Jenny went back to her new abode and went to bed. Strange as it was, she felt alone. She thought of Cat and, as much as she disliked cats, almost wished she were in bed with her.

Chapter 4

The next day, she asked William if she could borrow his car again to go to town. She went back to the bank and checked on her account, which was increasing by the usual $7,500 per month from her trust fund. Her savings had accumulated well over $200,000 over the last few years. She knew she was financially well off, but having so much money was completely foreign and confusing to her. Her banker had tried to advise her numerous times on what to do to make this accumulating wealth grow more than in a low-interest savings account, but she'd ignored his advice and walked out of his office. She withdrew $3,000 cash and transferred another $5,000 to her checking account.

After the bank, she went to her storage unit and gathered her boxes of books. Then off to the Apple store she went, buying a new laptop computer. Her final stop was a sports store, where she bought new running shoes, socks, a pair of winter running tights, a light running jacket, a new yoga mat, and a few other necessities for running and doing yoga.

Back at the bunkhouse, she unloaded the car and returned it and the keys to William. "Are you getting settled?"

"I'm getting so very settled, yes. Thanks. It's starting to feel comfortable and safe." But she was thinking, *I'm still not that sure I made the right decision about staying here.* "Give me a few days, and I'm going to get on with writing. I want to impress you."

He smiled. "We shall see. Take your time. No rush. Oh," he said as an afterthought. "Feel free to use my library, so long as you make sure to return my 'friends.'" He turned and walked away.

Jenny walked back to her new place and put away all her new possessions, made her bed, then organized and put her few books up on the empty bookshelves. William seemed to have bookshelves everywhere.

Dammit, I am accumulating "things": towels, linens, new clothes ... What am I doing? What am I thinking? It is not at all like how I have lived for years. But maybe it's okay.

The only other nice house she had ever been in was her grandparents' place in Denver, a large downtown penthouse. It had been wonderful, though it seemed cold with hard-looking modern furnishings. She had never felt as comfortable there as she already felt where she was now. Even though her grandparents had shown her love and kindness, she'd always felt out of place.

She slept a deep sleep that night with dreams of people around her, loving and caring for her, and she was able to feel love toward them, feeling warm and secure. She awoke in the morning with that sense of security remaining with her. She thought about it but really didn't trust that feeling; not at all did she trust it. Cat had somehow managed to sneak into the bunkhouse and was curled up by her, purring loudly. Jenny jumped out of bed and coaxed her to the front door, shoving her outside.

How the hell did this cat manage to get in my house?

She got up and did the yoga routine she had learned from Annie back at the Farm. Then she made coffee, sat down in front of her new computer, and froze. *What am I going to write about? I have no idea.*

She got up and found a half-filled Moleskine and a pencil. Then she curled up on the couch and began to write a poem about William.

The morning slipped away without much success with the poem. Frustrated, she ended up fooling around with her new laptop for an hour. Discouraged and feeling restless, Jenny decided to go for a run. The sun was out, the roads were dry, and snow was melting under the Colorado sun. The weather was again seasonably warm. Running always cleared her head. She changed into shorts, a long-sleeved top, and her running shoes. Then she went out, only to run into William, who looked like he was about to do that same thing.

"Hi, Will, I'm going for a little run. Looks like you have the same idea. Want to join me?

"You will leave me in your dust, I am afraid. I'm pretty slow these days."

"Well, I haven't done any running since last winter. Let's start, and we'll see how it goes, okay?"

She started out at a slow jog, and William had no trouble keeping up. The air was cool, fresh, and sweet.

"Don't get off your pace just for me," William said.

"Nah, this is a good pace for me right now. I'm feeling a little slow myself."

They ran a mile or so without talking. William asked, "Do any writing this morning?"

"Well, I started a poem, but my head wasn't in it."

"Just start writing words. Don't worry about what you are writing or where you are going with your words. Just write. Write about anything, like your experience the last few days, about something that inspired you when you were in the mountains this summer, what you saw, what you felt, encounters you may have had, the cabin that burned down. You never know what stories might be lurking there; every writer has times when nothing is there. We have all faced it. But writers just write, and sometimes when we get started, a story can take us to places we never expected. Get rid of that critic in your head." He trailed off, a little out of breath from talking and running at the same time; his pace slowed a bit.

Easier said than done, she thought and replied, "Thanks, Will. By the way, I really feel like I should be paying you some rent. You are providing me with real comfort. I've never had anything like this before; I can afford rent—I truly can."

"No, that wasn't our agreement. I have more money than I know what to do with. Royalties roll in every month. I can't spend everything I have, and I really don't care to. I really don't need rent money from you." Breathing hard, he slowed again.

"But William, it would make me feel better, okay? How about five hundred dollars per month?"

"Tell you what. Take that five hundred dollars per month and buy yourself a car. It will give you freedom to come and go as you wish without having to depend on me. I am gone once in a while for several days, even weeks at a time, leaving my car at the airport sometimes. Then what?"

Car, license, insurance, gas, service. Holy crap. More stuff, more responsibility. But it would beat hitching a ride everywhere I want to go. It would give me more freedom. Maybe I should buy a car.

"Maybe, William. Let me think on it. Never owned a car before."

At two miles, William wanted to turn around. Jenny had enough as well, and they headed back in silence. The only sound was their breathing.

She got to her bunkhouse, still thinking thought about it. *A car? More to take care of. More responsibility. I should do it.*

She walked over and knocked on William's door. "Sorry to bother you. Could I borrow your car to go into town? I thought about what you said. I want to look at cars."

William smiled. "Better yet, let me take you. I know some guys at the used car lot and might be able to get you a good deal."

"Not sure that I want a used car, William. I'm thinking new."

"Can you afford new? They are expensive."

"William, I have money, a lot of money. I can afford new, believe me."

"Well, then, let's just go shopping and see what we might find."

* * *

They drove through town to the south end, where all the dealerships were. On the way through, William veered left off the main highway onto Main Street, pointing out where his most recent ex-wife, Helen, had her yoga studio. He also showed her one of the local bookstores, restaurants, and other points of interest.

Jenny said she had walked down Main Street a number of times when she would go to the used bookshops to load up on books during the winter months when she stayed in the cabin. She had never paid much attention to the other stores, restaurants, and such.

"Helen and I are still close friends. We still really like each other, but we just couldn't live together. She wanted her space and was totally committed to her studio; and I was too controlling, wanting all of her time with me, not realizing how important her studio was to her. I have since come to realize how hard I was to be with. After three marriages and some counseling, well ... we still see each other often."

Jenny found it interesting that he was sharing this information with her. It was another thing to consider.

They came to the dealership, which had Subaru, Jeep, Chevrolet, and GMC. Walking around the lot, Jenny spied a gun-metal, gray Jeep Wrangler Rubicon. "That's the one."

By that time a forty-something, nice-looking man with a big salesman's smile approached them and greeted William by name. He introduced himself to Jenny as Tom Anderson. "Want to take this Wrangler for a drive?"

"Sure, I'd love to if it would be okay."

"Of course it's okay. Let me get the keys, and we'll give it a go."

After Tom left, she asked, "How do you know Tom?"

"Tom has sold me several Subarus over the years, and after a while, it seemed like everybody knows most everyone in Durango anyway."

Tom returned with the keys and opened the door for Jenny. She climbed in, and Tom got in the front with William in the back.

Jenny drove out of town, went down some back roads, came back, drove around town, and headed back to the dealership. Tom explained all the Jeep's bells and whistles as they drove.

"I'll take it."

Tom started out with his salesman's pitch. "Well, it's a really nice vehicle and—"

"I said, I'll buy it. What do I have to do?"

"Oh ... oh, okay, sorry. Let's go in and get the paper work going. When do you want to pick it up?"

"Now."

"It will take at least hour to get both the Jeep and paper work ready."

William grinning, grabbed Tom, held back a little, and had a quiet discussion out of reach of Jenny's hearing as they proceeded into the dealership. They went into Tom's office, and all sat down.

"William tells me this is your first car. Let me work on some numbers."

Tom left, and William asked, "Are you sure about this, Jenny? This Jeep is a lot of money. You said you never had a car before ... Are you certain about this? Maybe get a used one."

"Absolutely sure, William. Thanks for the concern, but I'm realizing that maybe it's time I started to grow up and quit avoiding my life. I love that Jeep. It will take me into places in the mountains and deserts I would never be able to get to. I love it."

Tom came back and quoted some numbers, which both Jenny and William went over carefully. They looked at each other and nodded in agreement. William posed a number of questions and seemed satisfied with all of Tom's answers.

Tom asked, "Will you want financing?"

"No, I'll bring you a check for the full amount ... if William will drive me to my bank," she replied, looking questioningly at William.

Tom looked at her, and then at William, with big eyes and a questioning look. Jenny just smiled, and William raised his eyebrows, rolled his eyes, and nodded.

"Let's go then."

Jenny went to her bank and got a cashier's check for the amount; they headed back to get her new car. Jenny's heart was about to explode with anticipation and excitement. She got the car with hard and soft tops, a full tank of gas, and instructions on all the intricacies of a four-wheel-drive high-tech machine.

William called his insurance company and explained what was happening. Jenny then talked to the agent, answering a number of questions, some of them needing William's help. Since it was now five o'clock, she promised to be in tomorrow morning to pay her premium and sign the necessary papers. The agent said she had activated a policy and that Jenny was covered.

Jenny said, "I want to go driving for a while. Thanks for all your help." She almost called him "Dad" but caught herself. "See you later."

She drove around for a while, checking out some of the outlying roads and then the town itself, enjoying her new freedom.

It was close to six, and she was ready for some dinner. She spied a pizza place downtown on Main Street. She parked, went in, and ordered a small pizza and a glass of wine. The she began checking the place out.

There were only a few people in the place, but more customers started coming in right after she was seated. She noticed a group of four women about her age at a table close by; they were talking and laughing. There were two tables of young couples, who were talking seriously and then breaking into laughter. There were some twosomes holding hands across their table.

Jenny felt strangely alone, something she didn't remember feeling for a long time. She got up, quickly paid her bill, and went to her car. There she put her head on the steering wheel and broke into sobs.

Chapter 5

The next day was Friday. She got up, went for a five-mile run, returned home, and began to write. Four hours later, she hit "Select all" and "Delete." She thought it was all just shit. Frustrated, feeling like crap, defeated and sad, she went to town for coffee and a few groceries. She also remembered she had to stop by the insurance agent's office and pay for her auto policy.

She found the insurance agent's office, paid her insurance premium, and went to a coffee shop named Raven's. There she got a latte, found a place on a nice sofa, pulled out her Moleskine, and began to write about buying a new car—and then continued writing about being alone. She realized the only person she knew in this town was William. She thought it might be all right that fate had introduced them. He was kind and generous, and he seemed understanding and supportive; and he had shared some of himself with her. He had taken her in and given her a wonderful place to live for the winter. But she didn't know how to deal with this; she had no experience of trusting anyone other than her grandparents.

Tears came again. She got up and left, bought what groceries she needed, and went back to her bunkhouse.

She heard a knock on her door. William was there with his usual congenial smile and said he and Helen were having dinner the next night in town. They would like her to join them.

"Ah, wow. Will, I don't know. I don't want to intrude. Where?"

"A nice restaurant we like. You wouldn't be intruding. We would love to have you join us. I have told Helen about you, and she wants to meet you."

"Oh, man. I've nothing to wear. Ah, maybe not, but a rain check?"

"Oh, come on. Go and get yourself something nice tomorrow. You can afford it," he said with a knowing smile.

"Really? You want me to join you in a nice restaurant. I've never been to a 'nice' restaurant except years ago with my grandparents. Not sure I'd know what to do."

"Oh, get over it. You will be fine. We are really informal in this town, nothing fancy. Maybe one step above dirty jeans but not much."

"So, let me sleep on it, and I'll let you know tomorrow."

"Good, I have already made reservations for three." He turned and walked away with a chuckle.

* * *

She had a wonderful dream that night of being a princess in her own fairy tale. Cat had yet again sneaked into her house, as she was becoming prone to do, hiding out somewhere and then slipping into bed with her. When Jenny awoke, Cat was by her head, purring.

Could I really be a princess and be beautiful?

After a short run, she went to town, stopped at her bank, got some cash, and went for a stroll down Main Street. She came upon a little boutique that had clothes in the window she liked, so she went in.

A young woman, about her age, came to help her. Together they selected a nice outfit. She paid for it and asked for a recommendation for a hair salon. The salesperson gave her the names of two places nearby. She left and proceeded forth. She had always cut her own hair ever since she left the Farm. She was pampering herself by going to a hair salon. It was something else she had never done before, and it scared her. She was living in a really nice place, she'd bought a new car, and now this. What the hell was she thinking?

She found the salon and went in to see about a cut. After waiting for twenty minutes, she was led back to a station, where a young woman greeted her warmly and asked her to sit. The stylist fluffed Jenny's hair with her fingers.

"Wow, who did your hair the last time? It looks like it was cut with a chainsaw. Sorry, don't mean to offend."

Jenny chuckled and said, "Actually, it was a knife, and I was the cutter. This is truly my first-ever time getting my hair cut by a real professional."

"Oh my God. I'm so really sorry. Open mouth, insert foot."

Jenny laughed. "Hey, no offense taken. It's just the way it was, so I'll be anxious to see if this turns out any better. Can you do anything for me?"

"Abslolutely. Let's get startd."

After the stylist got over the raggedness of her hair, getting it cut professionally was an enjoyable experience for Jenny. She liked having someone give her a shampoo, then gently cut her hair into a manageable length, still long enough for a ponytail.

She was finished and looked in the mirror. "Wow, you made me look great. Thanks so much. It's really nice."

"Thanks. Really I just evened it all out and gave it a little shape, is all. Glad you like it."

Jenny paid for the cut, thanked the woman—Claire was her name—and said she would be back. She walked down the street to her Jeep, feeling quite special.

She got back to William's house and knocked at the door. When he answered, she asked, "So what time, and do we go in together or separately?"

He stared at her. "My God, you look totally beautiful. I hope you realize just what an incredibly beautiful young woman you are. Sorry, excuse me, but you are—wow, okay. Ah, let's go in together, and reservations are for six. I will pick you up at five thirty. Helen will meet us there."

Jenny felt a warmth rush to her cheeks. *No one ever said I was beautiful.* She replied with a laugh. "Just got a nice haircut, is all. Did I look that awful before?"

"Of course not. You just look different, a good different."

"I'll be ready at five thirty."

* * *

She spent the rest of the afternoon trying to write and trying not to be anxious. William was at her door precisely at five thirty. She answered the door and stood there, exuding all her beauty she was always reluctant to show.

"Wow!" was all he could say. "Ready?"

"Totally." She walked to his car in her new tight jeans, a silky top, and a stylish, nicely blinged-out denim jacket.

William scampered around to open her door for her. Jenny suddenly felt like a real woman, a lady, someone for the right person to really pamper and care for someday. Maybe like a princess? It was a new feeling; it was a good feeling. It was all so new to her, and she liked it.

They drove to the restaurant, making small talk. There was no mention of writing, for which Jenny was grateful; they arrived shortly before six. They went in and were led through a quietly lit restaurant, which was already full of people, who were talking and laughing, eating and drinking. The smells of food cooking were wonderful.

They were shown to a table, where a beautiful older woman, with dark, bobbed hair with streaks of gray and intense blue eyes, was already seated. She got up to greet them, and her smile radiated true warmth, self-assurance, and love. She was tall, elegant, and very graceful in her movements, like a ballerina; she was impeccably dressed in stylish jeans, a silk blouse that matched her eyes, and a denim jacket with floral embroidery on the collar and sleeve cuffs.

"You must be Jenny. I am so happy to meet you. Will has told me so much about you. I am Helen."

Jenny couldn't help smiling, like her face would hurt. *She is so beautiful and elegant, radiating so much self-confidence.* She immediately liked her; she wanted to *be* her.

Jenny looked around the restaurant, noticing the long bar filled with younger people, who were socializing and laughing. They looked like they had just left work. There was a tall back bar that needed a library ladder for someone to reach the top shelves. There were exposed brick walls and a high tin ceiling with old-looking fans, groups of which were run with belts from a single motor. There were old black-and-white pictures on the wall she wanted to look at more closely.

She remarked, "This is a really cool place. I love the funky decor."

William said, "This was originally a bar back in Durango's early days. There was a shooting right outside in the street. Apparently the sheriff and town marshal got into an argument over gambling going on in here—the sheriff against and the marshal for. It escalated into a shootout. The owners wanted to recreate that ambiance of the time. Wait until you check out the restrooms."

Then came drinks and conversation about literature, life, health, youth, aging, and so on; Jenny felt included and important, her ideas and responses considered and accepted. She felt like an adult. It felt good. She immediately loved Helen, the first woman other than her grandmother. There were other women, but she had never been close to them: her estranged mother; a few of the commune women, except for Annie; and a few woman professors from her college days.

During the conversation, Helen said, "It is so wonderful the universe has brought you to us. I am so pleased to have met you and that you will be staying at Will's this winter. I hope we can be friends."

Helen asked Jenny about her yoga practice and training. Jenny replied that a woman at the commune had taught her, but that was the extent of her training, adding that she did try to practice regularly.

Helen invited her to come to her studio for her beginning yoga class; she would love to have her. Jenny smiled and replied that she would be honored to come. The three of them chatted on during their appetizers and dinner. Helen and Jenny got in some girl talk when they made a restroom trip.

The restroom was totally crazy, with the faucets made out of plain copper pipe and industrial-like valves. There were great vintage movie posters on the wall and dark lighting. This whole place was fun. The whole night was fun.

After dinner and desert, an aperitif, the night was over; good-byes and hugs were exchanged, and everyone proceeded home. Jenny couldn't remember feeling so happy, so accepted. No pressure, no strings. Helen even said they could be friends. But there was the writing thing.

A knot formed in her gut, and all the happiness faded; pressure and insecurity reasserted themselves. She said a good night and a thank-you to William and went to her bed and to a night when sleep wouldn't come.

Who was she kidding? She wasn't a writer, just a nonproductive trust fund kid and a drag on society and herself. She depended on her grandparents' love, support, and trust that she would do something with her life. But she wasn't. She knew it was wrong to ignore them, but she was so ashamed of the life she was leading. It was a life of isolation, fear, and sadness. She wasn't a writer; she was nothing but a failure. She finally fell into a restless sleep.

Chapter 6

Jenny woke up early and went for a run. William was outside when she returned and waved at her, but she pretended not to see him, went into the bunkhouse, and disappeared. She began avoiding William, feeling ashamed of herself, embarrassed to see him. She avoided any contact, just like with her grandparents.

After two weeks with no poems, stories, beginnings, or endings, there was nothing to show him for his kindness and his trust in her. She didn't deserve his kindness. She didn't deserve any of it. She was living a lie and needed to just leave, take her fancy clothes to Goodwill and get far, far away. She wanted to be alone, by herself.

Yeah, I have wheels. Why not grab some better gear at the secondhand store and head to the desert? I could hide away down south all winter and head up into the mountains after the snowmelt.

I could get away from all the pain of fear and self-doubt, and get away from all my emotional baggage, just get away from people and expectations I can never meet. I'm letting myself get too close. I cannot let that happen, but it already is happening. I like William. He's kind of like my grandfather, but I can't trust that he won't want something more. All men want something more, as I well know from experience. And then there's Helen. What does she want? Why would she want to be my friend? Why would anyone want to be my friend? I never had a friend. She doesn't even fucking know me.

She felt like crap, scared and vulnerable to all the forces unfolding all too quickly. All of it made her confused. Jenny felt like the recently fallen dead aspen leaves, like the dormant grasses around her house. She didn't think she could ever revive, ever flourish ... ever.

At the very least, she owed William an explanation, an apology, and a huge thank-you. Then she needed to get out. She couldn't live a lie anymore, and she was a lie.

She packed up her boxes of books and some clothes and necessities to take back to storage. Then reluctantly she went to say good-bye to William. Scared, her heart racing, she knocked on his door.

He answered, and she just stood there for a few moments, looking down at the floor. Finally she was able to say, "I'm moving out!" She dropped her face into her hands, crying her heart out, shaking with her pain. He just stood there and very gently put his arms around her and held her, like a small wounded bird.

They stood like that for a long time until her sobs slowed and turned into whimpers. Able to get her to let go of her death grip, William led her to the sofa. He got her a box of tissues and a blanket, and said he was going to make them some tea. "I think we need to have a talk."

She curled up, still whimpering and sniffling, feeling like a lost soul.

He returned ten minutes later, bringing them tea. He sat across from her in an easy chair, crossed his legs, and sipped his tea, waiting. She blew her nose and stared into space, unable to meet his gaze.

They were silent for some time, both sipping their tea. Finally Jenny started. Once she started, she couldn't stop. She told him everything about Old George, her uncaring parents, her subsequent wariness of people, her decision not to let anyone get close. She shared that she never felt good enough for anything; she felt like a failure. But she still avoided some of the deeper issues she couldn't find the courage or words to verbalize.

William listened, not saying a word, just nodding understandingly every so often.

She talked for almost two hours, pausing every so often to cry softly. William made more tea and brought in some snacks for them.

Finally she was done. She sat, still staring into space, and said in a hollow, weak voice that she would be leaving now. She thanked William for all his kindness and got up to leave.

William said, with some force, "Sit back down, Jenny! What the hell are you saying? I want you to know I don't want you to leave, especially not like this. You are in no shape to go anywhere right now. Also, as long as you are here, I want you to know that you are safe, that no son of a bitch will ever harm you under my watch. I may not have been the best of fathers, but one thing I did was protect my children, support them, and nurture them. I like you and enjoy having you here; please believe that. Helen adores you. We both are happy you are here.

"I *was* getting concerned that you were avoiding me. I just thought you might be working and didn't want to be bothered; that I could well understand. But hearing all this, it just makes me sad." He stopped, wiping away a tear.

"I don't know what else to say," he said. "I cannot believe your life, your abuse, and your rejection by those who should have loved and protected you. How did your brother survive?"

Jenny responded, "Number one, he was a boy, not a girl with little titties who was born just to please men. I guess somehow he was maybe able to tune it all out. I'm not sure what kind of shape he's in. Maybe he's been able to lose himself in medical school; maybe he's just put it all aside.

I saw stuff that went on with him too. I know he wasn't spared. I suppose, maybe someday, he might have to deal with his own stuff ... not sure. We've never talked about any of this with each other. I haven't ever mentioned any of this to anyone until now. I feel so ashamed, like such a fool, like my whole crazy life is my fault. I'm so sorry to dump all this on you. You're such a wonderful guy. You didn't need all this shit. I'm so sorry."

She choked back a sob and blew her nose.

William wiped another tear and said, "Trust me, Jenny. None of this is your fault. There is nothing to be ashamed of. You were abused and essentially abandoned by your parents and community. I am happy and honored that you felt you could share this with me."

He gave her a reassuring smile and continued. "I see that we have some rebuilding in store, getting you some self-confidence and assurance. I have a friend in town who is associated with the women's shelter. She is a good counselor. I hope you might consider checking her out. I will support you, and I know for certain that Helen will also. Please, please, consider our help."

She smiled weakly, "Thanks, Dad. Oh shit, I mean, Will. Sorry for that. You aren't my father. I'll consider your offer. I'm really tired. I think I need to rest. Thanks so much. Will, you're the best." She got up and started toward the door, muttered quietly to herself, "I love you, William."

"I love you too, Jenny, and thanks for calling me Dad. Haven't heard that in a long time. I liked it ... liked it a lot. I feel honored. I could come and sit with you if you want. Maybe try to give you some support? So you can get some rest?"

She looked back at him. "No, I think I'm okay. Thanks. I just feel really drained." She turned away and left, going over to her house. She was emotionally empty. There was nothing left.

Once in bed, her mind drifted to her brother, Michael, and she wondered how he was really doing. His few letters seemed full of scattered ramblings. He seemed angry, even hostile in his writing. He seemed angry with her; why, she didn't know. She felt sad for a moment and fell instantly asleep.

* * *

She awoke to a knocking on her door; it was eight o'clock the next morning. She got up and went to the door to find William standing there. "Are you okay? Just checking. I made us breakfast. Hungry?"

Jenny, still half asleep, tried to focus and think for a minute. "Ah, yeah, I'm starved. Let me wash my face and get dressed. I'll be over in a minute," she said with a weak smile.

"That sounds much better. Jenny. Sounds more like you. See you in a minute. Don't let our food get cold."

A few minutes later, she went into William's kitchen and found Helen sitting there; she jumped up and hugged Jenny for a long time. Jenny cried softly. Helen finally let her go, wiping her own eyes.

"William called and shared some of your story with me last night. We talked for at least an hour. Oh, Jenny, I am so sorry. You are such a dear, sweet girl; I just cannot believe what Will told me. I am in shock ... didn't sleep at all last night, thinking of you."

William said, "I am sorry, Jenny. Please don't be angry with me for sharing with Helen, but I was really upset. I needed to talk to someone."

"It's okay, Will," she responded with a quiet, shaking voice. She couldn't cry again; she had no more tears. "I do understand. I'm actually happy you did share with Helen. You both mean a lot to me. I want you to know that. I appreciate everything ... I really do. Thanks."

Food was ready, and they all sat and ate pancakes and bacon without much conversation. Jenny got up, cleared the table, and put the dishes in the sink. They then all moved with their coffee to the living area.

Helen started the conversation by saying, "I called a good friend Joan at the women's shelter last night and relayed a little of what Will told me, not mentioning your name or how I knew you. She and several women are counselors there, and they deal with this kind of thing all the time. They do both private and group sessions. She would love to meet and talk with you. Would you be up for something like that?"

"I'm not sure. I feel pretty raw and a little confused. I'm really, really scared right now. I don't know what's happening to me. I'm trying to digest the fact that I dumped all this on Will; I don't know what got into me. I never shared any of this, ever, and now you, Helen—I'm sorry to be such a bother with all this shit. I really am."

"Oh, honey, you are certainly no bother. We both think the world of you; we care for you and want to help. Please let us do what we can to help, please."

Helen and Jenny talked on with more detail about Jenny's story, and William excused himself, leaving the two women to continue without him. Helen and Jenny talked on well into early afternoon. Helen left to go back home but not until Jenny had made arrangements to see Joan at the shelter tomorrow at ten. They would meet at the yoga studio, and Helen would go with her.

Jenny left also and went for a long run. Her mind reflected on the events of the past two days. She thought about her despair, her sadness, and two people with whom she'd shared some of her deepest secrets.

I think I feel lighter, having shared some of the ugliness of my life. Neither Helen nor Will seemed anything but caring and understanding. As hard as it was, it felt good to unload. I am so blessed to have stumbled onto these two people. As Helen said, "It is so wonderful the universe has brought you to us ... I hope we can be friends." Helen wants to be my friend? I have never had a real friend before, ever.

Jenny slept with dreams of green grasses growing all around her in a beautiful meadow with birds and wildflowers just below groves of lush aspen trees.

Chapter 7

She awoke at seven o'clock to Cat's purring. The cat had sneaked in again; it was becoming a habit.

After putting the cat outside, Jenny put on some workout clothes, did some of her yoga routine, had a quick breakfast, and was at Helen's studio at 9:45, anxious and scared to death but determined to see this though. After talking with Helen at length yesterday, she felt some assurance that she might really have found someone who understood, someone she could trust, but she was still very wary and scared.

They walked the few blocks to the shelter, and Joan was there to greet them. Joan was a forty-something, pleasant-looking woman with hazel eyes and long auburn hair pulled into a ponytail. She was casually dressed in jeans, a pullover top, and running shoes; she looked fit.

Everybody in Durango seems to be fit, Jenny thought.

They went into her office and closed the door. Joan began by explaining what the shelter did: they had both residential women who were usually in danger from husbands or boyfriends and some who were non-residence. All were getting help with situations not too far removed from what Jenny had experienced, relying on what Helen had told her. Joan went on to say she would be happy to work with Jenny, that she also ran some group therapy sessions with women with similar abusive situations. All the situations were different, but the outcome of abuse was usually the same: fear, shame, guilt, lack of trust, lack of self-confidence, wariness, and solitude.

Jenny, very quiet, sat and listened; she became more at ease but still felt very frightened. *This describes me to a tee.*

Joan then asked Helen to leave; she wanted to talk privately with Jenny. Helen got up and said she would wait outside for Jenny so they could have lunch together.

Joan and Jenny talked until 11:45 and came out, Joan looking pleased but Jenny was feeling somewhat in shock, trying to smile. They all exchanged hugs, and Jenny and Helen went off to lunch.

It was a beautiful, warm, late autumn day, and they went to a restaurant with a patio so they could sit outside to enjoy the day.

"So," Helen started out, "how did it go with Joan? What do you think?"

Jenny looked out toward a mountain for a long moment and turned back to Helen. "I think I like her, what she has to offer. We briefly discussed my major phobias of fear and mistrust. I found out that I'm not so special and that even normal people may have the same issues but probably to a lesser degree. But on the other hand, mine are only the tip of a huge iceberg I'll need to come to terms with, given time and hard work ... some possibly very uncomfortable work. But I think I'm willing. I decided that I want to go ahead. She helped me realize that I've come to a turning point in my life. I can either choose to continue to ignore my past or face it and deal with it. But I'm scared. I'm scared to death, Helen. There are some things I don't know if I can ever talk about." She ended with a choke in her voice, and she looked away again toward the mountain and wiped away a tear.

"My first counseling session is the day after tomorrow."

Helen said softly that Jenny would have her and Will's full support, and they would do whatever might be necessary to help her get through it.

A server arrived and brought them menus, which they quickly looked over. They each ordered a chicken salad and a glass of iced tea. They enjoyed their food, the day, and the conversation with each other.

Chapter 8

Jenny arrived early for Helen's eight o'clock class, feeling nervous, like it was her first day in junior college. Helen was in the front foyer, greeting people, punching passes, or taking payments.

Helen welcomed her with her kind smile and a hug.

"So how much is class?" Jenny said.

"The first one is free, and we can discuss costs later. Go on in and find a spot for your mat. Then get out a blanket, a strap, and a block from the supply closet by the door."

There were several people already there when she arrived. Jenny picked a space in the back to be as unobtrusive as possible and unrolled her mat. She got a blanket, strap, and a block. She checked the room out: light wooden floors; white walls and ceiling; a few pictures of colorful, strange-looking people decorating the walls. There was a large statue of someone on a pedestal behind what, she thought, to be where the teacher would be.

Meanwhile, a number of other people arrived, some chattering away, others very quiet, as though they were entering another dimension. The group was mixed by both age and gender; there were several older women and two older men. A number of women were around her age, and several more men and women fell somewhere between those age groups. No one paid much attention to Jenny. A twentysomething woman walked over next to her, smiled at her, unrolled her mat, and sat, assuming an erect cross-legged position, which Jenny observed others doing. She followed suit.

Helen came in, and everyone fell silent. She walked to the front of the room, put her hands together, bowed, and greeted everyone with "*Namaste.*" To which everyone responded in like manner, all remaining seated.

This was all strange to Jenny, and she suddenly felt a little panic at what she perceived to be strange goings-on. Her teacher at the commune had gone through about six to ten different poses, and they were all Jenny knew. There had been no formalities, no "*Namastes,*" whatever that meant. Some sort of greeting? She suddenly felt way in over her head but held her resolve and reminded herself that she knew and trusted Helen.

The class was ninety minutes long. During the first seventy-five minutes, the instructor led the class through a number of different poses or asanas, the names of which, as she would quickly learn, were in Sanskrit. Some of the poses were stretching, some required some strength, and some were difficult for Jenny, especially the balance poses. She felt very clumsy. But Helen was constantly there, helping, correcting and encouraging her as well as others. Then they did something at the end called Savasana: lying on her back and relaxing her body for five minutes. Then everyone assumed the same sitting position as before class started, sitting erect with their hands on their thighs. Helen said this meditation would be on focusing, particularly on the out breath. Everyone simply sat quietly through this meditation time.

Jenny followed along and tried to focus on the out breath, but her mind was racing with thoughts and apprehension about her counseling session tomorrow.

Time was up, and all of them rose, rolled their mats, folded blankets, and proceeded toward the door, returning all the "props," as Helen called them. The woman who had been next to her smiled again and said, "I haven't seen you here before. New to yoga?"

Jenny smiled back and replied with a laugh, "So it showed?"

The woman replied, returning the laugh, "We're all beginners. We're all still learning. It's a process. Isn't Helen wonderful? I love her classes. My name is Kelly, by the way."

Kelly was about Jenny's age and height with a mop of dark curls and big blue eyes. She looked to be in very good shape.

"I'm Jenny. Nice to meet you, Kelly. Yeah, I have some yoga experience but nothing like this. Wow, I thought I was in pretty good shape, but I'm feeling muscles I didn't know I even had. What is that meditation thing? I knew some people a while back who meditated, but I really know nothing about it."

"Hey, want to get a cup of coffee down at Raven's? We can chat."

"Sure, but give me a minute. I want to talk with Helen."

"No problem. I'm off work today and have time. I'll wait out by the front door."

"Only be a minute." She went over to thank Helen.

"So, what do you think? I see you met Kelly. She is a regular. Nice woman."

"Just wanted to say thanks for your help and patience. Wow, I thought I knew a little but realize that I know nothing, but I'll be back. I'll have to first see how I recover from this session. And I've never had any instruction on meditation. I really wasn't too sure what to do. Can you teach me?"

"Love to. Can you come by the studio around one thirty? I will meet you, and we can talk."

"Sure. See you then. Thanks. Gotta go. I'm having coffee with Kelly."

"That's great. Have fun. See you soon," Helen said, smiling as she hurried out the door.

* * *

Jenny and Kelly went down Main Street a few blocks to Raven's Coffee Shop. They sat and talked for over an hour. Jenny realized she was letting down her defenses but truly enjoyed talking with Kelly. She was a physical therapist and worked with two other PT people, a physical trainer, and two chiropractors. It sounded like interesting work. She had been in town for two years, having moved here from Illinois, primarily for all the outdoor activities. She was a runner as well as a cyclist and a downhill and cross-country skier; she loved hiking and camping in the high country. Jenny was blown away by all she did.

Jenny selectively shared a small part of her background, saying she was from Northern California; she'd gone to college at CU and had moved here a while back. She had recently met Helen, wanted to be a writer, and was presently unemployed. Also she liked running, hiking, and camping as well.

Kelly went on to say that her father was a fairly well-known surgeon in Chicago. Her mom had taught school but now was a full-time manager of the oversized house where they lived in an upscale Chicago suburb. Plus, they had a huge condo on Lakeshore Drive. She was an only child. Her father had wanted her to be a doctor and had gotten her into the prestigious Princeton Medical School. But she had been tired of being a pampered spoiled child and had opted for physical therapy and sports medicine instead, a decision that infuriated her doctor father. It was another reason she'd moved out to Colorado: to be away from his domineering attitude. She liked being on her own, making her own way.

But her parents couldn't imagine that she could support herself and sent a monthly allowance, which she just put into a savings account. She didn't want to be known as a rich, spoiled, trust fund kid. She had a hard enough time making friends as it was.

Jenny thought, *My God, she's just like me, except she actually has a real job, a real profession. But not me. I'm just a trust fund kid.*

They talked about running, and Kelly invited Jenny to try trail running with her in the spring; there was a running club that had Wednesday night and Saturday morning fun runs, usually with beers and/or coffee and good camaraderie afterward. Would she be interested?

Jenny suddenly started to feel like she was getting too close. Kelly was a little overwhelming for her; she seemed nice but talked a lot. Jenny started to feel panicked, with a tightness in her chest; she was getting too involved with this woman and needed to leave. She cited writing as an excuse, saying she was working on her manuscript most days and sometimes even into the evenings. She said she appreciated the offer about running and would see her again at yoga but had to get going.

With that, Jenny got up, said she liked talking with her, and left the coffee shop in a hurry to get away from a situation she wasn't sure she could handle. She left Kelly still sitting and wondering.

I can hardly breathe. I liked talking with another woman my age, but why should I trust her? She's probably like everyone else.

As she walked back to meet with Helen, she thought about Becky, a girl she'd liked and gotten along with during her sophomore year in college. She remembered her five roommates during her freshman year, who'd moved out because they couldn't stand her aloofness, antisocial behavior, and sometimes downright-cruel remarks. Then Becky came along; she gave Jenny the space she wanted and needed, and she became a friend. *My first ever, or so I thought.*

She remembered that night. She'd been in bed, just dozing off, when Becky quietly slid in alongside her, leaned over, and put her hand softly on Jenny's right breast. Becky kissed her on the mouth, telling her she was in love with her. She wanted to make love with Jenny, and Jenny's response still echoed in her mind.

"What the hell are you doing? No fucking way. Get the hell away from me! I don't want to make love to you. I don't want you touching me. I trusted you, and this is what I get. Get the fuck out of my bed, you bitch."

Then, grabbing some clothes, she ran through the night to the union, sleeping curled up in a study cubicle. The next day, she cut classes and called a real estate rental agency, finding a furnished loft apartment about two blocks from campus. She moved all her stuff over to her new place, never seeing Becky again, never letting anyone else get close to her again during the rest of her time in college. She became a true loner, trusting only in her self-imposed solitude.

Chapter 9

It was close to one thirty when she got back to the studio to meet with Helen, finding her there. She smiled when she entered and went over and locked the door.

"I don't want us to be disturbed. Let's go into my office and have a seat."

Jenny liked Helen, but locking the door made her uncomfortable. She immediately felt trapped but took a deep breath and sat down.

I need to allow myself to trust Helen, I just have to.

Helen asked whether she knew anything at all about meditation. Jenny replied that she'd known some folks at the commune who did something like that, but her parents didn't. She didn't really know anything about it.

Helen gave her some rudimentary instruction about what meditation is: simply sitting quietly, calming your mind through watching your breath, just being with yourself for a length of time. She talked about how busy our minds can be, always chattering and keeping us occupied and busy. Then when we sit and elect to do nothing, our minds tend to go into overdrive, shocked to find that we're just sitting quietly and doing nothing. The busy mind is what meditation helps us to control; it helps us to regain focus, quiet, peace, and equanimity. After a while, by simply sitting, watching our breathing, and simply letting thoughts come and go, we can start to calm our busyness.

Then she went on to say that if Jenny was interested, there was a Buddhist group in town; it offered regular introductory classes that would give her more insight into meditation practice. She thought it was maybe a six-week course. She found a slip of paper and wrote down the phone number of a contact person to call along with the address of the Dharma Center.

"Thanks, Helen. I'm not sure about doing that right now. I gotta see how this counseling goes. I feel that I've got a lot on my plate right now, but thanks again. This helps. At least I won't feel so lost next time. Maybe I'll see if there's a class this winter, maybe after the new year."

They said their good-byes and shared a hug. Jenny left and went home. She spent the rest of the day at William's place, browsing through his library. She came across the section that held his books. She looked through several more and selected one that seemed interesting. She would try it.

* * *

Her first counseling session with Joan was at ten the next morning, the beginning of two sessions per week on Tuesdays and Thursdays. She got into town early and hit one of the local independent bookstores; she loved bookstores. She browsed through the literary section, looking for some early twentieth-century women writers. She found a book by Renée Vivien, *The Woman of the Wolf.* She remembered William mentioning her name. She read the first few pages and decided to buy it.

The woman at the cash register looked at the book, then at Jenny, and asked, "Are you familiar with this writer?"

"No, not really ... a friend mentioned her to me."

"Well, you are lucky. We've had this copy for a long time. It's out of print now, I think. The owner kept wanting to donate it to the library book sale, but I convinced her someone would find it. Apparently, that is you ... I guess we saved it for you."

"Wow. Nice to know. Thanks." Jenny paid for the book and left. She liked any bookstore, and this was one she knew she would frequent.

She arrived early for her appointment with Joan and began reading Vivien's book in the waiting room. Joan was running late, but Jenny really didn't care since she was totally absorbed in her reading. She loved Vivien's writing and stories. There was a beautiful, sensitive female approach to how she wrote. It was soft, loving, sweet, and passionate. She wanted to go into this book and never come back out, just stay hidden inside it forever.

Joan came out and apologized for keeping her waiting. Jenny replied with a smile that she didn't mind at all. But really she thought she was just postponing her inevitable commitment to this counseling thing. She took a deep breath and got up, following Joan into her office. She took a seat in one of two comfortable chairs and watched with dread as Joan closed the door. Even though Jenny knew Joan was there to help her, she still felt like the door was being closed on her tomb.

So now it begins, Jenny thought.

The first session laid some groundwork, and Joan spent time asking for more information about Jenny's background. She asked lots of questions without getting much, if any, response. During the second session on Thursday, Joan started doing some deeper probing with mixed results. Jenny, not so skillfully, danced around questions about relationships with her parents, talking about how she felt about her parents, about why she felt that way. Jenny was glossing over things and avoiding going any deeper than superficial answers. Even by the third session, Jenny was still treating questions as superficial by avoidance or denial.

Half way through this session, an exasperated Joan finally said, "Jenny, we need openness and honesty in here if this is going to work and you are not being totally honest or forthright with me."

Jenny dropped her eyes from Joan's gaze, head dropping, staring at the floor.

Joan continued, "Jenny, your injuries caused bruising, bruising on your mind and body. These injuries bruised your soul as well. We can heal the mind and body, but that will be only a superficial Band-Aid until we go deeper and salve the soul. To do that, you have to dig deep, get it all out, and then we can work on letting go. The only way is to talk about it, write about it, bring it into the open air … Make it real, face it head on, stare it down.

"You are at a point … right now. You can either elect to help yourself or stay stuck. I can't make it happen for you. I can facilitate, but I need you to cooperate if you want me to be able to help you."

Jenny was silent, staring downward, her breathing becoming nervous.

Joan asked, "You say you like to write? Have you ever kept a personal journal? Have you written anything at all about your parents, about your alleged abuse, about how you feel?"

Jenny looked up at her with her eyes but with her head still down, like a child being scolded. She just shook her head, saying quietly, "It isn't alleged. It was real."

Joan continued, "It was real? You haven't said one thing to me that would give me any idea any abuse ever happened. You have to let go; at some point, if you ever want to get rid of all you are carrying with you, you will have to talk about it.

"And I cannot imagine that you haven't written anything about your life, but I will take your word for it. Your homework from now on is to keep a personal journal of your thoughts, fears, worries, and anything from the past you're hiding from yourself and from me. Think you can do that? Think you can let go?"

Jenny nodded, still staring at the floor, feeling like she wanted to just melt into the floor and disappear. She knew Joan was right. She knew she had to get it out. She thought she might throw up. It was time to go.

Jenny walked out of the shelter, crying softly to herself. She was so scared to talk about what needed to come out, hidden so deep for so long, something she wanted forgotten, something that couldn't be forgotten. It was all so unspeakable, so shameful, so ugly. She knew it needed to come out. Now that it had been disturbed, she felt it growing like a cancer, a huge, hideous tumor. She just couldn't do it.

She went back to the bookstore and bought a new Moleskine she wanted specifically for journaling. She went to the coffee shop and wrote about her childhood for two hours, downing three cups of coffee in the process. She did as Joan had instructed and wrote about her abuse, wrote about things she had never allowed herself to ever think about, things she wanted to keep hidden. She wrote about Dory and what she'd done to her, what her Dory had made her do; about her father, who was always stoned, drunk, or both; about things that went on in the yurt when she was supposed to be asleep; about seeing her brother fucking ... fucking ... Dory when he was only fourteen fucking years old.

She had wisely chosen a place to sit in a corner, away from anyone who might see her crying softly.

So, okay, she had written out all the ugly crap hiding deep within her soul. It was to be done. Now, deep down, she knew she needed to talk about it. Joan was right; the journal was her vehicle to address these repulsive, shameful thing. Writing them down made them real, made them concrete. When she saw the words she had written, great anger rose within her, anger she had never felt before. She realized she wasn't a helpless child, that she was a grown woman carrying childhood abuse and guilt with her. She realized what a great weight it was. She reminded herself again and again that her life, as it was, wasn't working.

I can't keep hiding. I cannot keep avoiding people. I cannot keep avoiding my life. I'm tired of being a mountain hermit. I like the comforts I am enjoying while living in my bunkhouse. I like William and Helen; I like Kelly. I want to be able to trust people, to have friends, to see my grandparents and my brother, everything I keep avoiding and am fearful of. Okay, my next session with Joan is on Thursday, the day after tomorrow. I hope I can continue to feel as brave then as I am now. I'm going for it ... gonna get it done.

Chapter 10

Cat woke her up with some loud purring on Thursday morning. Jenny petted her and put her outside. She did some yoga, meditated, and went for a long run, trying to steady her nerves and gain some courage so she could say what she knew had to be said, but she couldn't calm her racing mind. She quickly showered but was too nervous to eat any breakfast. She hurried off to her session.

With great apprehension, she walked into Joan's office, removed her jacket, took a seat, and sucked in several deep breaths.

"Okay, I think I'm ... oh, shit. Here we go, Joan. Are you ready?"

"Go ahead, Jenny. I am here for you."

"It was Dory who I thought was my mommy, but she wasn't," Jenny began, drawing her knees up and assuming a sitting fetal position, her knees up to her chest, arms wrapped around them. She looked blankly at the wall with blank eyes, somewhere beyond Joan, and started speaking in a tiny, childlike voice.

"She touched me in my naughty place. She made me touch her in her naughty place. And she did the same with my brother. She told us to never, never tell anybody. Not anybody. It was like the naughty things I saw them do at night when they thought I was asleep. She made me do it a lot. I didn't like it ... but she wouldn't stop. I couldn't tell Daddy or anyone because it was a secret. I shouldn't be telling you. It's a secret. It's a secret that Mommy told me to never, never tell anybody. She would be mad at me for telling you. Please don't tell her I told you. Please! I saw her doing things like that with my brother too ... even when he was older. I hated her!"

Joan sat quietly for a few minutes, to let things settle, and said softly and lovingly, "Thank you for sharing your secret with me, Jenny. That had to be unimaginably hard for you as a child ... and now ... to share it with me. I will not tell anyone your secret, anyone, I promise. I would like to help you feel better about this naughty thing you think you have done. Please believe when I say that this wasn't your fault. There is nothing for you to be ashamed about. How old were you when she stopped doing this to you?"

"Thirteen. But my brother kept on. I saw them doing things the adults did to each other ... even when he was fourteen, fifteen, sixteen, seventeen. I got sick, ran outside, and threw up when I saw them doing that. I stayed away from all of them. I hated them!"

She stopped for a second, breathing hard, shallow breaths, like she had finished a hard run.

"Okay, Jenny, just relax and take a few deep breaths for a moment." They were quiet for a few minutes. Jenny's eyes regained focus, and her breathing finally slowed.

Joan broke the silence. "Is there anything more you want to say about this?"

Jenny sat still for a long minute and then shook her head very rapidly, uncurling herself, moving her feet to the floor, sitting erect in the chair, knees together, hands properly folded on her lap, her head and eyes downcast. She suddenly put her hands over her mouth and started retching; Joan grabbed the wastebasket for her, but it wasn't needed; there was nothing to come up since she hadn't eaten anything.

Calming down, slowly raising her sad teary eyes, she looked at Joan and said with a quivering voice, "Please don't hate me, Joan. I'm really a good girl. Please don't hate me. I didn't mean to do bad things. I really didn't! I never did those bad things again, ever. She made me. I thought she was my mother, my goddamned fucking mother. And then I found out she wasn't even my fucking mother. My real mother had died. Nobody even ever fucking told me. I fucking wish they were all fucking dead!" The damn cracked, and she broke into convulsive sobs.

Joan got a cool, wet washcloth; she went to sit beside her and wiped her face, placing the cooling cloth on her forehead. "Oh, my dear young woman, I could never hate you, never. Please believe me. You are so very brave and strong for sharing this with me ... for getting this secret out from your soul. By putting this out, you can begin to heal, begin to be the wonderful person that you really are. I am always here for you, even if we aren't scheduled. Just call me anytime if you need to talk, if you need anything. Promise me that."

Jenny nodded, and Joan sat holding her in silence for four or five minutes until Jenny had cried it all out.

Joan gave her some tissues. "This is hard business for sure, Jenny. That was a very big burden to be carrying around for so long. You are so very brave to get it out. Are you feeling okay? Can I get you some water or tea? Or anything?"

Jenny started to smile. "Yeah, water would be good. My mouth is really dry. Oh shit. I cannot fucking believe I told you this, Joan. Cannot fucking believe I finally told someone this fucking shit. Please keep helping me, Joan, seriously. And this is all the shit. Believe me, it's the worst of it, the things I have kept inside me forever. What about my brother? He's got the same fucking shit, Joan, the same fucking shit and more."

She broke into sobs again, choking out, "Sorry for the language. I'm just so fucking mad!"

"It's okay," Joan said, holding her until she finally got all the anger, fear, and shame washed out with her tears. She dried her eyes and said with a weak smile, "So where's my water, Joan?"

Joan responded with a big hug and produced a bottle of water from her fridge. Jenny almost drained the bottle.

Joan called out to the front desk and said she would be running over for a while, probably another hour. She and Jenny continued talking, continuing to sort through some other issues. How this woman, Dory, whom she always thought to be her mother, continued to abuse her. They talked about the incident with Old George when Dory had dissed her when she told her about it. That was when Jenny told Dory to "fuck off ... Never, ever come near me again, or I will kill you." Dory never touched her again.

Then Jenny said with fire, "I hate that fucking bitch for what she did. I hope she rots in fucking hell! Actually, hell is too good for her. There is no fitting punishment for that bitch. I hate her." She hung her head, looking at the floor, fuming. "I should have killed her. I should have stuck my knife into her fucking heart! I should have cut it out and ate it, the fucking bitch!"

Joan held up her hand. "Jenny, whoa, whoa. Let's take a breath. I understand your anger with the release of your trauma; you should be angry, very angry. You have a right to be as livid as you are right now. You have just shared something very profound, and you need to process it, which will take time. It will take time to come to terms with your anger and your grief, and yes, grief over what you have lost for so many years of your life. And forgiveness that may seem hard right now, but at some point, you will have to forgive yourself for thinking you should have done something different. And yes, at some point, as farfetched as it may seem right now, you will have to be able to forgive

Dory. I will always be here to help you as you move through this process. I promise."

Jenny looked up. "I guess I have a lot of work to do, don't I? And forgiveness? I'm not sure I can do it, Joan. Right now I am so pissed. I am so really pissed off. Bringing this shit up just makes me fucking crazy mad. I hate that fucking woman!"

"I know you do, Jenny. I know you do right now. This is only the first step, and it's a giant one. The rest will be easier now, I can assure you."

"I hope so ... this really sucks." She said she wanted to go.

But Joan kept her and talked with her a little longer until she felt she had calmed down enough to go.

Jenny thanked her, gave her a big, long hug and walked out into the Colorado sunlight, took a deep breath of late autumn air, and suddenly felt a thousand pounds lighter. She couldn't stop smiling and wanted to skip down the street singing. Instead, she went straight to Helen's studio, hoping to find her there. She was. Jenny went in and asked whether she had time to talk.

"Of course. You seem quite happy. What's going on?"

They went into Helen's office and sat. Jenny began telling Helen about her session and then continued with all the details, all of them. Helen sat there, listening intently.

"Oh my God!" was all she could say in response. "Jenny, I am so sorry. You poor, dear child. Such a horrible burden for you to have to carry for so long, such a horrible thing to do to children. I thought what I knew before was bad enough ... but this! Oh ... Jenny."

She got up, went over, and hugged her for a very long time. Jenny hugged her back, feeling a secure warmth she had never felt before, loving her like the mother she never felt she had.

"Please don't tell William. I'll tell him ... when I'm ready. Promise. I'm not ready to do it right now. But I needed to tell you. You and Joan are the only ones who know. Please don't tell him ... or anyone. Please?"

"I won't tell anybody, Jenny. That will be for you to do on your own schedule. I know he will understand; he cares for you very much. I promise I won't tell him or any other soul."

"Yeah, I know. Thanks, Helen. Thanks for being such a dear friend. I love you."

"I love you too, sweetheart."

"And please don't pity me or feel sorry for me. I don't want that; I don't need that. That's not why I shared this with you; I just wanted you to understand. Okay?"

"Yes, I understand. And thank you for sharing with me. I feel honored that you trust me enough to have done so."

Jenny got up to leave, and Helen said, "Hey, want to have an early dinner? Would be fun. My treat."

"Sure, love to, but please, I want to pay. I think I need to celebrate something, don't ya think? Let's do it up big!"

And Jenny grabbed her hand and led her to one of the nicest restaurants on Main Street, where they were seated and started with appetizers and wine.

Chapter 11

Jenny asked Helen how she had become a yoga teacher.

Helen said she'd grown up in Santa Monica, California, where there were any number of yoga studios around. She hadn't been much for high school activities, so she'd decided to try some yoga. One of the many studios was an Iyengar studio about two blocks from her house. She tried it and found she loved it, enjoyed the exercise and the serenity

Helen went on to say that she went to college at UC-Berkeley and found a studio close by, so she continued through her undergraduate studies and grad school to earn a master's in physical training. Then she worked in a gym in LA for about two years but wasn't happy with her work.

She happened upon an article in a yoga magazine about B. K. S. Iyengar's place in India, where one could go to become a certified teacher. She decided she wanted to do it and begged her parents to subsidize her again. They finally agreed, and she was off to India for about eighteen months. Everything about India and the school were exotic, magical even. She got her certification and reluctantly returned to the States.

She knew she wanted to get out of LA but had no idea where to go, so she headed east, exploring towns while traveling in her minivan, which was loaded with all her earthly possessions. When she hit Durango, she was out of gas and broke. She got a job as a waitperson in this very restaurant and searched for work as a physical trainer for over a year until finally landing a job at a local gym. She found out that people in Durango take fitness seriously. The gym allowed her to start teaching a yoga class, which filled up, eventually working up to three classes, beginner through advanced.

"I saved every cent I could with the dream of having my own yoga studio someday. About a year later, both of her parents were killed in an automobile accident, and being an only child, she received a sizable inheritance, her father having made a lot of money in real estate development. She found the storefront, remodeled it, and opened her studio.

Jenny asked, "So what is it with you and Will? You seem so good together ... I can tell that you both care a great deal for each other."

"I still care for Will very much. He is the best ever, but we are better apart than we are together. I was never married before, and I guess I wasn't prepared for what marriage entailed. I had my studio, and Will had his writing. He was already very successful and wealthy. He wanted to take a hiatus, to buy a motor home and travel around the country, maybe for a year or more. But I had my studio, and I loved what I was doing; I didn't want to give it up. I took a week for our honeymoon in Hawaii, but then I wanted to get back and settle in again with my new husband and get back to work.

"But Will was in a writing lull. Had too much time on his hands and was restless, constantly coming by the studio and just simply getting in the way. I tried to get him to start taking classes or help out or get involved some way, but he wasn't interested. He finally just became a little overbearing, bordering on being obsessive. I told him one day to just please get out and let me do my business. He got angry, and we had a big fight: the 'You love your work more than you love me' thing. I pushed him out and slammed the door in his face. I stayed in town that night with a friend. I couldn't sleep, wondering what I had gotten myself into. I questioned everything. Was I being selfish like he said? Had I made a big mistake in getting married? Did I really love him? I was confused. It had all seemed so right when we met and spent a year enjoying each other, and marrying him seemed so right. I finally cried myself to sleep about an hour before I had to get up to start my day.

"He called me at the studio that morning, furious. Probably had a right to be so. I had no clue how to deal with this sort of thing. I told him that I needed my space and my life, that I was forty-five years old and had no experience with marriage, that he had been married twice before, that maybe his being so overbearing was his problem. He hung up on me.

"I was scared and called Joan. We had a long talk, and she asked me if I wanted to make this work, which I did. I loved him, and we had such wonderful times together, but as soon as I said 'I do,' he took possession. Joan suggested couples and single counseling, which I suggested to him. He reluctantly agreed, and we went for about three months, but he gave up. He couldn't deal with it. I continued doing counseling myself for about a year. In the meantime, we separated. I had rented my condo, and coincidentally the lease was up about that time, so I moved back in. Two weeks later, I filed for divorce.

"We didn't see each other for a long time. Then one day he called me and asked if I would have dinner with him. I had been seeing this other man, Mark, for a few months by then but reluctantly agreed, and we met here. We had a nice, leisurely dinner and a good, long talk. He told me he had been clinically depressed after we separated. His doctor had him on medication for depression and urged him to get professional counseling, which he did. He began to see patterns he had in all of his previous marriages that essentially caused them to fail. He apologized and asked if we might be friends. While we were no longer married, he considered me his best friend, and he still loved me.

"And that is how it has turned out. We still see each other regularly, but I'm still seeing Mark. He knows about Will and isn't real happy about me still seeing him. I like Mark a lot, but ... I don't know. There's just some deep attraction to Will I can't get rid of. So there it is. I have probably bored you to death with all this."

"No, not at all. I did ask. Thanks for sharing this with me. I can understand better now. I am never falling in love, much less ever getting hitched. No way. It'll just never happen. There's no guy that I'd ever trust to get that close to. Something that'll just never happen."

"Oh, now, don't be so sure. You are a very attractive young woman; some really nice young man will sweep you off your feet someday."

"Bullshit!" Jenny replied adamantly. "I'll never let any guy get that close. Never, no way, no how!"

They had ordered their dinners and a bottle of wine, which arrived, and the conversation changed to lighter topics as they ate and laughed, enjoying their food and conversation.

Two hours later, Jenny paid the bill and got up, a bit tipsy. Helen noticed and insisted that Jenny stay the night with her, that she was in no condition to drive up the north valley. Jenny had a goofy smile and agreed. They walked hand in hand to Helen's condo.

Helen called William to let him know; he thanked her. She and Jenny chatted for a few moments and went to bed.

She lay awake, thinking about how she liked hearing of Helen's experiences of a life that seemed so much more normal than Jenny's, but she'd also had sad experiences, even tragic ones like the death of her parents. She thought of the women who she had seen and the shelter for therapy, there for their own sad experiences. She was beginning to realize all people had some drama in his or her life, that everyone had his or her own struggles.

It was already the second week in November. So much had changed for Jenny: William, Helen, Judy, therapy, addressing her past. Sometimes her head went spinning, and she felt guilty for feeling so light, hardly being able to stand the giddiness she was experiencing. Then there were other times when the darkness, the shame, and the anger resurfaced. She was experiencing some happiness for the first time she could remember, savoring it like the first taste of a good wine, but she dreaded her swings back to darkness.

Chapter 12

Jenny was trying to get to the morning yoga class at least three times a week. She was learning a lot, and she felt that somehow yoga and the meditations were helping her feel not only stronger physically but also stronger emotionally.

She was starting to connect more with Kelly; she found she enjoyed her company and girl chat. She started trusting that the relationship was platonic and that Kelly liked guys, not girls. They would usually go for coffee after yoga when they both happened to be there and if Kelly had some free time. Jenny thought she might have found a new friend.

The Friday before Thanksgiving, Kelly asked her to go to this great outdoor gear sale held a few times every year at the fairgrounds exhibit hall. She told Jenny that, living in Durango, she needed gear. Right after yoga, they jumped into Jenny's Jeep and went to the sale.

Jenny, under Kelly's tutoring, had a great time buying a down parka, a down vest, a pair of trail running shoes, two pairs of fleece leggings, a pair of waterproof pants, some warm socks, new long underwear, a fleece top, and, in one of her weaker moments at Kelly's prodding, snowshoes. Then, of course, she needed winter boots to wear. And gloves. And extendable hiking poles with big baskets to use with her snowshoes. And then a day pack with a hydration bladder. Lastly, two wildly colored stocking hats.

After over two hours of selecting, trying on, and laughing, she proudly paid for her purchases with her brand-new bank card. They carried all her new stuff to the Jeep. They went downtown to have coffee, laughing and being silly all the way.

* * *

Thanksgiving was the next week, and William was having dinner for some people, including Jenny. She was excited; she was actually looking forward to meeting some new people. She knew Helen would be there. William's son, Peter, was coming down from Denver. There were also another couple around William's age and two younger couples. She knew Kelly didn't have any plans for the day, so she asked Will whether she could invite her for dinner. Will was happy for her to do so.

She went over to William's place on Wednesday afternoon and offered to help out. Was there anything she could do? He had her check the silverware to make sure it was all wiped and polished, and then he wanted her to set the table. She had no idea how to set a table, so he showed her, and she proceeded, being very careful and proud of her work.

Thanksgiving Day came, and Jenny was at William's place early. Helen was already there with an apron on and a big hug for Jenny. Jenny asked, "So what can I do? I have never had Thanksgiving before and have no idea about anything. I want to help."

Helen put her to work with peeling potatoes, then cleaning and cutting carrots, and picking and cutting green beans. William had the turkey in the oven early, due to be done and carved for dinner at five o'clock. William was proving to be quite a chef, and Jenny was having fun working with him and Helen. Everything was well ready to go when guests started arriving around two thirty.

Both Jenny and Helen went to freshen up. William put out appetizers and drinks ranging from wine, beer, iced tea, and whatever mixed drinks anyone might want.

When Jenny and Helen returned, William was pouring wine and talking with people as they arrived. Everyone was in a good mood, talking and laughing. William called Jenny over to introduce her to two young men, Mark and Gary, whom she found out were partners. She liked them, and knowing they were together made her feel more comfortable and unthreatened. At this point in her life, William and her grandfather were the only two men she felt she could trust. The three of them were having a nice conversation when Kelly arrived, took off her coat, and ran over, giving Jenny, Mark, and Gary a big hug. She was excited to see them, and the conversation went on complete with silliness and laughter. Jenny was feeling happy and having a great time.

The older couple, Christine and Tom, seemed very nice. Jenny liked them both; then there was the younger couple, in their early thirties, Greg and Sara, both of whom she had seen at yoga but hadn't met. She stayed and talked, having some wine, heady with excitement. She had never been at a party before and was loving getting attention and being welcomed into a group of people.

At about three thirty, Peter arrived and was introduced around. He was like a younger version of William: tall and fit. He had a nice smile, a shock of dark hair, and dark, soft eyes. He was in law school and was due to graduate in spring of the next year. He joined right into the festivities and brought even more liveliness to the group. Like William, he seemed genuine and polished. Jenny decided he might be an okay guy like his dad.

By five, everyone was seated, Peter between Jenny and Kelly. The bird was carved, and everything was on the table, steaming hot. Wine was poured. William asked everyone to hold hands and to give thanks for whatever he or she felt thankful for.

Jenny's turn came, and she hesitated for a moment. "I am thankful to be spending my first Thanksgiving celebration ever with all you wonderful people. Thank you for being here, and thank you, William and Helen, for being such special and wonderful people. I love you both." Everyone sat in silence for a moment. Jenny used her napkin to dry her eyes, as did Helen.

Food was passed, and the merriment continued on until after the pumpkin pie topped with whipped cream, after-dinner drinks, and coffee. Festivities concluded around ten after everyone had helped to pick up dishes, clean up the kitchen, and put all the leftovers in the refrigerator. Good-byes, hugs, and 'see you soons' were exchanged.

Kelly came to say good-bye, a little drunk. Jenny noticed and asked her if she might want to spend the night. Kelly giggled and thought it might be a good idea. Peter was staying with William, so the three of them sat and talked well into the night, enjoying the last of the open wine, finally calling it a night around two o'clock in the morning.

Jenny started to feel a little hesitant about Kelly staying with her, an old fear rising, remembering Becky from college; nevertheless, they went over to Jenny's house, and Jenny made up the couch for her. They sat and talked a while longer, and both went to bed. Jenny, however, closed her door and wedged a chair under the doorknob. She felt safe and slept a sound sleep with dreams of being surrounded by interesting people and enjoying herself, being happy, trusting, and not being afraid. She awoke with Cat meowing, wanting to be let out of the bedroom.

* * *

They had both slept late. Kelly was off work that day, so she and Jenny had some breakfast and sat chatting over their coffee about yesterday's events. Kelly asked about Jenny's comment that this was her first Thanksgiving.

Jenny responded with more information on her childhood at the Farm. "No one ever celebrated holidays much. There were no traditional or religious folks there. Most were trying to escape from all that and their parents and all the middle-class stuff. There were some Wiccan people, and we had winter solstice bonfires as well as a summer solstice thing. It was weird: drums, whistles, flutes, all sorts of noise, and people dancing naked and some things I really don't want to talk about."

Kelly sat, reflecting on this for a few moments, and responded, "Holy shit, Jenny. I had no idea. What did your parents do?"

"Oh, hell, they joined right in. In reality, I had no parents. They were just some adult children I lived with, but trust me, they made sure my brother and I knew we were nothing more than a burden to them and that they couldn't wait 'til we left and were out of their hair. If it weren't for my grandparents, my brother and I would probably have been homeless in LA or somewhere, living on the streets, begging or whoring for survival," she said, her voice quivering.

"Holy shit," Kelly repeated. "Jenny, I can't comprehend it. That is so different from my childhood in upper-middle-class American suburbia north of Chicago with my domineering father. I can't imagine."

They both sat in silence for a long time. Kelly finally broke the meditation. "Hey, what do you think of Peter? He's really cute, and I think he likes you."

"Yeah, he's all right, I guess. I think he likes you too. He seems to talk a lot. Pretty much dominated the conversation last night, as I recall. Sort of a know-it-all."

Kelly laughed and said, "We were all a little smashed. Maybe he just talks a lot when he's drinking. Still think he likes you."

Jenny responded, "I really never had a guy who liked me. I was pretty reclusive in college and for the last few years since I graduated. I lived in the mountains in the summers and in an old cabin a few miles north of here in the winter, except it burned down and I sort of ended up here at William's. You're probably the first girl, or anyone, I might call a friend. Don't really know how to have ... or be a friend. Not much experience in the 'friend' thing."

Kelly said, "Really? You are one interesting girl. And, thanks for considering me your friend. I consider you my friend as well. But, I'm really not interested in Peter. I like this guy I have been doing physical therapy work with for his arm. He broke it in a bike crash, he's a really nice guy. His name is Matt. He's a mountain biker, competes nationally, wants to get on the USA Olympic team. He's really cute, and I love it when he comes in. I'm hoping he will ask me out sometime, but he seems a little shy. He wants to go back to school in sports medicine; he seems really smart. Graduated on a bike scholarship from Fort Lewis College. Maybe you and Peter and Matt and I could go out sometime," she finished, smiling.

"Well, Peter lives in Denver and is going back on Sunday, and Matt hasn't asked you out, so ... probably not going to happen."

"Well, we can always dream."

"Yeah, we can always dream, but I've a lot of other things to dream about other than guys," Jenny replied sullenly, thinking about her past.

"Yeah, I know. I'm sorry. I really am. But please trust me to be a friend. I can be a good listener and probably won't have much advice as you have so much different experiences than I ever could imagine."

"Thanks. I really don't need advice or pity, but sometimes it's nice just having someone to hang out with, someone who isn't associated with my drama. This whole thing seems to involve a lot of crying, I'm really tired of it."

"I have big, strong, welcoming shoulders that'll always be available."

"Thanks, Kelly, you're really great. I really appreciate you and your concern. Thanks. You're very special."

"Hey," said Kelly, "why don't you come into town tomorrow night? There's a new film at the indie theater that I want to see; we could go and have some wine and popcorn, maybe come in early, and we could catch a light dinner before."

"Sounds fun. Mind if I ask Peter to come? Might be nice for him to get out."

"Sure, ask him. It'd be fun. And you could get to know him better, hmmmm?"

"Oh stop. Just thought it might be nice for him."

"Yeah, right." She gave a coy smile. "Hey, gotta run. Lots of errands to do. Thanks for keeping me off the road last night. I was pretty goofy. And thanks for sharing. That's what friends are for. I really like you, Jenny. Thanks for being a friend to me." She gave Jenny a quick hug and said, "Come by my place around four thirty tomorrow, and we'll get dinner and catch the movie. See ya." She headed to the door.

"See ya," Jenny said, and the door shut.

It was now past one, and Jenny spent the next hour pondering what had taken place with Kelly along with her feelings, her confusion about friendship, about Peter, about yesterday. She wrote copiously in her journal, trying to unravel what was her life.

Chapter 13

Lately, Jenny had been thinking a lot about her brother and her grandparents. She felt ashamed of herself for being out of touch for such a long time. She thought about a letter she had received recently from Michael. His writing was ragged and barely understandable, his thoughts random, disconnected, and hard to follow.

Dear Jenny,

I haven't heard from you forever. Where the hell are you? I'm doing okay. What are you doing? I see our grandparents a lot. Are you hiding somewhere? Why are you not here where you should be with your brother? They are fine. School sucks. It's all about the girls, and they always get better grades and hate me. These stupid teachers like all the girls. Especially the girl teachers. The girl teachers always give me bad grades. Grandma and Grandma like me. Do you like me? The teachers do not like me. They do not respect who I am. I tell them stuff I do not like. Then they say I'm a bigot. They tell me maybe I should not be here. It's them that should not be here. Girls are not smart enough to be doctors like I am. Why are you not around here where you should be? I am your brother, and you should

not be away from me. Where are you? Your
post office box is Durango. Are you there?
Why are you there? No body respects me.
Maybe they need to be taught a lesson that
they should respect me. Maybe you do not
respect me like you should. I don't know.

Michael

The way he started out the letter seemed almost hostile
toward her for not letting him know where she was, and
then he wanted to know whether she was deliberately
hiding from him. Then he went on about how school was
so hard; it seemed all his classes were geared toward the
female student? And the female professors were picking
on him, giving him bad grades, and not appreciating him?
He seemed to be expressing a lot of anger and resentment,
making himself out to be a victim. Then he wrote something
about maybe having to teach them all a lesson on respect?

Everything about his letter disturbed her. Parts of it
frightened her. His writing was so scattered and cryptic, and
it certainly didn't seem to be written by someone in college;
how had he ever been admitted to college if this was the
best he could write? She wondered whether he was even in
college and in a premed program. Puzzled and a little upset,
she put the letter away, knowing she wanted to respond to
it—if nothing else, to let him know she was okay.

Having gone through college, she knew one thing from
her experience: she had never had any teacher single her or
anyone else out for any reason. If you worked and studied
hard, you were rewarded with good grades. For him to feel
so victimized didn't make sense to her, especially the part
about him thinking there was favoritism shown toward

female students. If anything, it was usually the opposite from her experience.

Her life was beginning to move to a better place, and she felt maybe it was time for her to reconnect. She wanted to see her grandparents and her brother.

She went over to William's place and asked, "Can I use your cell to call my brother?"

"Sure." Retrieving his phone from the kitchen counter, he said gently, "Maybe it is time for you to get your own phone."

She blushed. "Ah, yeah, I probably should. Thanks. I'll only be a minute."

She had Michael's cell number, which he had sent her in one of his last letters, and she punched in his number. He answered almost immediately.

"Hi, Michael, it's Jenny."

"Jenny, where the hell are you? What the hell's going on? Are you okay? I haven't heard from you in over a year, dammit! I worry about you. Is everything okay? Are you all right? Why aren't you here?"

"I'm fine, Michael. Better than ever, really. Better than I could've imagined last year this time. I'm sorry for being out of touch. I don't really have time to talk since I'm borrowing a phone, but I'm thinking about coming to Denver to see you and Grandma and Grandpa in the next few weeks. Could you come up from the Springs? Would that be okay?"

"Okay? That would be so great! I haven't seen you or talked to you in forever. Grandma and Grandpa would be so happy—it would just make them so happy. I see them a lot, and their first question is, 'Have you heard from Jenny?'"

"Okay, gotta go. I'll try to call you again tomorrow or Sunday. Love you."

"Ah, yeah? Yeah, sure—whatever."

She clicked off, thinking there wasn't much difference between talking to him and the way his letter read. She didn't feel very good about Michael's closing remark either, it seemed dismissive. *And what's with him wanting me to be there? Oh well.*

"Thanks, Will, and you're right. I really need to get my own phone. Any suggestions?"

Peter overheard her, having just walked in, and said, "Why don't I go with you, and I could help, if you want. I could give you some pointers."

Jenny thought about her and Kelly's date, and responded, "Sure, I'd love any help I can get, like, all the help I can get. I've no idea about technology, what to even begin to look for. Kelly and I are going to have dinner and a movie tomorrow night; we could go in to the phone store, then meet her and go out. Would that be okay with you, Will? If you want to, Peter?"

William smiled and said, "Sure, go ahead Peter. We have spent all day catching up, and we have tomorrow morning as well ... so go on. Have a night out."

Peter said, "Then I'd love to. What time? Phone store will be at least an hour, especially since this is your first phone."

"How about two thirty or so? That should give us plenty of time to meet up with Kelly at four thirty."

"Ready at two thirty, and we'll go phone shopping. See ya then."

She thanked William again and headed back to her house, considering what she had just done. *What the hell ... this was like ... what ... a date?* Was she getting too trusting? But it was William's son, and he seemed genuinely nice and sincere, and she thought she might like him. She liked a guy? She didn't quite know how to process the possibility of trusting a guy other than Will and her grandfather. But the more she thought about it, the more she felt okay about being with Peter. She realized she was trusting herself to make this decision and felt it was a good one. She smiled, sat down with her journal, and recorded it all down, processing it as she wrote. She went to bed early, still recovering from her late night. She was tired, sleepy, good, and at ease.

* * *

She was up early. Cat had sneaked in again and was purring her contentment; she would have to talk to William about her. *Darned devious cat seems to be able to be invisible when she wants.*

She went for a ten-mile run, came home and showered, had a bite to eat, read her latest book for a while, and wrote in her journal. Then it was time to go. She went over and got Peter, and they headed to the phone store. Peter suggested a wireless carrier both he and William used; it was reliable and had good coverage, none of which made much sense to technologically deprived Jenny. She had never had a phone, not even in college. She had basic knowledge on how to use a computer, but that was it.

They got to the store, and she went in to see an array of different phones, different sizes; some did this, some did that, and some did something else. Peter was partial to the Apple iPhone like the one he had and was explaining a little about it when a salesperson came to help. She went over the features with Jenny, who was familiar only with her Apple laptop.

"Okay, I like it. I'll take it."

They then went over various plans, and with Peter's help, she decided, and then it was a matter of paper work and getting everything connected and running. The salesperson went over all the basics, including where and how to get online help, and assured her she could come by the store anytime as well for any help she might need. All of this, surprisingly to Jenny, consumed well over an hour. Jenny bought a few accessories Peter had recommended, such as a protective case, a screen protector, and a car charger. She paid her bill and walked out, now connected to the world.

They went out, and Jenny asked Peter to drive so she could play with her new toy. They still had some time to kill so they went to have some coffee. She loved her new toy and only reluctantly put it away so she wouldn't be rude, but she did so only after first entering Peter's number, her first.

Jenny asked Peter about law school and his plans afterward.

"I would like to come to Durango after graduation and hopefully get an internship at a local law office and then study for the bar exam. I'm already beginning a search of various law firms. Dad knows a local lawyer pretty well, and together they are trying to help from this end. I'm feeling pretty confident. Dad is a very supportive father and is doing as much as he can to facilitate my getting to Durango."

And he continued to go on and on about law school until she finally interrupted him to get him off the law school thing by asking him about some technical aspect concerning her new phone.

After answering her question, he asked, "So, how did you end up in Durango?"

"Well, interestingly, I had no plans after I graduated from CU, so I went down to the 'ride board' at the union the day before graduation and saw a request for a passenger to ride to Durango and share gas. This guy had a pickup, so I could take all of what little stuff I had … I didn't have much. I gave most of it away except for some clothes and my books. Got ahold of the guy, and he agreed to pick me up Sunday morning, and we drove down here to Durango.

"Stayed in town for a few days, got a storage locker for my stuff, went to a thrift store and bought some backpacking gear, supplemented what I couldn't get there at a local outdoor store. Spent the summer backpacking in the San Juans." She continued with the rest of her years to the present. "Not much to show, is it?"

"God, I couldn't do that. Couldn't stand all the solitude. I'd be lonesome. I need action, stuff to do. That's why I like law school ... like the challenge. What did you do all day by yourself? Weren't you bored?"

"Hiked, read sometimes, wrote in my journal. It was okay. And I had a few challenges too," she finished trying not to be sarcastic.

"Yeah, but how much solitude does anyone really need? Didn't you miss people? Being around? Talking? Hanging with coffee and friends?"

She answered, "Ah, it was okay. I went into a town whenever to get supplies. It was okay."

"Just don't understand it. Interesting. So do you think you're going into seclusion again? God, like you are a nun or something, like in a monastery."

Jenny was tired of listening to him go on about her and directed him back to being a lawyer and his idealistic expectations about helping people. He said he was interested in law since it pertained to the Native American people. He had spent some time studying tribal law, especially the Southern Utes, whose governmental center was in Ignacio, twenty miles southeast of Durango, thus his desire to locate in the area.

Jenny realized all she could offer was her dream about being a writer. Other than her journaling, she hadn't written anything for weeks, months, even. Who was she kidding?

She was ready to leave and said, "Time to go and meet Kelly. We gotta go."

They met Kelly as planned, had a light dinner, and enjoyed the movie with a few glasses of wine and popcorn. They said good night, and Kelly headed to her place, and Jenny and Peter headed up to the north valley.

* * *

On the way home, Jenny mentioned she was planning to go to Denver to see her brother before Christmas.

"That would be great. We could maybe get together when you're there. I could meet your brother. Maybe we could go out for some drinks and dinner.

"Hey, Jenny, have an idea. I'm coming back down to Durango to spend Christmas break with Dad. Normally I would be with my mother, but she is going to be in London with her new boyfriend. So why don't you fly to Denver? I could pick you up at DIA and take you to your grandparents' place. You could spend your time with them, and we could drive back here together; it would be fun to have some company during the seven-hour drive."

"Ah, yeah, let me think it over. I haven't made any arrangements with anyone yet. I'm going to try to talk with Michael tomorrow and set something up. He actually lives in Colorado Springs for college. I'll call you and let you know one way or the other."

Peter walked Jenny to the door. "I had a nice time, Jenny. Thanks for asking me to come." He kissed her on the cheek, smiled, and walked over to William's.

She went inside, her cheek burning where he had kissed her. She felt a new sensation going through her, a sensation she had never felt before. She stood inside her door for a few minutes, considering what had just happened, not knowing whether she liked it. It was a nice feeling, warm like a luxurious bath. But it was also a bit unnerving to her; a guy kissed her: nicely, sweetly, respectfully. What to make of it? She didn't know. She went to bed, puzzled, but feeling warm and happy. She found her new best friend, Cat, snuggled in, waiting for her.

Peter left at noon on Sunday but not without coming over to bid Jenny a good-bye and asking her again to consider his offer about coming to Denver. She said she would be in touch. Peter commented again on having a nice time last night. She blushed, replying that she'd had a good time also, and thanked him again for his help in getting her new cell phone. They each said good-bye, and he was gone.

She thought about Peter's offer and didn't feel real excited about being a captive audience for seven hours in a car with him. She hadn't liked being confined in the pickup with that guy when she got out of college. She felt uncomfortable being alone with any man other than William, of course, who was fast becoming a father figure.

She spent the rest of the day and the next writing in her journal about the last few days, trying to process her emotions, especially Peter's kiss. Had it been just a friend's kiss, or did he really like her? Was it a prelude to anything more? Deep down she wasn't really sure she liked the idea, still very fearful of any kind of relationship with men. She'd had too many bad experiences with lies and unwanted sexual advances. She loved her grandfather, Dean; he was genuine and wonderful with all his love and support. But she didn't know whether she could ever trust any man enough for a relationship. By the time she had ended writing all her feelings down, she was emotionally drained.

Chapter 14

Jenny's first group counseling session was the Tuesday night after Thanksgiving. On Sunday she was already starting to get nervous about it. Her fears were starting again: fear of people, fear of being bullied again, fear of the ever-present shame. She again started questioning her trust in herself and the people she had become close to. She was getting close to more and more people, and she was beginning to feel weak and vulnerable.

Who was she to think anybody would ever be different from those who had abused or frightened her? Why did she think she could trust William, Helen, Joan, or Kelly? Or any of this counseling? Or this group session? Deep down inside, she knew better. In the last six weeks, she had changed. She knew it; she felt it. But all this sudden change in her life was unnerving. She felt uneasy about everything that was happening. She wasn't completely comfortable with it, but in many ways she cherished it.

She was also discovering something new about herself: resolve. She felt stronger in herself and in her belief in herself. Had she gotten that from all these people? It was confusing. She could do as she had before: run and disappear. Or she could stay, keep going, and see where it would all lead. She realized she had to save herself from herself, that she was her own worst enemy in many ways. To move forward into the life she was presently experiencing and what lay ahead of her, she would have to strengthen that resolve. She would have to take chances, and she would most likely get hurt again sometime. But William had three wives; Kelly had had two failed serious relationships; Helen, while married to William for a short time, still loved him. And they seemed so happy and caring, giving, and accepting. They had been hurt. Everyone apparently had some hurt, some baggage, but they had dealt with it or were dealing with it and not hiding away in the mountains. They were going on with their lives. They seemed to have functional lives.

She sat down Tuesday morning and began channeling these thoughts into her journal, which always seemed to help her better sort things through. She spent three hours writing, thinking, chastising, feeling scared, sorting through her emotions, fears, and desires. Jenny questioned everything, including all these new people in her life, especially Peter. She questioned her therapy and the childhood of abuse she had to face.

Could she ever be normal? What *was* truly normal? Was anything truly normal? She put her pencil down, closed the journal, pulled the elastic band around it, and looked out the window at the beautiful autumn day.

Fuck it! Screw it! I'm a big girl. If I can survive alone in the mountains, I can do this. I'm just tired of feeling this way. It's time to get on with it.

* * *

She put on her running clothes and went for a ten-mile run.

When she got home and cleaned up, she sat down with Will's book, the one she had selected a few days back. She read the first five chapters. It was like what she had seen in the other book she had skimmed back when she first met him. The writing was geared toward, what she considered to be, the lowest common denominator. The characters and plot were predictable, and she could see no redeeming value in spending any more time with it.

He said he wrote trash books, and he's right about that. If this is what he writes, will he really have anything to offer about anything I write? Of course, that's if I ever actually write anything. His writing is so shallow. I don't want to write like that. Should I say anything to him? What would I say? Best to say nothing.

By the time she needed to leave for group at six o'clock, she was so scared. All she wanted to do was to get into her Jeep and drive as far away as fast as she could. But she made herself go and get to the shelter precisely at six thirty. She hadn't eaten since breakfast, and she had no appetite. She felt sick to her stomach with anxiety.

She went into the shelter and the group session room. There were seven chairs placed in a circle. Two other women were there along with Joan. They smiled, and Joan motioned for her to come in and sit down. She could hardly breathe. She smiled back weakly and took a chair, sitting upright with her hands on her lap, staring straight ahead, making no eye contact. Four others arrived shortly, and the session began.

Joan smiled, welcomed everyone, and asked them all to introduce themselves, starting clockwise from her left. First was Shelly, then Ann, and Jenny was next; her mouth was so dry she could barely utter her name, which came out as a whisper. Joan came to her rescue and introduced her, and everyone said, "Hi, Jenny, welcome."

Jenny smiled, nodded, and whispered, "Thank you."

Introductions continued around to Mary, Barb, and Juanita.

Then Joan asked whether anyone had anything to share. Juanita started some observations from her week; she was discovering more about who she was, about how her past was affecting her less and less. She was feeling stronger.

Everyone nodded in approval and thanked her for sharing. All the rest shared stories and observations concerning their lives, including encounters, fears, anger, discovery, and even joy. Jenny listened intently to these women as they shared their stories of abuse, including their anger, pain, triumphs, failures, and fears. Everyone had shared, and it was Jenny's turn.

Jenny wanted to get up and run. All she could mutter was "A boy kissed me ... on the cheek."

Joan looked at her, nodded, and said gently, "Thanks, Jenny. Anything else you want to share about that? How did it make you feel?"

"I am confused about how I feel about it. I have never been kissed by a boy before. I have tried to understand ... make some sense of it."

Juanita said, "Your first kiss, Jenny, on the cheek? That sounds sweet and innocent. Do you like him?"

"I don't know. I guess so. I just met him at Thanksgiving. We hung out together Saturday and went to a movie with a friend. He seems really nice, but I just don't really trust men, only my grandfather and my father."

Jenny noticed that Joan quickly wrote something on her pad after that last remark.

Mary said, "All relationships seem to want to start too fast. It's best to take your time. Go slowly and let it unfold easily rather than too rushed but enjoy it. Discovering another person you like can be wonderful ... or sometimes not so much."

Joan interrupted, "Thanks, everyone, and thanks, Jenny, for joining us and sharing. It is eight and time to call it a day. I hope to see you all next week as well as see you all throughout the week. Peace and be safe."

Everyone got up and hugged each other, chattering away about unrelated topics. Jenny felt like such an outsider and was starting to leave when Juanita and Ann came over, grabbed her, and gave her a big hug. They told her how happy they were that she was there, that it took time, that this was the beginning of a process, and that it would just get better. "Hang in there." They looked forward to seeing her again next week. Then the others paraded over with hugs and similar encouragement.

Jenny had tears in her eyes and could only smile weakly.

Juanita, Shelly, and Barb were going out for coffee and asked Jenny whether she would like to join them. Jenny suddenly realized she was starving since she hadn't eaten since a late breakfast.

"I'd love to as long as there's some food. I'm starved."

They walked down to a little Asian restaurant. Jenny and Shelly ordered some food, and they all ordered tea. Jenny was enjoying herself, with everyone asking her about her life and she about theirs. They talked about where they were from, what they did, and whether they had kids. But they avoided anything serious; everyone seemed to respect that area as personal and off limits.

Jenny got home after ten thirty—fed, happy, and emotionally drained. She fell into bed, absent Cat, and instantly fell asleep with dreams that she and all these women were hiking together happily in the high country in bright sunshine and colorful wildflowers.

Chapter 15

On Wednesday morning, she got up and went to yoga class; then she headed back to her place and went for a run. She spent the afternoon reading; she was into D. H. Lawrence's *Lady Chatterley's Lover*. It was quite intriguing to her, but she was having a hard time understanding the sexual nature of the book and Lady Chatterley's emotions and feelings. She couldn't understand the idea of desiring a man; she just couldn't fathom why she might ever desire a man. Why would she? What would it mean?

She easily avoided any writing once again except in her journal where she explored her dream. She decided she really liked the support of the group session and found out she wasn't alone in her struggle; other abused women were struggling toward recovery the same as she. She felt comforted in that fact.

On Thursday, she went for her session with Joan.

"So what did you think of group?" was Joan's first question.

"Ahhhh, all right, I guess. I was really scared and uncomfortable, but everyone seemed so nice. I went out with Juanita, Barb, and Shelly afterward for a late dinner for Shelly and me and tea for the others. It was fun. I like them. They were really welcoming and made me feel better than I did at the session."

"I sensed your discomfort in the beginning, and I appreciated you sharing, as hard as it might have seemed."

"Yeah, it was hard. I hope I didn't sound hokey or stupid."

"Not at all. I found your comments interesting. First, the boy. Do you think you are ready for a boy in your life right now?"

"I don't know, Joan. It's all pretty strange to me with everything, as you already know. I don't really have any idea about any of it. I like him; he seems nice. William is his father. He lives in Denver. I'm planning to go up to see my brother and grandparents before Christmas. He wants me to fly up. He'd meet me at the airport and then take me to my grandparents. Then he wants me to ride back with him when he comes back here for Christmas break. I don't know. I'd sort of like to, but there are all these red flags from my past that are popping up. I don't know whether I am just being paranoid or what. I don't know. It all seems so confusing.

"And seven hours in a car with him ... alone. And he talks an awful lot. Might drive me crazy the way he rambles on."

Joan laughed. "Some people don't know when to shut up; believe me, I know. But my guess is, he was just nervous and trying to avoid any empty space."

Jenny continued, "Maybe, maybe just nervous. But Joan, you know, sometimes I wish I'd never stumbled on William's that night, that the cabin was there and I was just having a peaceful winter by myself. It would be so much easier. But, on the other hand, here I am. I'm feeling somewhat more social with people for the first time ever, and that feels good, really good. What do you think?"

"Well, I am not here to tell what or how to think. My job is to help you to be able to make your own decisions, hopefully good decisions, about what you want for your life, to help you get over your fears, your trust issues, and lack of self-confidence so you are able to deal with your past in a responsible, productive, and sane way, and move into your life that you deserve to be able to do.

"On the other hand, where would you be if you hadn't ended up at William's that night? I think you are beginning to get your life in order and should continue to do so now that you have started on this journey. As I said early on, this process can be a tough business, but I think you are a pretty tough girl.

"So, I want to ask you: do you think this guy is worth the risk?"

"I don't know, Joan. He's William's son, and I love and trust William. He's been so good to me. I want to trust Peter. His name is Peter—I like that name. He's nice, fun, interesting. He treats me so nice, and he's really good looking. Yeah, I guess I like him. But I have never really known any other guys except ... well, you know. And how can I know if I like the first guy I meet?"

"Well, Jenny, you have to start somewhere with men. I wouldn't be too concerned right now if this is Mister Right. I would say, if you feel good about him in your gut, trust that feeling and take a chance."

"Ahhhh, well ... yeah, maybe. I'll have to think about it. I don't want to make any decision right now, but I am leaning toward the Denver thing. But really, seven hours in a car with him? I don't know. Maybe it wouldn't be all bad, do ya think?"

"Give it some thought. If you want to talk about it later, just call me or make an appointment, okay?"

"Yeah, sounds good. Thanks."

"So, Jenny, I want to ask you something else you mentioned in group, that the only men you trust were your grandfather and your father. Please explain. I thought you hated your father."

"Yeah, I know. That must have sounded weird, but I was really thinking of William when I mentioned my father. I just love him. I wish he was my real father, not the piece of trash who is my biological father. I know it's weird. I accidentally called him Dad one time, and he said he felt honored that I felt that way and that he loved me as his own daughter." Her voice was shaky, and tears were forming. She put her hand to her forehead and turned away, sniffling.

Joan handed her a box of tissues and waited.

After a few minutes, she dried her eyes and blew her nose, continuing. "Sorry, it's just that I guess I really want a father, a good father. I guess I've sort of adopted William in some weird way. Is that wrong? Do you think I am totally twisted, wanting William for a father and then liking his son? Am I crazy? It all sounds so wrong."

She grabbed the tissues again and took a moment to dry her eyes and blow her nose.

"I don't think it is weird or twisted. I can understand you projecting your image of a father onto William. He is a truly nice man. I have known him for years. And apparently he likes you and feels comfortable and happy that you consider him in such high regard. This explains a lot to me. I know of no young woman who does not idolize her father—or in your case wants and needs a father to idolize. If William fills that void in your life and fills the need that you want as a father figure, I see nothing wrong in your adopting him. It would be nice if you actually told him you are adopting him. He would probably like it. And as far as you liking Peter, there is no blood relationship between any of you, so it is hardly incestuous, if that is what you are thinking. So that should not make you feel weird in any way. Okay?" She finished with a smile.

"Okay, Joan, thanks. That makes me feel better ... I think. But do you really think I should tell him? What if he freaks out?"

"I don't think he would freak out. I think he would love it. I know he is very fond of you. He has told Helen and me as much."

"Thanks, Joan. Whoa, hey. Time's up, I see. I gotta go. Meeting Kelly after she gets off work for a girl's dinner and chat. I want to tell her about Peter."

She got up, put on her coat. "See ya." She was gone, leaving a grinning, envious Joan behind.

* * *

Jenny met Kelly at a pizza place, where they got a seat and each ordered a glass of chard and began talking.

Kelly asked, "So what happened with Peter?"

"He kissed me good night, on the cheek."

"Oh my God. He so likes you."

"He wants me to fly to Denver and then ride back with him when he comes back for Christmas break."

"Oh, holy shit ... Ya gonna do it?"

"I don't know. What do you think I should do?"

"Oh, what the hell," Kelly said. "Do it ... It'll be so fun."

"I don't know ... It's really scary for me."

"But he likes you, and he's so cute."

"Really think I should?"

"Of course, you should, silly girl."

The server came. "Are you ready to order?"

"Oh sure. Ahhhhh, yeah. A medium vegetarian with ground beef. That okay?" said Kelly.

"Well, that's really not a vegetarian," said the waitperson.

"No, but we want the veggies and some ground beef. Is that gonna be a problem?"

"No, not at all. Thanks. I'll get it right in. And two more chards?"

"Yes, please."

She left.

Kelly asked, "So you gonna do it?"

"I really need time to think, Kelly. I have so much to deal with right now. I just don't know if I need something like a relationship with a guy of any sorts. Yeah, Peter's okay, but we just met. It's just that ... It's just that I just have so much shit to deal with." She hung her head in defeat.

"I'm sorry if I seemed too pushy. I can understand with all you've told me."

"Oh, Kelly, you really have no idea. What I've shared with you only scratches the surface, really only scratches the surface. Maybe someday I'll share more. Not right now, though ... not right now." She trailed off, looking beyond Kelly into somewhere beyond both of them, into another world.

Kelly sat quietly, watching her, concerned about her and wondering what things lay in her past.

Kelly said, "And I think I had it bad with my domineering father who wanted me to do this, succeed at that. I am still pissed that he considers me a failure because I didn't want to go to med school and be like him. He should have had a boy rather than me."

Jenny wistfully asked, "Do all kids have issues with their parents?"

"I don't know Jenny. I haven't a clue."

They went silent until their pizza arrived. They dug in and ate with some small talk, paid their bill, and said good-bye with hugs and parted.

Back home, Jenny wrote in her journal until past midnight, trying to digest her day and everything that had come down, especially Kelly's excitement over Peter and that Jenny should be so excited about him, when, in truth, she really wasn't. He was nice, but she felt he might be a distraction in her life, especially right now. It was almost too much.

* * *

Jenny spent her week waffling one way or the other. Somehow this thing with Peter was getting out of hand. She didn't like feeling pressured. She decided to talk to William and seek his advice. She went next door and knocked.

"Jenny, I haven't seen you all week. Are you avoiding me again?" he said with a big smile.

"Sorry Will, no, no ... I haven't been avoiding you at all, really. I've had just so much on my mind, so much to think about." She told him everything about Peter and about her meeting with Joan.

Then she went on. "Will, you have been so wonderful to me. Oh God, this is so hard, but I totally love you. I see you as the father I never had, and I ... I want to adopt you to be my father ... please?" She said this very rapidly, turned away, and started to cry.

William was silent for a minute while he fetched some tissues for her.

"I would be honored to be your adopted father, Jenny. You have come to mean a lot to me. I am grateful you entered my life."

She regained her composure, looked up with a weak smile, and said, "Thanks, Will. This healing and sharing and dealing with all my shit certainly use up a lot of tears and tissues, don't ya think?"

William sat for a moment. "Yes, it does. Sadly. I found that out the hard way also. Trust me when I say I can understand. Believe it or not, I used up my share of tissues as well. It's hard, but it will be worth it going through the pain ... to get rid of the pain."

They both were quiet for a long time, lost in their thoughts.

William finally broke the silence. "I would be more than proud and honored to be your adopted father. You truly are like a daughter to me, and yes, Jenny, I love you too."

She jumped into his arms and hugged him so tightly he thought he might choke.

"Oh, William, I love you so much. I promise I'll be a good daughter, I promise! Thank you so much. This means so much! You can't understand."

"I think I do. I think I do," he said as he reached for the tissues.

They sat for a few moments, and Jenny said, "Cat has been sneaking into the bunkhouse all the time lately. I like her and everything, but she's your cat. I feel like a cat napper."

William laughed. "Yeah, I know she's been visiting you. I think that she might have adopted you. I suggest you get a kitty box and some bowls for food and water for her. Also kitty litter. I can give you some food. Maybe she will be a shared cat. Sound okay?

Jenny laughed and replied, "Sounds okay to me if it's okay with you … Just was concerned."

William laughingly said, "I remember the first night you came here. You have come a long way—ah, with Cat, I mean."

Jenny picked up his double meaning and replied, "Yeah, Will, a long, long way."

He knew what she meant as well.

Chapter 16

Jenny met with Joan again on Tuesday and started off by saying, "I think I'm going to take Peter up on his offer. I have thought a lot about it, and it should be fun. I called my brother and my grandparents to let them know and got a flight to Denver tomorrow. They acted excited to see me. I'm really anxious but excited as well. They sound happy.

"I'm still a bit reluctant to be riding alone with Peter to get back. I know he's William's son and all, and I like Peter. He seems nice and all, but there's something I need to tell you about an experience I had once with a guy when I was sixteen and was out walking through the Farm. This guy was about my age, and he started walking alongside me, and we began chatting about this and that, ending up walking into the forest.

"It was a really nice day, and I was enjoying being with this guy. He seemed friendly and interesting to talk to. We went to a small grassy clearing, sat, and continued talking. The next thing I knew, he grabbed me and threw me to the ground. He was on top of me, trying to kiss me. He had a hand between my legs, rubbing my crotch. I screamed at him to stop, but he didn't. He kept on saying, 'Come on, Jenny. I know you want it. Don't be a prude. Come on. I want to fuck you. You're so hot. You'll love it ... You know you want to."

"I got a leg free and kicked him and caught him on his nose. He lost his grip, grabbing at his nose, blood immediately running down his face. I broke away, was instantly on my feet, and screamed at him, 'Go fuck yourself,' and ran away.

"He hollered, 'You fucking bitch, slut, cunt! You broke my nose! You bitch! You'll pay for this, you fucking bitch!'

"I never told anyone because I knew that no one would care. I was on my own. I cut off any association with all the kids in the commune, even my brother, as well as most adults. But I suffered the consequences: that guy told everyone what happened, that I was a bitch slut. And every time I was out, some of his friends, both girls and boys, said, 'Hi, bitch slut' or 'How's the bitch slut?' or 'Gettin' any fuckin' huh, bitch slut?'

"I stole some money from Dory, walked down to the mercantile store in the small town about two miles from the Farm, and bought a sheath knife with a six-inch-long blade. I was never without it.

"One day a guy was teasing me, then started shoving me, and I pulled out my knife and went for him, screaming, 'I'll cut your fucking heart out and eat it for lunch.'

"He ran away. From then on I was known as Crazy Jenny. I loved it and tried to live up to my new name by acting crazy, such as threatening people that I'd kill them and eat their beating hearts. People started avoiding me, leaving me alone. Hell, I never had any friends anyway, so I was fine with being solo. They were the crazies, the idiots, the bullies. I found solace in reading books and writing poetry and short stories about my fantasies.

"So, how's that, Joan? That was my fucking life. My earliest childhood memory was of the fights. I remember my father beating on my Dory, slamming her around, the bruises, the screaming, the crying, the fear. It seemed that was either fighting or sex, or abuse, and whatever other crap you might want to add it."

Joan was silent for a moment, considering all this. "How do you feel about all this now, Jenny?"

"How do I feel? How do I feel? I'll tell you how I feel. I'm so genuinely pissed off that I had such a shit childhood. I see other people my age that don't have all this shit, Joan. All this shit! I am so jealous of them and so pissed about the twenty-five years of me being so fucked up!"

"Jenny, I am sorry about your childhood. Truly, I am. But I think you know that you are not alone. Others have suffered the same things, abuse and bullying, along with the associated trauma. I also want you to know that you are not the worst case I have seen and counseled over the years. I'm sure that it doesn't make any of it any easier. You will survive. It's work, but you will survive."

Jenny hung her head. "Yeah, I know I will. It just all makes me so mad that I want to scream sometimes. I'm tired of crying."

Joan reached over and took her hand, saying softly, "I know you are, Honey. It will get better. Just hang with me. We'll get through it. We will. I promise. One more thing I want to talk about before you go is about your grandparents. How long has it been since you have seen them?"

"It's been over two years, the years I've been hiding away from everything."

"I think it will be very good for you to see them."

"Yeah, I know. It's way past time ... They did so much for me, getting me away from the Farm, supporting me through college, their ongoing support. It's been so long. I think they will be mad at me for seeming so ungrateful. I'm pretty nervous to go see them.

"I guess I got so wrapped up in escaping from everything after college that I just cut off all communication with them. Then, as time went on, I became ashamed and afraid to contact them. I was ashamed that I wasn't doing anything with my life. What could I tell them? 'Hi, Dean and Susan. Thanks for helping me become a reclusive, homeless bum.

All your support and caring really worked.' I sort of tried to stay in contact with Michael through letters," She trailed off.

"I doubt that they will be mad at you, Jenny. My guess is that they will welcome you with open arms and a lot of love. I will be waiting to see how it all goes. Anything else?"

"I think I covered enough, and more. Thanks, Joan. You're the best. I'll keep you informed on how it goes."

With that, they both got up, exchanging hugs and good-byes, and Jenny left for home.

Chapter 17

William took Jenny to her ten o'clock flight the next day. She relaxed into her short flight to Denver and began thinking about her grandparents, about how they had saved her. She remembered that it was about a week before her eighteenth birthday. She'd been walking across the compound and ran into the mail sorter, who said there was a big envelope in the mail for her.

She was surprised, since she'd never gotten any mail in her whole life, and ran to the mail room and, out of breath, got her envelope. She sneaked outside the compound where she could be alone and carefully opened it; here were birthday greetings from her grandparents, including fifteen new $100 bills. There was a note urging her to come to Denver and see them. They added that they would help her get into college if she wanted. This was exactly what she needed, a ticket to escape.

That night she stealthily put a few things in an old bag. She didn't sleep at all but lay awake, waiting in anticipation until right before dawn; then she sneaked out of the place that had been her home for eighteen years. She'd hitchhiked before from the commune to a little town about two miles away, so she knew how to get a ride. She had made a sign that read "Sacramento" and caught rides in a few old farm trucks, with a woman salesperson and lastly two young women about her age. She was in Sacramento shortly after noon.

She asked everyone for the best way to get to Denver. Suggestions were to hitchhike or take an airplane, bus, or

Amtrak. She found the Amtrak station and bought a ticket to Denver. The next train was scheduled to leave the next morning. She found a room in a nearby motel, flopped down on the bed, and wrapped her arms around herself in a self-hug and giggled. She was free, she was giddy, she was scared, she was happy.

It was mid-afternoon, so she went out and wandered the streets of Sacramento. Finding a sports store, she bought a few new clothes, a day-pack, and a water bottle. Then she found a bookstore and bought two brand new books. She never had a brand new book before. To her, it was like finding a treasure.

Checking out of the motel early in the morning, she had a big breakfast at a diner and strolled to the station, enjoying the new day, her second day of freedom.

She got to the train station, found out where she needed to wait, filled her new water bottle, and sat, reading one of the new books she had bought.

The train arrived at ten thirty. She boarded and found her seat, barely containing herself with the excitement and also the fear she felt. It was a big buzz of energy. The train left at 11:09. She would get to Denver thirty hours and twenty-nine minutes later: early evening the next day

The train pulled out, and she went back to her book but soon became mesmerized by the passing scenery through the Sierra Mountains, Truckee, Reno, then into the Nevada desert.

Nighttime came with a restless sleep. Then there was morning: Salt Lake, the Rocky Mountains, Denver. It was over too soon. She wanted to do it all over again. She could never have imagined so much land, such big cities, such freedom.

The train arrived at the Denver station, and she got off with her pack, found a phone booth, and called the number her grandparents had included in their note.

A short time later a black Mercedes pulled up into the loading zone, and a handsome older couple got out, anxiously looking around.

She didn't remember what they even looked like, not having seen them for fifteen years, but she knew it was them. They must be in their early sixties. Her grandmother, Susan, was about Jenny's height, with bobbed gray hair, slim and healthy. Her grandfather, Dean, was probably a little over six feet with a full mop of gray hair, cut long so he could comb it back to hang over his shirt collar. He too looked very healthy. She remembered how they had almost smothered her with hugs, kisses, and tears of happiness.

They drove to a high-rise condo building, went into the secure parking garage, parked, then took the elevator to the penthouse. Jenny stepped into what she perceived to be such opulence that she never could have imagined it in her wildest dreams. She was used to the plain, simple communal living where there were only basic necessities of life: a communal shower, a communal outhouse, and small cabins—in her case, a small yurt. There were art, fine furniture, views of the city—it was amazing. She walked around, just looking.

She remembered them telling her about the private investigator from San Francisco they had hired about two years before. It had taken him about three months to find her and Michael.

Jenny then thought about them telling her Dory wasn't her mother, that her real mother had died at childbirth, devastating her father. She had been so upset, her whole world turned upside down. It had been built on lies, had crashed around her.

Then she thought about how they had supported her, helping her to get her life going. Now, she was feeling she had completely failed.

The plane landed in Denver. She was out of security at eleven thirty and met a smiling Peter at the baggage pickup. She got her bag, and they headed into the city. Peter took her to her grandparents' high-rise, and she made him come up with her so he could meet them. They took the elevator to the penthouse and got out to find Dean and Susan waiting expectantly, running to her and both hugging her, almost squeezing the breath out of her.

"And who is this?" Susan asked, going over to Peter.

"This is my friend Peter. The man whose house I am renting is his father. Peter's a last-year law student here in Denver. We met over Thanksgiving. He picked me up at the airport, and I'm riding back to Durango with him when I leave."

Susan and Dean went over and shook hands, welcoming him.

"Oh, Jenny, we thought you would stay with us through Christmas and New Year's," Susan said wistfully.

Dean said, "Come on, Susan, Jenny has her life. Let's enjoy her company while she's here and not pressure her."

Jenny smiled gratefully at her grandfather and said, "Peter has to run ... I just wanted him to meet you."

Peter said, "Great to meet you both. Have a great time together, and I'll pick you up on the morning of the twentieth."

"Yeah, let's be in touch if anything changes. Call me to give me the time you want to leave, and I'll be ready."

With that Peter said his good-byes and disappeared into the elevator.

"Let's have some lunch. We hope you are okay with some cold cuts and sub rolls. We have iced tea, water, or coffee if you want," Susan said.

"Sounds good, and iced tea will be fine."

They sat down at the table and made sandwiches. Susan also served lettuce, sliced tomatoes, and some chips and fruit.

Jenny looked at both of her grandparents and said, "I'm so deeply sorry to have been so neglectful of you for so long. I feel very ashamed. You have done so much for me. You have shown me so much love. I'm sorry. Please forgive me." She dropped her eyes.

Dean replied, "Jenny, we figured you had your reasons. Yes, we worried about you. But Michael shared your few letters with us, so we knew you must be okay."

"I'm sorry. It was wrong of me."

"Let's just write it off to experience."

She raised her eyes, reached out, and held Dean's and Susan's hands. "Okay, but there is really no excuse. I was just very thoughtless. Thank you. I love you both so much. It won't happen again. I promise."

"Then let's eat," Susan said and then went on to ask, "So, is Peter a boyfriend?"

"Not really, just a friend. He's really nice and great to hang out with. It's really no big deal."

"He seems nice ... and a nice-looking boy," Susan added.

"Have you seen Michael lately? How's he doing?" Jenny asked, hopefully changing the subject.

Dean responded, "Ah, yes, Michael. I'd have to say we are a little concerned—actually, very worried about him. He stopped by about a month ago. He seemed strange, unfocused; it was hard to talk to him. He said he was having a hard time in school; then he kept saying it wasn't his fault, that everyone was against him."

Susan joined in, "And he didn't look good. He was very thin and had dark circles under his eyes, like he had been studying too hard or maybe hadn't been getting enough rest. We kept asking him if he was okay and if we could help."

Dean said, "And then he started to be a little hostile toward us. He told us it was none of our business and left abruptly in a little huff. We haven't seen or heard from him since."

Jenny thought of his last letter to her, of how disjointed it had seemed. "I have talked with him about me coming here. He's coming up from the Springs, and we're planning on going to dinner tonight. I'm excited to see him again. Will you come with us?"

Dean answered, "Thanks, but we think it will be nice for you two to have some time to yourselves. We will have time with you the next few days. How about you Jenny? Tell us what you have been up to. Are you working?"

Jenny was about to start telling them about everything she was dealing with but thought better about it. They were already worried about Michael and didn't need to be also worried about her, too.

"To be honest, I have spent a lot of time and effort in trying to be a writer, but so far, that hasn't worked out very well for me. I'm renting my little house from a nice man who is a published author, and he's helping me. I've been wanting to get myself gainfully employed. I have time, time that I'd like to be working, doing something. I just haven't a clue what. I want to take a break from trying to write. I want to start exploring after the first of the year to see what's out there that I might be able to do. I really love living in Durango. I have met some nice people whom I cherish and love. I'll certainly keep you posted."

Her grandparents nodded, as if in some sort of quiet agreement, or maybe it was in despair at having an unproductive granddaughter.

The conversation had come to a lull. Susan got up to clean away the dishes, and Jenny jumped up to help. The conversation drifted around from this to that for the rest of the afternoon. Jenny was informed that she and Michael were to be the primary beneficiaries of their will, to which Jenny responded that that was wonderful, but she expected them to be around for a long, long time.

It was getting late, and Jenny excused herself to freshen up and get ready before Michael arrived. She finished right before he arrived.

Chapter 18

Michael got off the elevator, and Jenny was struck by how truly pale and gaunt he appeared. She, like her grandparents, thought he looked very unhealthy.

"Jenny, you look great."

She had her arms outstretched, expecting hug, but none was forthcoming from him. He smiled sullenly at her and greeted Dean and Susan.

"It's so great to see you, Michael, just great."

They all sat and talked for about a half an hour, and Michael got up. "Hey, we have reservations in about ten minutes. The place is close by; we can walk, but we should move on."

Michael seemed more than a little disengaged in the conversation. It was making Jenny uncomfortable and she again asked her grandparents to join them, really wanting their company, but they again declined.

Michael and Jenny went down to the street and walked about a block to the restaurant. On the way, Jenny was asking Michael about his life and getting little information in return. They got to the restaurant and were seated, each ordering drinks.

Jenny asked, "So why did you stay at the Farm so long when you could have left?"

He countered, "And why did you leave so quickly without a good-bye or anything? You just all of a sudden were gone, disappeared. Nobody knew what happened to you, but personally I sort of liked it there. I stayed for two years after you left. Then I decided I wanted to go to college and came to Colorado. At least I said good-bye to Mom and Dad. That's more than you did!" He ended with a note of sarcasm.

"Well, Michael, I left because if I stayed there one more day, I would have died."

"Oh, Jenny, get over yourself! You were always a prude, always by yourself. No wonder everyone called you a 'bitch slut,'" he said with a laugh.

She felt an old chill run down her spine, not liking where this all seemed to be going. She started to feel wary, hating that term, hating everything connected to it, and her brother seemed to think it was a big joke. She wasn't about to back off.

"Yeah, I was a loner because of all that bullying bullshit I had to put up with. That's why I'm now in therapy, trying to get my life back after all the fucking sexual abuse from that bitch, Dory. I so hated her for what she did to us. So don't act like it was all a big joke. It wasn't! You might have thought it was funny, but I sure as hell didn't."

"What the hell are you talking about? Dory was great to us. Sexual abuse! What the hell are you talking about?" he said, laughing.

"Dammit, Michael, how can you even say that? You were there! You saw what she did to me. I saw what she did to you. What don't you get? Did you like fucking her, like her playing with your dick, making you have sex with her when you were, like, fifteen? I saw it, Michael. I was there. I was part of it all! Remember?"

"Awe, Jenny, Dory was good to us. I don't know what the hell you're talking about. And therapy. What's up with that? You were always such a drama queen. God, just get over yourself. I should probably take you and knock some sense into you." His voice rose.

Her blood now turned to ice. He was just like their father.

114

"Oh, fucking knock me around like Julian did to Dory? Beat her or fuck her along with all the other sex shit that went on. You want to knock me around, you skinny-ass piece of shit? You are just fucking like them. Do you beat up your women too? Is that what gets you off? I'm out of here! You're so in denial, and you are sick, Michael. You are a sick fuck, just like the rest of them were." She started to get up.

But Michael was already on his feet, knocking over his chair and kicking the table, their drinks falling onto the floor. He screamed, "Fuck you, you bitch slut! Just fuck you little cunt! You go to hell! I'll kick the shit out of you. Teach you a lesson, you stupid fucking bitch. All fucking women are nothing but stupid whores."

He grabbed his jacket and was gone out the door.

The server rushed over. "Are you okay, hon? Do you want me to call someone?"

Jenny shook with anger, bordering on tears. "Thanks ... I'm okay. I'm so sorry for all that. Here, this should cover everything." She handed her a wad of bills. "I probably need to leave. I'm really so sorry for all that, really. I apologize to everyone for my brother. It's just a little sibling problem."

"Shouldn't you call someone? Are you sure you'll be okay?"

"I'm good. Thanks, I'll be fine. I'm only a block from where I'm staying with my grandparents. I should be fine. Thanks. I appreciate your concern, and I'm really sorry."

She got up, put on her coat, walked outside, and heard Michael from the shadows. "Okay, you bitch slut! I'm going to teach you a lesson right fucking now, you fucking bitch! Run and hide, and I'll find you ... you bitch!"

Jenny saw him starting to come toward her and quickly ducked back inside the restaurant before he got to her. As soon as she got back inside, he stopped, waved a fist at her, and shouted something she didn't quite hear. He disappeared into an alley.

She got out her cell and called 911.

"Nine one one, what is your emergency?"

"It's my brother! He just went crazy. He's threatened to beat me!"

"What's your name and location?"

"My name is Jennifer Morse. I'm hiding in the Bomber Café on the Mall ... on Sixteenth. I'm really scared!"

"Help is on the way. Stay where you are and do not confront him. I repeat, stay away from him! Is there anyone else around you?"

"Yes, I'm in the restaurant, and there are a lot of people in here. I'll stay in here. I should be okay. Thanks! I'll be here."

The same waitress saw her and rushed over. "What's going on? Are you okay? Can I help?"

Jenny started to shake even more and dropped her phone. "I'm scared. He's just crazy! He threatened me, said he wants to beat me."

The waitress picked up her phone, handed it to her. "You'll be safe in here."

Two men standing close by overheard. One said, "Trust me. We're here for you. You're safe. He won't dare touch you."

Others from the restaurant were now gathering.

Within minutes two police cars arrived, light bars flashing. Two uniformed officers came in, and Jenny and the waitperson went to meet them.

"Hi, officers, I'm Jennifer Morse. I made the call. It's my brother.

We had an argument, and he just went nuts and threatened me. I'm scared ... really scared. He ... he just went nuts!" she said, still violently shaking.

The waitress added, "I saw and heard a lot of what went on. He was really being crazy. He threatened her and got up and stormed out. She paid the bill and left but then rushed back in, calling 911. Apparently he was waiting for her outside."

"Thanks, miss. Jennifer, can you describe him?"

"He's about six foot, thin, wearing a brown leather jacket and jeans ... no hat, dark-blond hair. He's my twin."

The officer radioed the information to two other uniforms in the street, who immediately dispersed to look for Michael.

"Let's go out and sit in the car where it's quiet and more private so I can ask you some more questions."

The other officer was getting the waitperson's name and her statement, and a number of the patrons came up to give information as well.

"Jennifer. It's Jennifer, right?" he asked gently.

"Yes, but please call me Jenny." Her voice now shook as well. She was starting to cry. The officer called for a female officer to get to the scene.

The female uniform arrived moments later and sat with Jenny, getting her statement and asking her more questions about Michael and their relationship, about where he lived and what had precipitated the event and some other details. Then she offered her a ride back to the high-rise, which Jenny thankfully accepted.

It was only a little over an hour after she and Michael had left when she rang the security buzzer, was let in, and got off the elevator into the penthouse. Her grandparents were both reading. "Home so soon? Where's Michael?"

Jenny tried to respond but just fell into the sofa and started shaking again, crying with uncontrollable sobs.

Her grandmother came to her, sat, and tried to console her. "Jenny, dear child, what happened? What is wrong?"

After a few minutes, Jenny was finally able to get herself together and said, "It seems like every time I'm here, all I do is cry. I'm really sorry."

"Don't be sorry, darling. What happened? Was it Michael? Did you have a fight?"

"I don't know if I can tell you, if I want you to hear what happened. It was awful! Michael was just awful. I should never have come. I so wanted to see you and Michael, but he's just like Daddy. He hates women, thinks we are stupid and need to be hit and slapped because we are stupid." She started to cry again. "I'm not stupid, Grandma! I'm not stupid. Do you think I'm stupid, Grandma?" She moaned. "I never should have come, Grandma. I'm making you and Grandpa upset just be being here. I make everything so awful. It's all my fault."

Her grandmother held her, at a loss as to what to do or say. Finally, she said, "We are so happy you came and are here; we wanted to see you. You are definitely not stupid; you are a very smart young woman. You cannot be responsible for Michael; we can't possibly imagine what your childhood was like. We really had no idea but are starting to get a better picture as all this unfolds. We both love you so very much; we do love you, more than you can imagine. We want you to feel safe, and you are safe here. You will always be safe with us. I promise you that."

Jenny sat up, looking at Susan. "Thanks, Grandma, I love you both ... you're wonderful to me and have saved me in so many ways, ways you can't ever imagine. I love you."

Dean asked, "Jennifer, would you want something to eat, if you're able? I am guessing you didn't have dinner?"

"Thanks, Grandpa, I am starting to feel hungry—starved actually. Could I have a glass of wine first, please?"

"Of course you can. White or red?"

"White, please, and some of those cold cuts would be fine. Please, I don't want to trouble you. Please don't make a fuss."

She had two glasses of wine, a big sandwich, and some chips. She was feeling better. It was then that she told them everything about her last two years and her therapy. Then she went into some of her childhood but not sharing anything about her sexual abuse, sparing them and herself from that. Dean and Susan were visibly shocked and silent.

Dean finally said, "Jennifer, we had no idea. And therapy? What can we do to help? Can we do anything? Can we help pay? Is this therapist any good? Do we—"

Jenny held up her hand to stop him. "Grandpa, I'm really doing okay. My therapist, Joan, is wonderful. I have support from some wonderful people I've met, some really close and dear friends. And I can afford to pay from your generous support. Right now, it's Michael I'm worried about. I've learned a lot in the last few months. What I saw tonight—"

Dean said, "We will do whatever we can to help both of you. If you ever need our help for anything—"

"I'm really okay, Grandpa, really I am. I'm really tired right now. I know it's only eight thirty, but if I could be excused, I really need to rest."

Good-nights and hugs were exchanged, and she went to her room and took a long, hot bath, trying to wash Michael and his anger off her. It took a long time.

Chapter 19

She was in her sweats, ready for bed, and decided to call Joan. She needed to talk about the disaster with her brother. She made herself a cup of chamomile tea, curled up in her bed, and called. Joan answered the second ring.

"Hi, Joan, it's Jenny. Can you talk? I need to talk to you. I really do."

"Yeah, sure, Jenny. What's up?"

And Jenny told her about all that had happened earlier, everything in detail. How frightened she was of her brother. How she just wanted to be back home.

Joan was quiet for a few moments. "Okay, here's what I think. First off, we need to get a restraining order against Michael. From what you have told me, he seems like a loose cannon, and you could possibly be in serious danger. With the report you have given the police and that many witnesses, it shouldn't be a problem to get one. I will start on it first thing tomorrow morning. You can sign it when you get back here."

"But won't that just make him angrier?"

"Jenny, he's already angry from the sounds of it. This is abuse, Jenny. This is bullying—pure, plain, and simple. He is an abusive man. He fits every profile of an abusive man. You could be in danger, serious danger. Jenny, I have dealt with abused women for over fifteen years. I know! You are sounding exactly like the abused woman you are in so many, many ways. Yeah, he will be angry, maybe angrier being served with a restraint. So let him. Secondly, get back here as soon as you can. We have a lot of work to do, actually a lot more work than I thought. Are you riding back with Peter?"

"Yeah, but not for three more days."

"Then try to get a flight out tomorrow. Have your grandparents take you to the airport. You need to be with someone at all times until you are through security. Please trust me on this. You could be in danger. He most likely could be stalking you. You stood up to him, and that really pisses guys like him off. You made him feel powerless. He wants his power back, and he needs to beat you up, or do worse, so he can feel strong again. Trust me! He could be very dangerous."

Jenny had stiffened up and wasn't relaxed anymore. Her heart raced, and her breathing quickened. Talking to Joan had made her realize even more how much danger she could be in. She wanted to be back home in her little house, with William next door. She knew he would protect her.

"Okay, Joan. I'll see what I can do about getting home tomorrow. Thanks. You are the best. I'll keep you posted. Love you."

"Yes, please keep me posted. Love you too."

And they cut off their phones.

Jenny immediately called Peter, who answered groggily, "Yeah, hello?"

"Peter, it's me, Jenny. Did I wake you? Sorry, it's late, I guess. I wasn't paying attention to time. It's been a crazy night. Hey, my plans have changed."

She gave him a short version of the night's drama. "I'm going to try to catch a flight out to Durango tomorrow. I'm really scared, Peter. I'll see you in Durango."

"Whoa, wait, wait! Wait a minute. Flight out? This guy is threatening you? No way! I'll pick you up tomorrow at eleven, and we'll head back. I can get everything done here that I need to in the morning, and we can be out of here. We'll be in Durango tomorrow night and have dinner together at The Tavern. No problem."

"Wait, Peter. I thought you had finals and stuff. I can't ask you to do this."

"Bullshit, Jenny! No argument! I can seriously get everything finished up and organized to be out of here in the morning. I'll be there at eleven. Be ready. I was really sort of killing time because I wanted you to have time here with your family and not rush you. I am really sorry all this happened. Really sorry."

"Thanks, Peter. Okay then, I'll be here and ready at eleven. See you then. And thanks so much, Peter. I owe you one."

She cut off, crawled under the covers, and thought of Peter. She liked that he seemed concerned and protective of her. It made her feel secure, and her heart swelled, thinking about it. She really was starting to like this guy. Jenny slept well, dreaming of Peter and her having a candlelight dinner together when he told her he was in love with her.

Morning came, and she was up early, missing Cat and her early morning purring. She did some yoga, meditated, packed her bag, then went out to the living room, where she found her grandparents having coffee and reading the morning's *Denver Post*.

Susan greeted her with "Good morning, Jennifer. There's fresh coffee. Did you sleep okay?"

"Thanks. Yes, I did." She went to the kitchen, poured herself a cup, and went in to try to explain that she was leaving at eleven and why. Peter was going take her back. They were understandably upset and concerned. She told them about her conversation last night with Joan and went on to try to explain all the implications of what was happening, including the danger and her fear.

"But Jennifer, I can't believe Michael would ever hurt you."

"I know, Grandma, but it's not a chance I'm willing to take. I saw way too much violence between Daddy and Dora. I know what it can be like. I don't need it in my life. Please believe me. I've seen and talked to some of the battered women at the shelter. It's never pretty."

"We understand," Dean said. "It is not easy for us, but we trust your judgment. We hate to have you leave. It is just that we want to spend some time with you, be with you, and enjoy your company."

"I know, Grandpa. Me too. We'll be together soon. I promise. I'll be back.Why don't you come down to Durango? There is so much I want to show you. I want you to meet William and my friends. We could ride the train to Silverton when spring comes. It would be so much fun."

"We'll plan on it, Jenny, this spring."

"I so want to, just to have you—" She stopped, her voice shaking, and she wiped a tear. "My real family. I love you both so much. I miss you so much already." She hugged them both like she would never let go.

Chapter 20

It was right at eleven o'clock and the buzzer rang. It was Peter. Dean rang him in. He came off the elevator and went immediately to Jenny. "Are you okay, I worried about you all night. This thing with your brother scared me. Are you sure you are all right? He didn't hurt you?"

"I'm fine, Peter, really. He didn't touch me. It was a real ugly scene, though, really ugly. I really appreciate your concern."

He turned to Susan and Dean. "I'm sorry. I didn't even say hello. I was just so concerned about her. I was scared. She is a really special friend."

"No worries, Peter," Dean said. "It is good to see you so soon again—too soon, really. We were hoping to have more time, but we are understanding more and more about what is going on. We hope to see you again. Please stop by when you are back in town. You are always welcome here."

"Thanks, Dean. I appreciate it, and I will endeavor to do so."

"That would be nice. We could talk about the law. I was an attorney for all of my life, and it would be fun to talk."

"That would be great. I will look forward to it. We have to get on the road, Jenny. There is some weather coming in, and I want to get over Wolf Creek Pass before it hits. Time to rock 'n' roll."

Good-byes were said, and they were in Peter's Subaru and heading out of Denver west on 285. It was a beautiful day with bright sun on new snow as they drove through the foothills up to Kenosha Pass. There was some idle talk about the end of Peter's semester, about Jenny's grandparents, and about Dean being an attorney. They intentionally avoided talking about Michael.

Jenny and Peter were coming up to Buena Vista and decided to stop for a potty break and get some coffee and snacks. Jenny offered to drive, but Peter insisted that she just sit back and enjoy.

They had been quiet for a long time. Peter looked over at her. "Jenny, I like you. I really like you a lot, and I, well, I guess I want to see you, maybe like more than friends. I really feel clumsy right now—duh—but dammit! I really want ... well, I—"

She reached over and put her hand on his. "I know, Peter. Thanks. You're the most wonderful guy I have ever known or ever expected to. Right now all I want to do is to get to know you better and to savor every moment. Okay?"

"Yeah, exactly what I wanted to say. Ah, thanks. I want to be with you. Let's see how it goes. No strings. Okay?"

"Yeah, let's see how it goes."

Jenny felt her heart open with a wonderful warmth that flowed down into her belly as an unknown, never-before-felt tingle. *Was this what D. H. Lawrence was trying to describe, what Connie, Lady Chatterley, felt? It is a good feeling. I like it.*

She felt so close to Peter right then and reached over and put her hand on his neck.

They rode in silence, listening to music, until after Salida, when Jenny broke the meditation. "Peter, there's some things I need to tell you, things you need to be aware of right now. I hesitate to tell you, but—" She paused for a moment to drum up some courage. "I have a boatload of baggage that I'm carrying with me, a *big* boatload, maybe several boatloads.

I'm dealing with a lot of shit. I was sexually and emotionally abused as a child by the woman I thought was my mother.

"Michael's my twin, and yeah, I now apparently have him to deal with. Looks like he's in way worse shape than I am. I could go on, but that is pretty much it in a nutshell, the short version. I just want you to know what you are getting into with me. I may not be everything you think I am. You are dealing with a very vulnerable and insecure girl—yeah, in many ways a damaged girl.

"I want you to know that you can bail right now before it gets more involved. I'd rather have you say right now that I might be more than you think you can handle. We all have our limits. I know.

"So please, think about this and give a lot of consideration to what I am telling you. I'm not kidding! This is some serious shit I am coping with. I intend to keep going with counseling and so on, but there are no guarantees. I hope someday I'll be better and be done with it, but ... no guarantees."

Both of them were quiet for a long time; then she added, "Just don't lead me on and then break my heart. I don't think I could handle that. Seriously, I don't."

Both were again silent for a long while. Jenny silently prayed that she hadn't frightened him away. *He needed to know. Yes, he needed to know.*

Finally, Peter spoke. "Wow. I knew there were some things from your past. My dad alluded to it but no details. I appreciate you telling me. And, to be honest, you have given me a lot to think about. I really like you and want to spend time with you, but, I ... I don't want to hurt you either, especially after what you just told me. I don't know. You have so much to deal with. I would like to be of help. I don't know if I could help or just be a hindrance.

"Please, let's enjoy our time while I'm here over the Christmas holidays. Let's, let's—oh, hell. I don't know, Jenny.

I just don't know. It has to be scary for you. I can't imagine how hard it must be for you. I just don't know. It's scary for me right now. I don't want to get in the way. Let's leave it to rest until tomorrow at least and talk again so I can think it over. Okay?"

"Okay, yeah, sure ... tomorrow," she responded and was quiet, mulling over his response. It wasn't what she had hoped for at all. She realized he wasn't ready for her.

After a quick stop in South Fork, they started over Wolf Creek Pass just as it was starting to get dark. The pass was clear, but they ran into light snow west of Pagosa Springs, and it got heavier as they drove toward Durango.

Jenny said, "I think we should skip our planned dinner in Durango and just head up valley and get home. This isn't looking real promising. What do you think?"

"Yeah, it's just going to get worse. There are some protein bars and apples in a sack on the seat behind your seat. I'd like one of each, please, and please help yourself."

"Thanks. Yeah, I am getting hungry," she said flatly and turned and grabbed the sack. Both were quiet again while they ate their dinner.

It was nearly a whiteout by the time they got up to William's compound. They got out, and Peter walked Jenny to her door. He looked at her and gave her a little hug, kissing her on the cheek. "You are the best, Jenny. You are a strong woman. I'm really sorry for you, sorry for everything. See you tomorrow." He let go, turned, and walked to his father's house.

She went inside, closed the door, and stood there, leaning back against it. She let her bag drop to the floor and sighed, replaying the last two days in her mind, especially the ride home, what was said and what wasn't. It was what wasn't said, what could have been said, that weighed so heavily on her. *He feels sorry for me? Gotta think it over? Screw him!*

Finally she walked into her bedroom, kicked off her shoes, undressed, and fell into bed, emotionally drained.

She dreamed she was wandering on foot, lost in a terrible snowstorm; it was night, pitch black, very cold. She was freezing; she knew she was going to die. She saw lights coming toward her closer; then she saw it was her own Jeep. It stopped, the passenger door opened, and she looked in and saw herself driving. "Get in, Jenny. I will save you."

When she got in, it was so warm; she knew she would be okay. They drove off into the night sky toward the dawn, breaking over the mountains. Jenny awoke with a start, peeking out her window at the dawn breaking over the mountains.

She lay there, confused about where she was. Was her dream real, or was this real? Finally, her head started making sense out of where she was and that she was dreaming, but it was so real. Then everything about the past few days erupted slowly in her head, like a bad movie in slow motion.

Chapter 21

Jenny checked the time. Eight thirty. It was late for her. It was Friday; she had missed yoga. She wanted to see Helen and talk to her; she needed to see Joan. She desperately needed to see Joan. She jumped out of bed and found her phone but with a dead battery. "Damn!" She hooked it up to the charger, undressed, and went into a long, hot shower, again trying to wash it all away. Finished, her phone was charged enough to call Joan. The receptionist answered.

"Hi, this is Jenny Morse. Would Joan have any time to see me today?" she asked desperately "I really need to talk with her. Please say that she does! Please?" She ended with more of a call for help than a request.

"Ah, let's see. Yes, she has an hour at eleven this morning. Will that work for you?"

"Yes, yes, thank you so much! Yes, thank you! I'll be there."

She got dressed and made some coffee and toast with peanut butter for her breakfast, not remembering how little she had eaten yesterday. She was already too preoccupied with wanting to remember everything. She got her journal and wrote everything she could remember, bringing it all back to life. It made her very sad and frightened about her life, about Peter, about her grandparents, and especially about Michael. It was already ten thirty. Time to go. She grabbed her jacket and phone, and raced out the door, almost knocking over Peter on her way out.

"Hey, good morning. How are you doing? Have time to talk about yesterday?"

"No time right now. Gotta go. See ya later."

She was in her Jeep and gone, leaving a confused Peter standing on her porch with his mouth still mouthing words that weren't there.

She broke the speed limit all the way in, arriving for her appointment at 10:45. It turned out that there hadn't been that much snow overnight, and roads were already clear, melting dry under the Colorado sun at an elevation of seven thousand feet.

She had so much she wanted to talk about, to get some answers for, and to find some help processing it all. It was more than she could deal with.

Joan popped out of her office about five minutes later. "Hi, Jenny, you made it back."

"Yeah, around eight o'clock last night, later than we planned with the snow. Oh, God, I am so happy you have time. So much happened, so much to talk about. I don't know where to start."

"Whoa, slow down. I can skip my lunch hour if I need to; I wondered after your phone call, so tell me what's going on."

Jenny went into some greater detail about her brother and their ill-fated dinner date.

"That does not sound very good, very scary. I called our attorney this morning about a restraining order. He was going to call the Denver police and have them fax him a copy of the report. He hasn't gotten back to me yet. What else?"

Jenny talked in length about her grandparents and that they were so good to her, that they might come and visit. Then there was what she dreaded to talk about or even think about: her conversation with Peter and his response.

"Well, Jenny, it was very brave of you, and you did the right thing about informing him about your life. I can't imagine it was easy for you to do. And his response, as you describe it, doesn't surprise me at all. You are a lot for him to handle. The beginning of any relationship is usually very heady and sometimes very disillusioning. I am sure he had already put you up on a pedestal as being perfect in every way—flawless, pure, like the proverbial fresh flower. What you told him had to shatter any idealistic notion he was carrying around; that he came over when you were leaving could be a good sign."

"Or a very bad sign."

"Yeah, possibly. Let's hope not. From what you have told me about him, he seems grown up and mature. That is good. You should talk with him when you get home, if you can, to save yourself from worrying more than you already are."

"Yeah, I'll call him before I leave for home and see if he has time or even wants to after I shrugged him off this morning."

She was about to continue when Joan's phone rang. "It's our attorney." She picked up, listening intently for about five minutes. Then she thanked him. "Will you fax me a copy of that report? Good, I'll watch for it." She cut off and looked at Jenny for a moment. "It is worse than we thought, Jenny. I am sorry to have to tell you this, but Michael has been arrested and is in jail." She then related what she'd found out about Michael's interaction with her grandparents.

"Apparently, your grandparents had just finished lunch and were about to go out for the afternoon when their buzzer rang. It was Michael. They let him in, and he charged out of the elevator, screaming at them, looking for you. I guess his language was very profane, and he was completely out of control.

"Your grandfather told him to leave, but Michael just continued on, going into bedrooms, looking in closets, just being nuts, screaming he was going to kill you for calling the police.

"Your grandmother was on the phone, calling 911, and Michael started for her when your grandfather grabbed him and put him on the floor with his knee in his back and holding his arm like he was going to break it.

"Your grandfather held Michael, who was screaming profanities at both of them, until a few minutes later when two police officers entered and cuffed Michael. One of the officers dragged him to the elevator and was joined by two more officers. The three of them took him away, with Michael still screaming, totally of control. The first officer asked your grandparents about what all happened. They explained everything to him, including last night and what happened to you. The officer said they were aware of that and had been keeping an eye out for Michael. He was being arrested and would be charged with assault and making serious threats of bodily harm. Your grandparents agreed to press charges against Michael. The officer said that they would be notified of what was going on and also gave them his card, ending by saying Michael would be booked and held until court on Monday. They could call the station any time to check on his status."

"Oh shit! Are my grandparents okay? Are they all right?"

"Yes, somewhat shaken up emotionally, I suppose, but they weren't physically hurt or anything. They are fine. But it gets even worse. Hang on— this won't be easy for you, but there were five outstanding warrants for Michael down in the Springs. He apparently attacked and beat five women, severely beat two of them so bad they had to be hospitalized: four students and one of his professors. The police had a BOLO out for him. He was hiding out in Denver for the last few weeks, flying under the radar, until all this came down with you and your grandparents. He is not being a model prisoner at all. He can't seem to help himself by keeping his mouth shut. He was just going on about how you and your grandmother are nothing but 'stupid bitches' that need some sense knocked into them, how those stupid girls in Colorado Springs were 'bitch whores' who didn't appreciate how great he was. They deserved to get slapped around. Didn't anyone realize that he was helping them to understand how to please their men?" She trailed off, looking at Jenny.

"You were very lucky. We don't know what is going to happen to him right now, but I would say he is definitely not well and needs a lot of help. He shouldn't be let out of incarceration. I would have to say that he needs to be institutionalized rather than imprisoned. We'll have to wait and see. In any case, we should have no problem getting you a restraining order against him, which may be moot, because he may not be out from behind bars for a while, maybe quite a while."

Jenny seemed to be looking right through Joan, out into some other place. *Shit, this is all my fault. If I hadn't gone to Denver, none of this would have ever happened. I should have never gone. I just messed things up.* Finally she refocused and asked, with panic in her voice, "So, is there anything I can do to help him? He's my brother! He needs my help! I need to go back up to Denver and see what I can do. Maybe if I could see him ... talk to him."

"No, Jenny! No! Right now, there is nothing you can do. Nothing. I repeat, nothing. You need to stay here and get yourself grounded. You are in no shape to do anything but try to help yourself. I can understand you wanting to help him, but there is nothing you can do. Understand?"

"But I could tell them it was all a mistake, what happened with me, tell them I lied, tell them none of it really happened."

"Jenny, there were—how many witnesses?—who corroborated what happened at the restaurant? Then there was what happened with your grandparents, not to mention the warrants from Colorado Springs. Jenny, there is nothing you can do. Get that into your head. I am sorry. I am truly sorry, but there is nothing. You. Can. Do! Are you hearing me? He is in trouble. But you have to think of yourself first. It is not your fault. None of this is your fault."

"Yeah, Joan, I know, I know. It's just, everything is so crazy. Everything's falling apart. Everything I am trying so hard to make better just gets worse. I ... I ... I'm just so, so mixed up with everything: my life, Peter, Michael, everyone. I just want to run away. Everything was so much better when I just was with myself. I was able to keep the demons away. Now they are eating me alive." There were tears running down her cheeks.

Joan handed her some tissues. "This is hard, Jenny, very hard. We talked about that early on. I think I said it might get worse before it gets better. It has definitely gotten worse. Those demons have had a long time to grow, fester, and get strong, but you are stronger, much stronger, and we are not going to let them run you out of Dodge. We will conquer those darn demons and get through this together. Please, please believe me when I say this, but we will. I promise. Okay?"

"Yeah, thanks, Joan. Yeah, I know what you are saying is true. I appreciate the faith you have in me," she said, smiling weakly. "I probably need to leave. I've taken up most of your lunch break."

"That's no problem, but I want to be sure you are okay. Don't do anything stupid on me now."

"I won't. I promise. My head is feeling more clear. I want to try to catch Helen. She's always good at grounding me."

"Okay, get out of here then. Please call me and let me know how you are and if you talk to Peter. Promise. Either promise me, or I'll send the sheriff after you. He's a personal friend and will do what I ask," she finished, smiling.

"I'll call for sure then," she bantered back.

"Great. I will be anxious to hear how you are doing."

"Thanks, Joan. Thanks so very much for ... for everything. Love you."

"Love you too, sweetheart. Love you too. Don't forget group session Tuesday night."

"See you Tuesday for our session and then group." Jenny grabbed her coat and was out the door.

Jenny hurried to Helen's studio, hoping she was there and not at lunch. When she got there, the door was open, so she poked her head in. "Helen, are you here?"

"Yes, I'm in the office. Come on in, Jenny. I thought you were in Denver until Sunday."

"Oh, Helen, so much has happened. I just spent since eleven talking to Joan about all the shit that happened. So much shit seems to be coming down on me I think I need an umbrella. Have you had lunch? I'm starved. I need to talk."

"I haven't eaten, and yes, I am starved also. Let's go." She got up and grabbed her coat, and they walked out.

It was a lovely day out, unseasonably warm after last night's snowstorm. People were walking around in shorts.

"Shorts in December. A little excessive, don't you think?" Helen said.

"Yeah, but it is such a warm day. Maybe too warm?"

"Very dry. All we really had was that freak snowstorm in early October. Not much since. Even the mountains don't have much. It will make for a dry summer unless we pick up some storms after the first of the year. Just have to see."

They got to The Tavern, their favorite lunch restaurant and were seated; each ordered water and a glass of wine.

"So, Jenny, what's going on?"

Jenny leaned over and started to unload. It was easier the second time. It seemed more clear and more manageable. The server returned with their wines, and they ordered quickly without even looking up; Jenny continued nonstop. Helen sat, listening intently with her eyes wide, amazed as the drama was unfolded to her.

Finally Jenny concluded, "And that's about it. Yeah, that's about it, I guess. Everything is all so messed up. What should I do Helen, especially about Peter? I thought I might really like him, and it's probably over before anything even really started. Oh well, maybe it's really for the best. A guy in my life is just another added thing to have to deal with. There's just so much right now."

"I know what you are saying, but one positive thing is that he was there to talk to you this morning, so he must not have totally given up on you."

"Yeah, I know. I really cut him short. I was in such a hurry to get to my meeting with Joan. Maybe I should call him. What do you think? I'll be back home in an hour. It'll wait, I guess."

Helen said, "You have so much on your plate. I think maybe if you look at it in pieces, if you can break it up: Michael, Peter, your grandparents. Maybe you could deal with one piece at a time. Just a thought."

"Yeah, good advice. Makes sense. I'll give it some thought. But to change the subject, I want to find a job, find something to do. I have too much time. All I seem to do is sit around, writing in my journal and worrying about everything. Do you have any suggestions? I don't really have any skills. A degree in rhetoric and literature, and camping for two years, doesn't say much."

"What would you want to do? What do you enjoy?"

"I don't know. I thought I wanted to be a writer, but my head is so messed up that when I sit to try to write something, poems or prose, all the uglies are there, banging around inside. I can't stay focused. I need something external to keep me on course, I guess."

Their food arrived. They each ordered an iced tea, took a moment to start eating, and continued.

"How about trying to get something in a sports store? There are at least five or six in town. You are very active and athletic."

"I could try, but I'm not sure I can deal with people that well. I still feel really uncomfortable around strangers. I get scared. I guess I need a lot of reassurance. Not sure I would get that working for somebody that doesn't know me or my history, and if they did, they probably wouldn't hire me. I still have so much to work out."

"Well, would you feel comfortable working for me, at the studio? Vicky is leaving after New Year's. She and her husband are moving to Denver. He landed a new and better job up there. I will need a replacement."

"Wow, that would be great, but I can't teach yoga. I have no creds at all. And I don't want to leave here right now to go to India to study yoga. Good idea, though, and thanks for the offer."

"Now just wait. First of all, you don't have to go to India to study. There are several schools here in the west that you can go to study and get certified to teach. Plus there are any number of workshops you can go to for more advanced training and practice—that is, if you really get serious about yoga. But we won't worry about that right now.

"What I was thinking is that you could do the beginner's classes. There are three a week. I would move Sara to the intermediate level. She would like that. You are a quick study; you are already at the intermediate level, and I can teach you what you need to know, if you are ready for some hard work and a quick learning curve. I would need you to start in early January. The pay isn't spectacular; it's a percentage based on the number of students in your class. I have several good books I can lend on yoga, body structure, and musculature."

"Wow, can I let you know, like tomorrow? This sounds wonderful. I'm not sure about teaching a group, but I guess everybody would be busy doing their yoga, that I would just be a facilitator. I don't know. Let me think on it tonight."

"Tomorrow would be fine."

They were finishing up; they paid their bill and got up and left. They said their good-byes and went their separate ways.

Jenny got home. She was drained from today, from Denver, from the ride back with Peter, from everything. She was tired and felt really cranky, so she went for a run. Fifteen miles later, she was home. The run and a hot shower had washed the day away.

She wanted to return some books to Will's library and went over. No one was home, so she went in and replaced them on the shelves. She was on her way out when she noticed a sheaf of papers left on the coffee table. It looked like an outline, so she snooped to see whether Will was starting on a new book. She started to read it and thought her head was going to explode.

Fuck, this is about me, all about me, my life, stuff I told him! What the fuck? He's writing a book about me. Me! That fucking bastard! Stealing my life for one of his trash fucking books. Lying bastard, saying he wanted to help me. I'm so stupid. Fuck these people. I'm done!

She ran back to her house, slammed the door, and fell on the floor, pounding her fists in anger, and sobbing. After her immediate wave of anger abated, she lay there for a long time, considering her options, what she should do. Who was she able to trust? Helen? No, she would be in Will's camp. Joan? Probably. Kelly? Maybe. Peter? No way.

There was a knock on her door. She ignored it, but the knocks continued, and then the next knocks and the next. Finally, she said, "Go fucking away! I want to be fucking alone. I'm tired. Just please go the fuck away!" She heard who ever it was walk away, their footsteps crunching on the gravel drive.

That night she dreamed of being in the mountains, alone in her solitude from last summer, and the whole world disappeared and everyone in it. She was wonderfully alone, by herself, no one in her life. It felt good.

She awoke late. "Shit. It's eight o'clock. I'm becoming a slacker." She shook herself awake and started to do some yoga; then the knocking started. "Dammit, please just go away."

"Okay all ready," she heard Peter yell, and it was quiet.

Thank you, she thought and continued for an hour, having a breakfast of an orange and a peanut butter sandwich and coffee. She curled up on her couch with her journal and started to put her thoughts down. Her first words were "I am feeling overwhelmed and feel like I am suffocating. It seems that every time I start to trust someone, I get screwed!" She stopped and reflected on what she had just written.

Then there was another knock on her door, and she heard Will. "Jenny, are you okay? Peter told me some of what went on. Do you want to talk?"

Jenny went ballistic. She flung open the door. "You fucking bastard! I saw your goddamned outline yesterday. You're writing a book about me? You son of a bitch! How fucking dare you! You are a lying cheat just like every man I've ever come across! Get the fuck away from me!"

Started to slam the door in his face, but he caught it. "Jenny, let me explain. I was writing that outline for you. I thought maybe you could do your own story, like a memoir. It was just a thought to try to help you start writing. Truly!"

"Bullshit! I thought I could trust you, and you betray me like this. You could have told me, goddamn it! We could have talked about it. Please leave me the fuck alone! I have to think."

"But Jenny, please—"

Now she was screaming. "Get the fuck away from me! Just go the fuck away! Leave me alone!" She turned away and started toward her bedroom, hearing the door close and footsteps walking away.

She sat, trying to calm herself down, and came to a decision.

Fuck 'em all! Time for a road trip.

She got dressed, packed up some camping gear, grabbed the passport she'd gotten when she thought she might go to Europe after college, and wrote a note. "Out of town. Don't wait up. Fuck you all." She stuck it to her front door, threw her stuff into her Jeep, and headed south toward Arizona.

Fuck 'em all. I'm so outa here. Fuck Peter, fuck Michael, and everyone else. Fuck Christmas! Fuck New Year's! Fuck everything! I am fucking tired of everybody, everything. I need just to be alone.

She turned off her cell phone, found some vintage rock on the radio, and cranked it up.

Somewhat calmed down by the time she got to Durango, she decided to stop at Desert and Mountain Outfitters, and bought a water filter, some freeze-dried food, two water bottles, a new backpack stove and fuel, a large cooler, a few other necessities, and maps of Arizona and New Mexico.

"Heading out? Where to?" the cashier asked.

"South, the desert. Just me and my Jeep."

"Make sure you take an extra can of gas and water if you are heading out in the desert very far. Don't get stranded.

And tell somebody where you are going and when you will return."

She considered this and asked where would be a good place to get some gas and water cans.

"I'd try the four-wheel drive accessory place south on Highway 3. You'll see it, right on the left side ... sort of a used-car lot too."

"Thanks." She paid and started to leave.

"Safe travels and have fun. Wish I were going," he said with a chuckle.

Jenny smiled back at him and left, threw her new gear into the back, and headed to the accessories place. She found it easily and went in, told the saleswoman what she thought she needed. She ended up buying a gas can, a water can, a heavy-duty jack, a Thule top storage box, and an outside rack to mount the gas and water cans, the jack, and the Thule. She decided against a front winch, which was suggested. She paid her bill and waited while a mechanic mounted it all. An hour later she was headed west on Highway 160 toward the Four Corners and Arizona.

Chapter 22

The vast emptiness of the Diné (Navajo) Nation swallowed her up; it helped clear her mind, her anger, her frustrations. She stopped in a little town called Kayenta for gas and a potty stop. She was curious about the interesting rocks she saw behind a ridge to the north and asked a person at the gas station. He told her it was Monument Valley. She should go up there. It was beautiful. But she had gotten a late start and wanted to keep going. She got to Flagstaff in late afternoon and stopped again for a break. She checked her map; she could make it to Sedona right after dark, which she decided to do. Flagstaff was too big and busy.

An hour later she was in Sedona. She found a motel and had some dinner in a Mexican restaurant.

After dinner, she walked around the town for an hour or so, went back to her room, and wrote in her journal about where she was, where she was going, and why. She read until ten and went to sleep.

She slept deeply, dreaming about being somewhere in a place of red stone and meeting a strange man who took her to a magical place where she saw herself as a glowing, rainbow-colored orb that flew over a spectral desert sea.

Waking around seven, she did some yoga and went for breakfast. The day was already warm with a bright sun soaking into the red landscape that surrounded the small town. She was feeling in a funk and had lost her interest in camping out. She felt alienated, listless, lacking of energy and motivation. She walked the main street, still feeling pissed about all the people and problems she'd left behind. She had walked this street last night, but now, even though it was Sunday, it was coming alive with some stores opening now for business. It was very much a tourist town with T-shirt and souvenir shops everywhere and shops selling rocks. *Who would buy rocks?*

She continued walking, looking in shop windows, checking out a bookstore, but she was feeling so sad and depressed. She finally went back to her room and fell asleep. She woke and read for a while. She didn't feel like eating, so she crawled back into bed and lay there awake, tossing, her mind racing.

I was such a fool. How could I have gotten involved? I was so stupid to trust anyone.

Then she felt sad and lonesome, remembering the nice times she recently had with everyone. How happy she was then. She thought of how pissed she was at Will, her brother, everyone. Then how crazy and confused she was feeling. She was starting to panic. She remembered her sleeping pills and antidepressants Joan had wanted her to have. She had seen the doctor Joan had sent her to for a checkup early on. She knew she had them in her toiletries. She found them, and as much as she hated drugs, she reluctantly took the prescribed dosage and went back to bed. Her mind slowly stopped running wild. She calmed down and fell asleep into a dreamless night.

Her funk continued the next day. She went out for breakfast and was starved from not eating the night before. After she had eaten, she walked down the main street again. She noticed she was in front of a rock shop. She noticed a woman had just opened up, and she went in.

There were all sorts of rocks, tapestries on the walls, a display rack of incense and holders; there was an area with statues, one she recognized as being similar to the Buddha at the yoga studio. There were several shelves of books. She wandered about, curious about it all.

A fortysomething woman, with long dark hair streaked with gray and wearing a long, flowing, silky, purple-pink dress, appeared from the back.

"Hi, how can I help you? Looking for anything in particular?" she asked with a warm smile.

"Not really looking for anything in particular. I was just interested in your place since I have never been in a rock store before."

"Well, we have stones," the woman corrected her. "Are you familiar with crystals and the energy some stones have to offer?"

"Really? Ah … no, ah, not at all. Don't know anything about stones or energy."

"Come over here and let me show you some things."

She took Jenny's hand and led her to the rear of the store. She showed Jenny a clear stone, about six inches tall and maybe two inches across the base. It had six sides and was tapered to a point.

"It's beautiful!" Jenny exclaimed. "Wow."

'This is a quartz crystal, a very nice one. Now let me show you this." She handed Jenny a smaller version of the same stone with a five-inch very light chain attached to the base with a small rounded version of the clear stone on the other end. She told Jenny to hold the round stone with the tips of her fingers with the pointed one hanging down.

"This is called a 'pendulum.' Now hold it over this one I just showed you. Hold it as still as you can, and let's see what happens."

Jenny felt sort of funny, but she obeyed, holding it as still as she could. Slowly the crystal on the end of the chain began to wiggle and then to started moving in a clockwise direction around the larger crystal on the counter. It moved faster in an increasingly larger circular motion.

"Oh, hon, it likes you. You make it happy. Look how strong the pendulum is spinning. That is a huge circle of energy. Here, let's try it on this one." She got out another out.

Jenny tried it and got the same circular motion, but it wasn't nearly as strong. She tried yet another, and the pendulum started going counter-clockwise. The woman snatched it away. "No, no, no, not this one for sure."

"So, this all very interesting, but, so, why would I ever want a crystal? What are they good for?"

"Well, they can be used for healing, for focus during meditation, for clarity and help in making decisions, just to name a few things."

"Hmm. Interesting ... very interesting."

"I also do readings and energy healing. Interested? I see some things in your aura. Are you having any difficulties with some things from your past ... and present? Maybe?" the woman asked with a warm smile.

Jenny considered this. As weird as all this was, she found herself feeling unusually comfortable with and drawn towards this woman.

"By the way, my name is Amanda."

"I'm Jenny. Nice to meet you, Amanda. So what does a 'reading' accomplish?"

"Well, I can see areas that may need clearing or healing or both for that matter. I could then help clear away any issues that might be blocking you. I do see some dark spots in your aura."

Jenny was somewhat familiar with auras, energy fields that emanate from the body, but wasn't familiar with anyone ever being able to see one. *Holy shit, if she only knew.*

"So, want to give it a shot? Try it out. We can see what happens."

"This isn't like fortune-telling or anything, is it?"

"No, no, not at all. It's just about clearing away negative energy."

"How much money are we talking about?"

"Since you're a first timer, I'll do a reading and clearing for one hundred dollars, and I also want you to have that crystal. It likes you, so I'll throw it in. I want you to have it. Is that okay?"

"I guess so. Let's do it. What do I have to do?"

"Let me put up my 'Closed, Be Back Soon' sign, and we will go into the back room."

Jenny began to feel a little nervous about this whole thing; she felt herself beginning to perspire and wanted to leave. It seemed a little woo woo for her. But, at the same time, she was excited about a new experience, something that might take her mind off the anger and confusion she was feeling. Something about Amanda made her feel good, so she decided to hang in with it and see what might happen.

Amanda led Jenny into a nice, quiet room in the back of the store. Amanda lit some candles and asked whether Jenny minded incense. "Some people are allergic. I like it. Helps clear any bad energy in the space."

Jenny said it would be fine. She was already feeling a calm warmth in her solar plexus; her breathing relaxed, and her busy mind became very quiet.

Amanda asked her to lie down on a long, padded table like a bed, except it was higher. She got Jenny comfortable with a pillow and some support under her knees.

"Now, Jenny, just relax and breathe normal. This won't hurt, I promise."

Jenny was very relaxed by now and closed her eyes; she felt a nice warmth wash over her. All was quiet for a time. Jenny knew Amanda was moving about. She never felt any touching, but somehow she sensed Amanda's hands moving above her. Something, like a feather, was caressing her. She felt herself calming down to the point that she was totally relaxed; her mind was clear, like sometimes when she meditated.

Sometime later, Amanda said very softly, "Okay Jenny, I am seeing some sort of terrible trauma in your past, like a dark cloud that you carry with you. Would you like me to release this negative energy from you?"

Jenny was so relaxed she found she could barely talk, mumbling. "Ah, sure. Clear everything away. Please."

By this time, Jenny's breathing was so slow and shallow that it was almost imperceptible. She felt a lightness come over her, something she couldn't remember ever feeling before, almost like she might float off the table.

After several more minutes, Amanda said very quietly and softly, "Okay, Jenny, there was a lot of trauma. I cleared away all that I could. But there was a lot of dark stuff. I don't know if I got it all. I cleansed your aura as best I could and gave you healing energy to your body, mind, and spirit. I did what I could. Whatever has been bothering you should be hopefully mostly gone, but there was a lot and might well be more. You might want to come back. Take your time and come out front when you are ready; no rush. Excuse me. I need take a moment to go and cleanse myself now. I'll see you when you're ready." Jenny felt Amanda leave the room.

She lay there for over ten minutes, trying to get some movement into her body. It was like she was paralyzed, but she also relished the total peace she was feeling and didn't want to disturb it. Finally, she was able to sit up, turn, and get her feet down.

She opened her eyes, taking a moment to try to get some focus, get some bearing. She didn't know if she could walk. Her whole body felt like rubber.

Holy shit! What was that? My head is spinning. What just happened?

Finally, she was able to get up, regain her balance, and walk carefully into the main store.

Amanda was there, smiling. "Are you okay? Here's a bottle of water. Make sure to drink plenty of water today and tonight. Lots of water. How are you feeling?"

Her head was still spinning. She took the water, opened it, and drank half the bottle. "Thanks. So what the hell just happened in there? It was amazing … I think."

"Jenny, please excuse me for saying this, but I have never seen as much stuff as you are carrying around. It was so stuck, but I managed to move it and hopefully got rid of it for you, at least as much as I could. If I might ask, did you have a bad childhood? Don't answer if you don't want to."

"No, it's all right. Yeah, it wasn't the best. Pretty much sucked, actually, but wow … I can barely stand up, much less walk very well. Whatever you did, it was amazing."

"Thanks. It's what I do," Amanda said, smiling. "Just take your time. Sit for a while. I need to open the store back up. Excuse me."

She came back, got out Jenny's new crystal, wrapped it in soft paper, and placed it into a nice box. She then explained how to work with a crystal: how to cleanse it with saltwater or exposure to the full moon, how to charge it with intention, and how to use it for healing and meditation.

Jenny then asked about the pendulum she had used, and Amanda explained how to use it to help make decisions and detect negative areas in your body or aura. She talked about how Jenny needed to check every so often on what direction a "yes" might be to make sure it was clockwise or counterclockwise. Sometimes it changed, but most generally, a yes was clockwise. She explained how to track energy patterns in the body if and where negative, or positive, patterns might be. Then she recommended a book to Jenny that explained everything in greater detail.

"I'll buy those as well, and I will pay you for the crystal. You don't have to give it to me. I want to make it right with you."

Amanda started to protest, and Jenny raised her hand. "No! Just tell me how much this all comes to."

"You are a tough customer. Won't take freebies. Okay. Ah, total comes to ... how does one hundred fifty dollars sound? Okay?"

"I still think you are shortchanging yourself but okay. Thanks Amanda. That was a great experience," she said, handing over her bank card.

"So are you going to be around a while?"

"I was planning on going out into the back country to do some camping and hiking, some exploring."

"This is a very high-energy area. Energy vortexes abound. Come here a second." She dug under her counter and gave Jenny a little stone hanging from a waxed cord. "Wear this. It will protect you from any negativity out there. There is some nasty stuff as well as the good. This will help."

"What do I owe you?"

Amanda held up her hands. "Nothing. Come back and see me before you leave the area. I would like to see how you're doing, maybe do another cleansing if you want. I would like to make sure I got all the bad stuff out of you. Okay? Promise me."

"Yeah, I'll come back for sure Amanda. Thanks. I would really like to see you again. You're great."

She smiled. "Thanks."

And with that, Jenny left and felt like she was floating down the street. The weather was pleasantly mild, though the nights were fairly cold, getting down to the thirties. She decided she was ready to go out and camp for a few nights, even though the nighttime temperatures were chilly. She had updated her sleeping bag to a heavier winter weight, so she felt she would be comfortable. She found a tourist information kiosk and talked to the woman working there, asking about back roads, where to go, places to camp, and things to see.

The woman was helpful, giving her a detailed map and showing possible places. She gave her several brochures and a guidebook that covered the joys and dangers of back-country travel.

Jenny left with her materials and checked out of her room to find a place for lunch. It was already well past one o'clock in the afternoon. She found a nice, quiet café with outdoor dining. The sun was warm, and she wanted to be outside. She ordered a light salad and iced tea, and she began to look through her new information, planning where to go.

The server came with her order. Jenny stopped her and asked her about vortexes.

The girl replied, "They're everywhere around here. Where are you planning to go?"

Jenny showed her several options she was considering.

The girl pointed to a spot. "I'd go there. I've camped there a few times, and it's amazing. I had the most incredible dreams and experiences there."

"Like what?"

"It's hard to explain. I'd just go and find out for yourself."

"Okay, this might be a silly question, but, so, really, what is a vortex? Everybody I talk to here talks about vortexes. Please?"

She laughed. "They are apparently high-energy areas in the earth. Sensitive people can read them and tell you where they are. I heard they are caused by energy lines in the earth, or 'ley lines' as the locals call them. I'm not sure, but I know when I am out there. I can feel different energy things. Sort of weird. I'm from Arkansas, and I visited here three years ago and never left. I love it here for other reasons as well, just generally a lot of interesting people, a lot of new age types. Know what I mean?"

Jenny nodded. "Yeah, think so. Yeah, thanks. Been good talking with you ... thanks." But she hadn't a clue, having no experience with all this energy stuff.

The waitperson replied, "Yeah, have fun and enjoy. Nice talking." She turned and left.

Jenny stopped her and ordered six sandwiches and a quart of potato salad to go.

She ate her lunch, got her to-go food, paid her bill, and left. She walked to her Jeep and started to head out to her chosen road, excited to enter into a new adventure.

Chapter 23

She stopped at a grocery store and got some ice for her cooler, some fruit, some frozen burritos, and six bottles of chilled wine. She turned on her cell phone for the first time since she had left. She had six calls and three texts from Will, four calls from Helen, and four calls and four texts from Joan. She looked at Joan's texts first. They all said the same thing: "Jenny, please call me. We are all worried about you. We must talk." Will's read, "Jenny, so sorry. Please call. Where are you? I am worried about you." She listened to the calls that all expressed concern, worry, and love.

Love. I'm not sure I even know what the term means anymore.

After considering all three of them and realizing that it was Tuesday and she would be missing her therapy session and group, she needed to call Joan. Also, she felt Joan was the one person she might trust.

Joan answered immediately. "Jenny, my god, where are you? We are so worried. Are you all right? What's going on?"

Jenny told her everything: where she was, how overwhelmed she felt about Michael. Then she spoke about seeing Will's story outline and about the betrayal she felt—the anger and the sadness.

Joan listened and responded, "I can understand how you must feel, Jenny. I have talked with Will, and he's really upset. He thought his outline would be a great surprise, but now he realizes he should have talked with you first. You need to talk with him, Jenny. Please call. He really feels bad."

"I'll consider it, Joan. Right now, talking with you is all I think I can do. It's just everything with my brother, Peter, Will—it's just all too much. I need a break for a few days. Tell everyone I'm okay. I'm on my way out into the desert to camp for a while. I'll be in touch when I get back. Thanks, Joan."

"Just please call Will, okay?"

"Yeah, maybe when I get back."

"Now, Jenny!" Joan said more forcefully.

"Yeah, okay, I'll call. Thanks again. I'll call you again in a few days." She ended the call. She didn't want to talk to Will but gritted her teeth and punched his number.

He answered immediately. "Jenny! Where the hell are you? What's going on? I have been trying to call you! We've all been calling you, wondering what's happened to you."

"Will, I am still really pissed off at you for that goddamn outline I saw. I feel really betrayed by someone I trusted to … I don't know, just someone I thought I could count on to be honest and caring. But, but … how could you do that, Will? How could you? My life is my own fucking story! Not yours. For you to assume to think you can write about it just really pisses me off. Get your own fucking story!"

William listened without saying a word. When she finished, he just said, "I understand how you can feel this way. It was wrong of me. I should never have done that without first talking with you and getting approval. We could have worked together on it … or maybe not at all. It was a bad idea. I was wrong, and I am deeply sorry. Please don't hold it against me. You are so special to me. It breaks my heart that I made you so angry."

Jenny listened and felt a tinge of compassion rising inside her. "I am sorry too, Will. Maybe I overreacted, but with my brother and that mess, and then seeing your outline, it just pushed me over the top. I was feeling too overwhelmed and just needed to breathe."

"I understand, Jenny. I apologize for everything. Where are you? Are you coming back?"

She told him where she was and what she was planning but gave no indication of when she might return, because she hadn't a clue. She would be back when she was back.

"Take your time and please come back safely. Tell someone where you are going. Please do that for me, okay? Hopefully you will be back here for Christmas so we can all be together. I am planning on having a big dinner."

"Don't know about Christmas. Today's the first. So Christmas is like in, what, three weeks? Have to see. Right now I can't guarantee anything. And yes, I will tell someone before I venture out anywhere. Oh, I see I have calls from Helen too. Please let her know I'm okay. See you. Bye."

"I love you, dear, sweet girl. Be careful."

She answered with a flat, "Yeah."

They both clicked off.

She didn't bother to tell anybody where she was going. She didn't really care. But she had filled her water and gas cans; she had food and wine.

She started out of Sedona on the highway west for about ten miles. Finding the road she was looking for, she turned off onto a rough road she had to navigate very carefully and slowly. It required some serious focus on driving her rig and avoiding the huge holes and large rocks that were everywhere. But it was fun. About two hours later, she got to a place she thought was where she wanted to be. She wasn't really sure, but it looked good enough.

Jenny found an area well off what was loosely called the "road" and parked. She unloaded what she needed: her tent, sleeping pad, sleeping bag, cooler, and cooking gear. She set up her tent and put in her pad and bag inside. She got out her little camp chair, poured herself a glass of wine, sat down with her journal, and wrote about her day. She finished, sat, and thought about everything that had happened again, pondering it all: strange, very, very strange indeed.

Then she thought back to Denver, back to Durango, back beyond Durango, beyond, beyond. She suddenly realized none of it mattered: Peter, Michael, William, Helen, Joan, her grandparents, her bogus mother, her father, the abuse, her whole past. It was as if it all were a dream of some sorts, like her past was only an illusion, just an illusion. There were no demons; there was only emptiness. She remembered everything, remembered all the people, but she felt free of it all, like it was all there, but it didn't matter in her present state of being. She felt a little awestruck. Then she went back to what happened at Amanda's store and what she had said: *"I have never seen as much stuff as you were carrying around. It was so stuck, but I managed to move it and hopefully got rid of it for you."*

Got rid of it? How? What got rid of it? It was all still right there but just didn't seem so important right now. She got out her new crystal and looked at it, handling it. It felt wonderful. It made her feel good to hold it. Then she rewrapped it, placed it carefully in its box in the Jeep, and locked it.

It would be daylight for another hour or so, so she went for a short walk through the rocks, scrub oak, and piñon. It felt wonderful to be here. It was different; she was feeling different. Her life was becoming different. She felt new ... like the last few months, and everything, everyone, had made a difference.

She thought about her father. She knew Dory wasn't her mother, but Julian was her biological father. She knew from Michael that he was in prison for something somewhere, probably in California. She wondered whether she would ever see him again.

Jenny went back to her camp and found a guy standing there: ragged, long haired, unshaven. She could see he had kind, dark eyes. He was about her age, as best as she could determine. Her red flags immediately went up and were waving in a strong wind.

Chapter 24

"Hey, this your camp? My name's Chris. Would you mind if I camped over there?" He motioned with his head to a place by a huge rock. "Don't want to be a bother or be in your way. I can move on if you want, but this is a favorite spot of mine. Sorry I look a mess. Been out camping for two weeks."

Fuck, what does this guy want? It's a whole billion acres out here, and he wants to camp here. I just can't deal with having him anywhere near me. I'm gone!

"Yeah, hello, and knock yourself out. It's a huge place. I was just leaving as soon as I break camp."

"You don't have to leave on my account."

"I was leaving anyway. No bother. I have to get back." She busied herself with breaking her camp, avoiding looking at him. She loaded her Jeep and within ten minutes left with that guy watching and scratching his head.

Dammit. Why did some stupid desert bum have to show up? Ruined everything. Dammit, it's getting dark, too late to find somewhere else to camp. The day is ruined. I'll just go back to town.

Forty-five minutes later, she pulled into the motel she had stayed at over the last few nights, feeling vulnerable, insecure, and sad.

If I was in the mountains, I could camp thirty feet off a main trail, and no one would know I was there. Out here, it's too open.

The next morning over coffee, she started looking over her maps for other locations she might try, especially looking for places more out of the way. She sat for a while, writing in her journal about yesterday and about how afraid she'd been when that guy showed up. She always felt braver and stronger than that. She thought once more about everything that had happened with Michael and her grandparents, with Will and Peter. Then there was yesterday; she'd had to escape rather than hold her own. It was close to noon, and she had some time to kill, so she decided to go by Amanda's shop again and say hi.

She walked in and came face-to-face with the same guy who'd been at her camp last night. He looked just as shaggy as the night before.

"Oh, hi," he said. "I remember you from last night."

Amanda appeared. "Hi, Jenny, you're back so soon? I thought you were going to be out for several nights. Oh, I'm sorry, Jenny. This is a good friend of mine, Chris Holdsworth. Chris, this is Jenny ... I'm sorry. I forgot your last name."

Jenny felt her cheeks flush with embarrassment.

Oh, holy crap. This creepy, shaggy guy is a friend of Amanda's. This is getting weird.

Jenny stuck out her hand. "Hi, Chris, nice to meet you."

He looked at her. "I'm curious why you bailed last night. You looked pretty well set up to just pull stakes like that. I'm really sorry if I scared you off. I am truly pretty harmless. Just ask Amanda."

Jenny looked at Amanda, then at Chris, not knowing what to say. The best she could muster up was "A girl can change her mind, can't she?" Then she added, "It's a long story."

With that, she turned and started to leave. "Good seeing you. See you later. I'm going camping."

Chris said, "Wait up a minute, Jenny. If I scared you, I want to apologize. Why don't you let me buy you lunch to make up for it?"

Jenny turned, about to turn down his offer, when she saw Amanda smile and give her a *You should definitely accept his offer* nod.

Jenny considered the invitation another moment and said, "Yeah, sure. Why not? Thanks." She looked back at Amanda, who smiled and nodded her approval. Jenny smiled back and gave her a look that read, *I'm holding you responsible for whatever might happen.*

She didn't feel at ease with this guy. Even though he appeared to be a friend of Amanda's, she didn't really know Amanda either. She wouldn't be alone with him, so she felt somewhat okay. She would do the best she could to survive this lunch.

Both Jenny and Chris bid Amanda good-byes, left, and walked down the street to a café Chris liked. They went in and found a table. Once seated, Chris was first to speak. "So, Jenny, where are you from?"

"Up by Durango."

"Durango? Been there. Nice town. That's the place with the train?"

"Yup, that's the place."

"So, what are you doing around here? Come for some new scenery and warmer weather? Or are you another energy freak like I am?" he said, laughing. "I've hung around Sedona for the last few years. Love this place. Work with a landscaping outfit to support myself so I can spend as much time as I can being out here in this amazing place. It's like my home out there."

"It seems interesting as I keep hearing. I got into town a few nights ago and have already met some very strange and interesting people, starting with Amanda, the server where I had lunch a few times, and now you."

He laughed. "Amanda? She's the best. I've known her since I moved here. We're great friends; she's one of the first people I met when I got here. Man, she so helped me unload a ton of stuff from my last job in the Silicon Valley. Burnout at twenty-three. I don't plan on being a desert rat forever. Guess I'm sort of like the rock climber dirt balls and the ski bums who are up in your area, huh? Right now is my time, and I am enjoying the ride.

"So, what was the real reason you left so quickly last night? I'm really sorry. I would have just kept on going if I knew I scared you. I was headed back myself. Caught a ride in early this morning."

"Let's just say I haven't been having the best few weeks, and my nerves are pretty raw and on edge. And yeah, you did freak me out when I saw you there. Something just told me to leave. And I was pissed off that you showed up, but hey, it's a free desert, I guess."

The server came and took their order. Chris continued, "Well, I apologize again. I'll tell you what. Let me get home, clean up, and repack, and I'll go out with you. I know this place really well and can show you all sorts of cool places ... my present to make up for ruining last night."

Jenny hesitated, thinking this was something she definitely shouldn't do. Her negative reaction must have showed, because Chris said, "If you're still worried about me, Amanda will give me a good reference. I'll head to my place after lunch, and you can go and talk with her. If you still don't want to, I'll understand. It's just that it's not every day that I get to invite a beautiful woman out into the desert.

A beautiful woman! He thinks I'm beautiful? I remember Will saying that, but that was different. I don't know this guy at all. To go out to the desert with him is just not a good idea. He's probably like Old George. Wants me to play with his cock.

Trying to get out of the situation gracefully, she said, "Thanks for the invite and flattery, but I don't think it's a good idea. Maybe I can call you or text you?"

She got Chris's cell number but avoided sharing hers. The rest of the lunch was spent in quiet, with Jenny not knowing what to say and Chris not pushing any more conversation. He paid for the meal and headed home to his place. Jenny walked back to Amanda's.

Amanda was waiting on a customer, so Jenny looked around her store at all the stones and other things she had for sale.

After the customer left, Jenny said, "Okay, Amanda, what's going on here? You're giving me those signals. Are you trying to be a matchmaker?"

Amanda laughed. "No, just helping things unfold as maybe they should. I see you and Chris being very close friends, possibly more. I see you both would get along well together. That's all. What do you think of him?"

"Well, he seems okay, I guess. I've never been really tuned into guys. Just my brother, and he's a mess. So, this Chris wants to go out camping with me and show me around? I'm not real comfortable around men and don't want to go out alone into the desert with a strange man. Doesn't seem very wise. I think it's a bad idea. It just seems too scary. I don't even know him, and even if I did, I'd still be nervous."

Amanda said, "That's understandable, but I've known him for almost four years. I can truly say he's one of the most genuine, sensitive, and kind men I have ever met." She smiled dreamily. "I wish I were twenty years younger. He's explored this desert for as long as I have known him, and he does know quite a few interesting places out there. He's taken me to several. It's up to you, but I'd talk to him, see what he has in mind."

"You seem to think pretty highly of him. Maybe you'd like to go with me. It would make me feel more comfortable."

"I wish I could, but I've got a lot of online orders to fill and get sent out. I just can't right now."

"Yeah, I understand. Maybe I'll just head out by myself."

"Just go out for a few hours with him. No camping. He's a good guy."

"I'll think about it, maybe call him and see. Thanks, Amanda. I'll let you know."

"Good luck and hope to see you soon."

Jenny left and called Chris as she walked toward her Jeep. He picked up quickly. "Hello?"

"Hi, Chris, it's me, Jenny. I am willing to consider your offer but only for a short trip. No camping. Can I meet you somewhere?"

"Hey, that'd be great. I just got out of the shower. Why not come by here, if you want? It's close, and I'll be decent by the time you get here. Here's the directions—"

"No, I don't want to go to your place. Maybe meet at the convenience store on the west end?"

He chuckled. "Have it your way. I'll be there in about fifteen minutes."

Jenny got to her Jeep and went to the convenience store. She didn't see Chris there yet. *What am I thinking? I can't do this.*

She turned around quickly, tore out of the parking lot, and headed back into Sedona with her head down so he maybe wouldn't see her if they met on the road.

Back at her motel, she called Joan, who was tied up for the next hour with an appointment. The receptionist would have her call as soon as she was finished. Jenny got her journal and tried to decipher her feelings about Amanda and Chris and where she was and whatever it was she thought she was doing here. Why not just leave and go somewhere else, into the desert, as she had originally planned? It seemed like every place she went, there was something that caused her trauma.

Forty-five minutes later, her phone chirped. It was Joan. "Hi, Jenny, what's up?"

Jenny explained everything that had happened with Amanda and Chris and told her how mixed up and frightened she felt.

"So, Jenny, do you think this guy is dangerous?"

"No, it's not that. Amanda seems nice, and they're friends. I just don't know what to do. And I don't even know why I'm concerned about this. I don't know why I'm even considering this. God, Joan, I just get so confused sometimes. There's Michael and Peter and everything. It's all crazy."

"I know, I know. This has been hard for you, especially with Michael and all, but tell me this. What does your gut say?"

"My gut? It wants to go. He seems nice. He has soft, kind eyes and a warm smile. When he talks to me, he looks quietly into my eyes. He seems really nice and knows a lot about the desert here. He wants to show me around some of the energy spots, or vortexes, as the locals call them, but my head says, *No, no, no. He could be dangerous, and who knows?*"

"Okay, Jenny, here's what I think. Obviously I know your trauma and I fully understand your fear of men in general. However, I'm not saying do this, but I think it might do you some good to go on a hike with him. Give it a shot. Keep it short. Sometimes our guts tell us to do something, and our rational minds think otherwise. You are at a place now where I think you need to start exploring outside your fears. It might be a good thing, as scary as it might be, to start to break out of the cocoon you've had wrapped around yourself for so long."

"But Joan, what if he turns out to be a bad guy? I have no experience with guys. I don't know how to evaluate them, trust if they might be good or bad. I wish there was someone else who could go too. I asked Amanda, but she's busy with her business."

"We all face fears and have to take chances sometimes. I had a fear of heights when I moved to Durango some years ago. I met some women who convinced me to go out into the high country to hike with them. Some of the trails were pretty precarious, but I survived after crying several times. I've even skydived. I still respect heights, but I broke through that fear."

"I know what you're saying. I'll think about it. I was supposed to meet him, but I bailed out, couldn't do it. Maybe he won't want to now," she replied, half hoping that would be her way out.

"Has he called you?"

"I purposely didn't give him my number."

"So, are there any places you could go to that might have others out hiking as well?"

"I could call his friend, Amanda, and ask. See what she thinks."

"Think it over, Jenny. At least call him back and talk with him about it. You might want to explain your fears—not in great detail, of course."

"Yeah, I'll think about it. I'll let you know."

"Call me anytime. I mean that. Don't ever hesitate to call. Okay?"

"Thanks, Joan. How was I so lucky to connect with you? You've helped me so much already. Thanks."

"That's what I try to do. Be careful and call."

They both bid their good-byes and clicked off. Jenny lay back on the bed and considered all Joan had said.

I'm a big girl. I can't spend the rest of my life being afraid. Why not?

She called Amanda, telling her a watered-down version of what was going on and trying to give only general information about her fears of being with men. Amanda seemed to understand and reassured Jenny that Chris was a decent sort and would never do anything to ever hurt anyone.

She thanked her and clicked off, then punched in his number.

"Hi, Chris, this is Jenny. We were supposed to go hiking. I sort of missed our date. I'm sorry."

"Yeah, I waited for you for a while and finally went home. Are you okay? Everything all right?"

"Yeah, I'm okay. Thanks. Maybe tomorrow, if you're still up for it. Is there anyplace we could go where there would be other people? Maybe someplace close to town? I would feel more comfortable until I get to know you better. Would that be okay?"

"Perfectly understandable. I know a place like that. Usually some others are out there, even this time of year. Maybe at ten tomorrow morning. Bring some lunch and water, and we could have lunch out there."

"Okay, ten then. At the convenience store?"

"This place is on a different road out of town. Can I stop by your motel, and we can go from there?"

"Only if I can drive," she said, feeling that if she drove, she would have more control. She also felt the reassurance of her knife on her belt.

"Absolutely. I'll see you then."

Jenny lay back on the bed, considering what she was doing. Her head said, *Are you crazy? What are you thinking?* But her gut and her heart looked forward to the next day. This whole situation was extremely confusing and uncomfortable for her. She went out for a quick dinner and headed back to write about the day and everything that seemed to be changing inside her.

In the morning, Jenny was up early. She meditated, did some yoga stretches, and went out for breakfast. She checked her water and packed her day pack with some trail mix and protein bars. Then she took a deep breath and waited for Chris to show, which he did at exactly ten.

Chapter 25

He drove up in an old Toyota pickup and parked a few spaces away from her Jeep. When he got out, she noticed he had cleaned up and shaved off his beard growth; he was a really good-looking guy. He had long, dark hair, now in a ponytail, and he looked to be quite nicely built. She immediately compared him to Peter. Peter was okay, but Chris was more than okay. She felt a little something happen deep inside, a little surge of warmth. While it was a good feeling, she chose to dismiss it.

"Hi," she said. "Ready?"

"Sure. Let's go."

They got into the Jeep, and he gave her directions to a place just a little north and west of town, a parking area with several other vehicles already there. Seeing them there made her feel better, but she still had butterflies in her belly, not knowing whether they were fear, excitement, or maybe a bit of both. They hefted their day packs on and got ready to go.

Jenny was the first to speak after a quiet drive to the area. "So, lead the way. Show me your desert."

"Walk alongside me so we can talk. The trail's wide enough here. Again, I apologize for upsetting you, which I know I did. I know I looked pretty ratty that afternoon when we first encountered one another. I apologize again."

"It's okay. I just wasn't expecting to see anyone else out there. I'm used to being in the Colorado mountains, where I seem to be able to avoid anyone else. You just threw me off guard."

"Again, sorry. So tell me a little about yourself."

"Well, I keep telling myself I want to be a writer, but writers write, and I'm not writing anything at the moment, so ... I guess I'm presently being a desert rat or, in my case, a mountain rat."

"A writer? Me too. I graduated from UCLA five years ago. A double major: journalism and creative writing. I landed a job right after graduating, up in Silicon Valley for a tech outfit. I was pretty excited, but after I found out my days were going to be 'eat, sleep, and work' with never a free moment, my excitement quickly waned. I literally spent all my waking moments in meetings, writing copy, and grabbing a sandwich at my desk. Granted, there were a lot of perks: a gym, meditation room, game room; I never had time to enjoy any of them. I was a good writer; they loved me, but I felt burned out right after first year there, so I resigned. They hated to see me leave, offered me a substantial raise. I was damned productive, but I was also dying inside ... and out, for that matter. I looked at myself in the mirror. Didn't believe how sallow and gray I looked. I was gaining weight and was, I guess, just numb.

"I'd saved every cent I made from a very lucrative salary. Really my only expense was rent, very high rent, and bus fare. I didn't own a car. So I got rid of what few things I owned except what would fit in a backpack and hitched east and ended up here. I never left—I love it here.

"I'm filling journals with notes about all my adventures: the people, the quirkiness, the places, the desert. I'm sort of working on it now, turning it all into a book, maybe several books of fiction. I've the plots set for several stories and numerous characters already outlined. I have the first chapters for my first one down and have been circulating it to various agents. I have one that seems interested and is talking to a few publishers, but so far, nothing is for certain."

"Wow, Chris! You're doing it! I'm embarrassed that I ever said anything to you. I just can't seem to get anything going—no ideas, no possibilities, even. I'm a failure before I even get started."

"Now wait a minute, Jenny. Do you journal at all? Do you write down your thoughts, your experiences? People you meet? People you know? Things you see? Everything, anything, can be an influence for a story. Just build an arsenal of observations and experiences, and make some into some short stories. Short stories are a great place to start and can lead you to longer stories, even novels."

She said, "I understand what you're saying, really I do. But I've never even really thought of it that way. I always looked at everything as my own private drama. I guess I have never thought anything of what I see or do as anything interesting or important story material."

"But Jenny, we are where stories come from, from our experiences, our view of the world around us, our own fantasies about that world, and the characters we create to populate our world. It's a lot of fun just making shit up as we go."

She laughed. "You actually make it sound fun. But I just get lost in my crazy reality and really don't see how anyone would ever find it the least bit interesting."

"Yeah, I know, but you'd be surprised. So okay, I blathered on about myself way too long. Please tell me more about yourself. Tell me everything."

Jenny started talking and told Chris a short, guarded version of her history: that she grew up in California, went to college in Boulder, and was living in Durango, skipping over anything about her problems. By then, they had met several other people along the trail, which made her feel a little more secure.

After hiking a few miles into the desert, she felt a stillness that was a total absence of any sound: no breeze, no animal sounds, nothing other than the sound of their footfalls, her breathing, their voices, and maybe the far-off call of some bird. The desert was rocks and sand but alive with sage and piñon pine. Now, after walking without talking for another mile or so, Jenny felt like she was almost in a meditative state of being.

Chris broke the silence. "Here we are at the place I wanted to have you see ... and possibly feel. I found it to be a pretty high-energy spot."

"One of the famous vortexes?"

"You might call it that. Let's sit over there." He pointed to a flat rock alongside a low cliff wall.

Following him over, she sat with him on the rock. The desert fell away to the west, and she looked out over the vast landscape until it faded away into the horizon. The air was cool, but the sun-warmed rock made it comfortable to sit and bask.

"Do you meditate, Jenny?"

"Yeah, I have at yoga class and some other times. Why?"

"I always like to sit and meditate at these places. It can be pretty amazing. Want to try?"

"Sure, why not? Then a little lunch."

Closing her eyes and taking a deep breath, she easily entered into a state of quiet bliss like she had never realized before. Her mind opened into a spaciousness of light, her breathing became shallow, and she simply sat in peace. Shortly, she had a very clear image of her and Chris somewhere, like in a field of light. They were both dressed in white and holding hands, looking into each other's eyes and smiling blissfully. She stayed with that image for what seemed like hours.

She heard Chris's voice whisper, "Jenny, it's time." She slowly came back to reality, opening her eyes to what was, to her, a new, wonderful, beautiful day. She sat for a minute, bringing herself back into reality, then looked over at Chris, who was still sitting there with his eyes peacefully closed. She knew she had heard his voice, but he was still far away somewhere.

She said softly, "Chris, it's time."

He wiggled a little and slowly opened his eyes, turned, and smiled. "How was that?"

"Nice, very nice," was all she said, remembering her vision, now more confused than ever about whatever it was she was doing here with him.

Chris checked his watch. "Oh my, we've been here for a little over an hour."

Jenny raised her eyebrows. "Really?" It had felt like five minutes.

After a little snack of protein bars, trail mix, and some water, they headed back to the Jeep.

"Thanks for bringing me here, Chris. It is beautiful. I don't know if that was a vortex, but it was the nicest meditation I've ever experienced. Usually my mind is racing, filled with a grocery list of thoughts. At that place, my mind just went completely quiet. I really loved it. Thanks."

"Hearing you say that make me happy. We could go out again tomorrow."

"Yeah. Maybe." She silently pondered the request. *This was a nice experience. Chris was helpful and nice to talk to. It was an interesting place and a wonderful experience. But I don't want to commit to anything until I can resolve this vision of Chris and me that's burning in my brain.*

They spent the rest of the hike lost in their own thoughts. On the way back to town, Chris asked again whether she wanted to go out again tomorrow, to which she responded the same. "Yeah. Maybe. I'll call you tonight."

As soon as she dropped Chris off at his truck, she left to go to Amanda's, hoping it wasn't too late to catch her. It was right at five thirty when she got there, and a Closed sign was being hung. She ran up and knocked. Amanda noticed her and unlocked the door for her, letting her in and then relocking it. This made Jenny feel trapped and uncomfortable. She took a deep breath. "Can we talk for a minute?"

"Are you okay? Something wrong?"

"No, I'm fine, just confused about something that happened. Hey, I'm hungry. Can I treat you to dinner?"

"That would be nice, but you don't need to do that."

"I want to, so please?"

Amanda agreed to join her, and they left for a quiet restaurant Amanda knew about a block away. Out of the store, seated with drinks ordered, Jenny felt more comfortable and told her about the day and her meditation vision. Amanda listened quietly and seemed nonplussed by her story.

After she finished, Amanda said, "That's very cool, don't you think?"

"Not really. It makes no sense, but it was so real. I'm not sure what I think."

"Well, Jenny, I deal in this sort of thing in my work all the time, among other things. But visions like that do have meaning. What I see is that you and Chris have a spiritual connection of some sort. I saw that when you two were together at the store. There are all kinds of connections, and there are many books written about them. I don't know whether or not you have much faith in this sort of thing, but I do, and I'm serious about it. I've seen lots of things of this sort. However, it's totally up to you to do as you choose. But I think that it might be good for you to explore that connection to whatever degree you might be comfortable with."

"Truth is, I'm not comfortable around men. Okay, I was abused as a child and am dealing with it all right now. It's like a festering sore that has recently come to a head. I'm in counseling. I just get so scared."

Amanda was silent for some time, staring blankly somewhere beyond Jenny. Finally she focused, put her hand on Jenny's, and said, "I knew there was something bad when I did that session with you. I am so very sorry. I'm really sorry. Is there anything I can do to help? Anything at all?"

"I don't know what. Whatever you did that first day seemed to make things different somehow. Things didn't seem so bad afterwards."

The conversation was interrupted when their food came. They then spent their time talking more about themselves and their backgrounds. Jenny knew she was always careful about what she shared with others, but she detected Amanda was doing the same, glossing over a lot of her past. Finished, Jenny paid, and they bid each other good night.

Back in her room, she cleaned up and spent the next hour writing in her journal about the day and the strange things and people she was encountering in this strange place. Before she went to sleep, she called Chris and made plans to go back into the desert the next day.

Chapter 26

Chris took her to a new, more remote area, and Jenny was surprised by how much more at ease she felt being with him this time. He was thoughtful, kind, and respectful to her, reminding her of William when they had first met. (She still wasn't sure about how she felt about him now.)

They hiked for miles on a trail that followed different terrain than yesterday, through some canyon areas where he showed her ancient petroglyphs. It was fun for Jenny. She found Chris nice to be with. They chatted on about writing along with many topics about their lives and the stunning area they were hiking through. Jenny learned a lot more about him than he did about her, however. The trail ended back at the parking area about six hours later. There were no vortexes or meditation stops.

Both tired and hungry, they decided to have dinner together when they got back to town. Seated at the Mexican restaurant they chose, they ordered drinks and food.

"So Jenny, how long are you going to hang out here?"

"I don't know, maybe a few more days. I'm not wild about being back in Durango for Christmas. My friend, the guy whose house I live in, is planning a big deal, and I'm not really wanting to be there. Presents and all? I'm just not into it. I'll probably move on somewhere to camp, maybe farther south."

"Well, don't get me wrong here. I'm not trying to be pushy or anything, but I have an offer. I like being with you. I enjoy your company and would like it if you would hang here for a while. You could stay at my place. I'd sleep on the couch, and you could have my bed. I promise—everything will be on the up and up. I'm not trying to be too forward or anything. I will respect your space and maintain a proper distance. We could do some writing and spend time in the desert, and you wouldn't have to pay for a motel room. If you don't want to, I understand. I just enjoy your company. Please don't think I'm being stupid. Oh, crap! This all sounds so stupid. I'm sorry. Maybe just forget it."

The vision she'd had of the two of them flashed in her mind as well as the talk she'd had afterward with Amanda. What was happening to her?

"It wasn't stupid, Chris. Actually, it was a nice offer, but I'm not ready for a relationship. Aren't there any girls in this town you go out with?"

"There are, but they all want to get serious, get married and have babies. Or there's the opposite, others who just want to party all the time. I'm not tuned into either right now. But you're different, not threatening either way. You're just Jenny, and you're fun to be with. That's all. Promise."

She smiled. "Somehow, I think that might be a compliment. I have not been out with many guys—hardly any, for that matter. So I'm not sure how to react to your offer. But to be perfectly honest, it sounds scary to me. So let me think on it. Okay?"

"Yeah. If you do, great. If not, that's okay."

Drinks and food came. They ate without broaching the subject again. They split the bill, and Jenny took him back to his truck.

Jenny said, "Hey, we have a hot tub. Want to come and soak your tired muscles for a bit? Maybe in an hour to let dinner settle?"

"That'd be awesome. I'll go shower, grab my trunks, and be back in an hour then. Thanks."

175

"I'll meet you in the lobby at seven then."

He left, and she went to her room and cleaned up. She found her two-piece that Kelly had insisted she buy, and sat and thought about this strange journey she seemed to be experiencing, trying to make sense. She liked him and felt comfortable around him, which she thought was strange considering her phobias of men. But did she trust him? Becoming muddled in her thoughts, she decided to call Joan and seek her counsel. Joan answered after a few rings.

"Hi, Joan, it's Jenny. I'm so sorry to bother you in the evening like this, but I need to talk if you have a few minutes."

"Of course I do. What's going on?"

Jenny told her everything that had happened since the last time they talked, including her vision. Joan paused for a minute, and Jenny could almost hear the wheels turning in Joan's head. She responded with "Wow. I wish you were here so I might read you better than long distance, but knowing you as I do, my advice is not to take this offer. If you like him, give it time. You don't need any more trauma in your life right now. The desert hikes you have been doing sound fine, but take it slowly. Okay?"

"Okay. Hear what you're saying. I will. Promise."

"When are you coming back?"

"Not sure yet. Maybe after Christmas."

"You know, Will is planning a big Christmas dinner."

"Yeah, but I'm really not into the holiday thing. Just as soon not be there right now."

"Well, I talked to him a few days ago, and he is hoping you will be there."

"I'm sure he is. I'm still not sure how I feel about him right now, if I even want to stay in his bunkhouse anymore."

"Jenny, I don't want to lecture you, but you need to let that go. It was a misunderstanding on his part, and he deeply regrets that he upset you. Call him again and just talk. Try to let your anger or whatever go."

"Okay, maybe tomorrow. I need to let you go. I'm taking up your time when you need to be not working. I'll say good night and thank you so much for everything. Can't wait to see you again and get back to the group session."

"You are being missed by everyone. And thank you for sharing. It must be getting easier."

"Yeah, it is."

"Good night Jenny."

Dammit, it's after seven. He'll wonder where I am. Hope he didn't already leave. She raced down to the lobby and found him sitting and reading a book, looking quite at home.

"Hi, sorry I'm late. I was on the phone and lost track. You ready?"

"Yeah, show me the way."

"What are you reading?"

"Rereading actually. *A Moveable Feast* by Hemingway. Ever read it?"

"I did in college. Pretty good book but pretty much a guy's book. Not sure I'd read it again."

"Understandable, but I enjoy his style, sparse and to the point, a break from the more flowery romantic style of the belle epoque. I'd have loved to live in 1920s Paris and hung out with all those great writers and artists. Wow."

Jenny didn't care that much for Hemingway and let the subject drop. They were at the hot tub, which was outside and adjacent to the indoor pool so they could jump in it to cool off. There was no one else there.

She asked, "Would you want some wine if I ran back to my room? I have a bottle of Chardonnay in my mini fridge. It'll only take a minute."

"I'd love some. Can I help?"

"No, it's only a bottle of screw-top wine and two plastic glasses. I'll be right back."

She appeared in a few minutes and opened the wine, pouring each of them some.

He pulled off his tee shirt as she slipped out of her sweats. She checked him out and was liking what she saw, well-muscled arms, broad shoulders and chest, a flat belly and a slim waste. She didn't know much about guy's physiques, but his was looking pretty nice to her. She felt a now familiar warmth arise in her.

They slipped into the 104-degree water directly across from one another. It felt great to be soaking under the stars in a clear desert night. They soaked in the ambiance of the night and each other.

Jenny felt something deep within her, a warm, comfortable feeling of peace. She realized how much she liked being with Chris. It felt right for her, and she hadn't even tasted her wine yet. Her decision was crystal clear.

"Chris, I'll bring my stuff over tomorrow, if your offer still stands."

Chapter 27

She checked out of her room and drove to his little house from the directions he had given her last night. It was a small rustic cabin nestled in cottonwood trees by a creek. He answered her knock, opening the door for her, and escorting her in. The inside was surprisingly updated, neat, and tidy other than the dirty dishes in the sink. Still, she was impressed. In many ways, it resembled her bunkhouse; it was a little smaller but with a similar layout.

"Welcome to my humble abode."

"Nice little place, Chris," she said. She noted his writing desk with a laptop, yellow tablets, and a large china cup storing pens and pencils; then there were the bookshelves. "You look pretty well read ... and pretty neat for a guy."

He laughed. "Ma Holdsworth didn't raise me to be any old slob."

Jenny laughed, thinking that, while he seemed like a nice enough guy, he didn't seem as self-assured as he had been last night.

"Can I get you something? Iced tea? A beer? Wine?"

"Some tea would be nice but only if you have some made, or else just water, please," she replied.

"I'll make some tea then. It'll only take me a minute."

"Please, just have water then," she insisted.

"Okay, but I could make tea."

"Water will be fine."

He brought in glasses of water and motioned for her to sit. She sat on the sofa, and he sat opposite.

He said, "Do you maybe want to go out camping for a few days? Maybe tomorrow? There're some places we could go to that we can't really do justice to in a single day. The weather's supposed to stay reasonable warm."

"God, Chris. Why are you so determined to get me camping in the desert?"

"Because I know you'd love some of these places I have in mind, and I ruined it for you the first time. I just feel like I owe you, like I want you to really enjoy more of the beauty and mystery of it. I want to share it all with you."

"Maybe. What about today?"

"It's a little after noon already, and I have to get myself organized. Maybe for three days?"

Jenny felt a little rushed but really wanted to go out and spend time camping, and Chris knew places, having already taken her to some amazing spots. "Okay, let's do it."

"Great! You'll love it. I know you will."

"I have food in my cooler. It would be good to add to it, with you tagging along," she said, half serious and half in jest. "One more thing. I sleep with this under my pillow," she said, brandishing her knife. "So no funny business! Understand?"

Chris's eyes grew big, and he could only respond with "Understood!"

Jenny said, "As I said, I have a cooler full of food, if you like frozen burritos, which aren't frozen by now, and deli sandwiches. I also have fruit, chips, and wine. We can go out this afternoon and stock up with what else we might need."

"Well, yeah, sounds good. We can eat here tonight, maybe have the burritos? Another dinner with a beautiful woman."

Jenny felt her cheeks warm up. *Dinner with a beautiful woman? No guy has ever said that to me ever, not even Peter.*

She pretended to ignore his last comment and turned away so he wouldn't see her blush. "I'll get what I need for tonight and the cooler from the Jeep."

"I'll help with the cooler," he said as he followed her outside.

They unpacked a few of the cooler items into his fridge and left for the grocery store for supplies and more ice. They returned and organized the food, and Chris put together what he needed in his pack while Jenny busied herself by looking over his large collection of books. He must have had every book Ernest Hemingway wrote as well as books by other classical writers of the late 1800s through present day authors.

It was getting toward late afternoon. Chris finished with his pack and asked her whether she wanted a beer. She declined the beer but would like a glass of wine. She went to the fridge and selected a bottle, and Chris got two glasses. Jenny grabbed some crackers and cheese, which Chris offered to cut and serve. They sat in the great room across from each other and relaxed with their wine and snacks.

They sat and ate the cheese and crackers, talking about books they had read and liked. They finished the wine, and Jenny felt a little tipsy. "Hey, I'm really hungry. I'm ready for a burrito. How about you?"

"Sure," he said, getting up and heading toward the kitchen. "I'll nuke the burritos in the micro." After he got the burritos going, he set out plates and some forks. "Hey, you are great to talk with, Jenny. You are smart and interesting. I truly enjoy your company. Should I open more wine?"

He thinks I'm smart ... and interesting? Be careful. You know it is most likely bullshit. You've had plenty of bullshit. Just be careful. Be careful! No more alcohol.

"Ah, no thanks. I don't want to get wasted. I'll get some water."

He looked at her for a moment. "Sure. Ah, sorry. Just trying to be sociable. The glasses are in the cupboard next to the sink."

She found a glass and poured some water. The burritos were done. He put them on the plates and motioned for her to sit at the table. When she sat back down to eat, Chris waited for her to start, a courtesy she noticed.

Hmm, he seems polite enough. Maybe I'm just always being too paranoid. Will I ever be able to be completely comfortable around a guy? I don't know.

They ate in silence, both hungry, neither wanting to make any small talk. Finished, they picked up and put everything away. Jenny started to feel strange and distant from everything. Suddenly, the man and the house became too much for her; everything started closing in, and panic filled her. She had difficulty breathing.

She blurted out, "Chris, this just isn't going to work! I can't stay here. I have to leave. Sorry." She started to gather her things.

Chris said, "Why? Did I do something to upset you? I'm sorry, I just—"

"No! Nothing you did. Just me. I'm sorry. I'm just not very social. I can't be here. I need to be alone."

"But Jenny. What? I don't understand."

"Just fucking leave me alone! Just, just, please, just—" And tears started to come. She grabbed what she could and ran out to her Jeep, dropped everything, leaned against the car with her head in her hands, and cried.

I'm so fucked up! He didn't deserve that. He was just being nice. Why couldn't I just let him be nice? Why can't I just trust that some people are just trying to be nice?

She felt him lean in beside her and place an arm around her shoulder. No words, just an arm; not holding tight, just being gentle. The touch felt reassuring. She cried it all out, leaning her head on his shoulder. No words, just some physical comfort. She liked the tenderness she felt from him right then.

She said, "I'm sorry, Chris. You are a nice guy and didn't deserve that. You are just dealing with one fucked-up girl. I should probably go now. I'm sorry."

"It's okay. Anything you care to talk about?"

"Thanks. But you don't want to know, Chris. You don't want to know."

"Hey, try me. I got big shoulders and a good ear. And I don't judge. It hurts me to see you so sad."

All she could say was, "I was smothering, dying. I needed to escape from Durango for a while, and I ended up here. Yeah … ended up here in Sedona." She trailed off and paused for a moment. "And I then I ran into Amanda, and then I ran into you. Now you're seeing what a crazy person I am. There are things I can't share with you, things I could hardly share with my therapist even a month ago. Yeah, now you know. I'm in therapy because I'm a crazy, antisocial bitch. I sure can't unload my shit onto somebody I just met. So, have I shaken up your world? Scared you? Ready to be rid of me?"

"Hell no, Jenny, not at all. What I'd really like is to get to know you better. My offer still stands. I'll stick with you. You seem to be a strong woman. Wow. Seriously, you're great. Okay, sorry, I'm being a jerk … but I mean it when I say you're great. Okay?" He fumbled with his words.

"Yeah, okay. But Chris, you don't really know me at all, and I don't know you. You're just some hairy guy who appeared at my campsite. You have no idea whether I'm great or whatever else you're conjuring up in your fantasy.

"But you're forgiven for being pushy, and thanks; in some ways I need to be pushed out of my own drama. Thanks. So many others I've met seems to pity me or be scared of me, like this guy, Peter. I told him half of what I told you, and he went all, like, 'Well, I need to fucking think about all this. I don't fucking know. I'll let you know.' He's studying to be a fucking lawyer. He's just like a lawyer. I don't want a fucking lawyer who has to consider whether or not he can deal with me ... I want someone who knows about me and doesn't give a shit because I'm more important than my history." Her voice was rising, and she was getting really pissed the more she talked.

"Whoa," Chris interrupted. "Slow down, Jenny. No need to get so upset, really no need. I'm right here, and I don't care about your history, only who you are, right now, right at this moment. I appreciate you already, even though we just met. I like hanging out with you right now, not yesterday, not a week ago, a month, a year, or whenever.

"I've just met you, Jenny, and you don't make me want to think for a moment about whether or not I can handle you or your history. I really don't care. All I see is what I see, and that is a really nice, interesting woman I'd like to know. Okay? And I'll shut up now."

She sat for a moment, digesting what Chris had just said. She felt a new warmth rise from somewhere deep within her, a warmth that ran from her heart down into her belly and into that place between her thighs. She felt desire, a lustful desire, some something she had never felt before.

Was this what Lady Chatterley felt for Mellors? Lawrence's description fit her exact feeling? It was so new; she knew she was blushing like a beet. Thankfully it was dark, and he couldn't see how flushed she was; she felt it had to be apparent.

"Jenny, are you in there? Are you okay?"

"Oh, sorry. I'm spacing out, sorry. What did you say?" Chris asked again, "Are you okay?"

"Yeah, I was just thinking about something."

"Want to share?"

"Ah, no, not really. It was nothing."

They stood there for a while longer, enjoying the quiet, clear night. She looked up through the trees. The stars were brilliant, so brilliant; they seemed so close that she could reach out and touch them. But the temperature was dropping, and Jenny began to shiver.

Chris said, "Let's go back in where it's warm." He reached down to pick up the things she had dropped. "You still want to leave? I'll get your cooler."

"If you don't mind a crazy lady being around, I'll hang out on your couch like we talked about. Okay?" She looked up at him with a smile it was too dark for him to see.

"I don't mind if you don't mind hanging out in a desert rat's house."

Chris helped her back inside, made space for her in the bathroom, and got out fresh towels for her. She unrolled her sleeping bag and spread it on the couch. Chris went into his bedroom and closed the door.

Jenny was about to get herself ready for bed when she remembered her pendulum. *Why not try it and see what happens?* She rummaged through her things and retrieved it. She held it like Amanda had showed her and asked for a yes direction. It wiggled for a moment and began to move in a clockwise rotation. She stopped it and then asked about staying for the night alone with Chris. It again wiggled for a moment and began to move in a clockwise rotation; the longer she held it, the harder and faster it rotated. *I take that as a definite yes.* She then asked about camping with him and got the same results. As weird as all this seemed, she felt better, more confident, trusting what she had just experienced. She got herself ready for bed and crawled into her bag. She was asleep as soon as she closed her eyes.

* * *

They were up early and headed out to the desert, where they ended up spending the next three days camping and hiking. Chris showed her some of his favorite haunts. She was, indeed, loving the desert and some of the energy places Chris took her to. They made her buzzy. At two of the places, in particular, they stayed for a while and meditated together. No visions, just quiet, peaceful experiences.

They spent their time hiking and exchanged more information about themselves: their thoughts about life, books they had read and, of course, more about writing. Chris kept encouraging her to do at least a short story to see how it would go for her.

After another wonderful day together, Jenny was feeling calm and happy. She really liked Chris: being with him and talking with him. She found him as Amanda had said: genuine, sensitive, and kind, along with being interesting and good looking. She actually was beginning to feel safe being with him. After eating a freeze-dried dinner and killing a bottle of wine, Jenny asked, "Chris, will you sleep with me tonight?"

"What? No! No! No! This not what I'm about, Jenny. That was never my intention with you. I really enjoy your company, but we don't need to do anything like that. Each to our own tent."

"Just shut up, Chris. Just shut up and listen. Don't make this harder than it is for me." She noticed her hands were shaking and began talking very fast. "I've never slept with a man before. I don't want to have sex with you. I just want to be close to you, to feel your warmth, to hear you breathe next to me. It's hard to say what I'm trying to say. I don't know how," she stammered. "I've never had any practice. You're the first guy that I ever wanted to share a night with. I know I just met you a few days ago, but I really like you. I feel good about you, even though you might well be a serial killer, and if you are, at least I would die happy that I shared at least one night with a guy I like. Please don't think I'm nuts. I like you, Chris. Please don't dis me! Oh shit, this's really hard."

"Awe, Jenny, I'm not dissing you, but I've been out here three days. By now I'm dirty and must smell like a goat. I would welcome your company, and I promise I'll respect your wishes. But let me think on it. Truth is, this is scary for me, too."

She gave a nervous laugh. "Yeah, I'm probably getting pretty gamy as well. Think about it for a while, and if you decide to, you can bring your bag over to my tent. It's bigger."

They sat for a while in silence. Jenny now had mixed emotions about her offer but still wanted him to say yes. It was getting chilly in the early desert night. Jenny said, "I'm chilly and ready to get into my bag. Did you decide anything?"

"Yeah, I'm thinking I'm up for it if you still are."

"My invitation still holds."

"Okay, then," he said and got up to fetch his sleeping bag and pad.

He came back and put his stuff in her tent. She felt that warm tingle again in that area between her thighs grow into total lust. She realized she did want to have sex with him. She really did. She had never felt such desire. She thought she might finally understand Lady Chatterley. *But, no, not tonight. Maybe never.* But she was excited that she could feel, and she wasn't afraid. She didn't feel shame, only desire.

She'd never had sex with anyone. She had seen things, and since her parents had been useless for much of anything, she had elected to talk with Annie about sex when she was twelve years old. Annie was a good confidante and explained to her about what happened between men and women, about how beautiful it could be with someone you loved. She went on about her first and only love who died in the latter years of the Vietnam War. She moved to the Farm afterward to lose herself in her grief. She never moved on or found anyone else.

She was feeling cold and she had to pee. She excused herself and went off into the dark and came back to find Chris ready to light a little pipe.

"Want a little hit? It'll help you sleep."

"A little hit of what?"

"Just a little pot."

"I've never tried it. What'll it do?"

"Just mellow you out but no more than a little hit, especially if you never tried it before. Okay?"

She was beyond worrying about much of anything right now and said, "Sure."

He showed her how and handed over the pipe and lighter. She followed his instructions, then coughed and sputtered. "Gaaaak! That was harsh!"

He laughed. "No problem. Yeah, it can be pretty harsh the first time."

They each took another hit, the second being easier for her. He put his stash away and said, "Man, look at the stars, so beautiful, so clear, no city lights out here. It's so amazing."

She had been so wrapped up in her chill that she hadn't paid attention. She looked up.

"Wow, just like my nights in the mountains—so clear, so beautiful. It always makes me feel so small and insignificant."

"Truly so, but we're all children of the universe. We are not insignificant but an integral part of this wonderful creation we are part of, and we all participate in the constant creation and recreation just by being who we are."

Even though she was chilled, she sat there for a while longer with him. Jenny pondered Chris's philosophy. She was starting to feel a little strange, very mellow and very tired. She got up and moved toward the tent. He followed. After initial clumsiness, boots off but fully clothed, they each got settled into his and her respective sleeping bag.

Jenny said, "Chris, will you kiss me good night?"

"I would be honored." He reached over and gave her a peck on the cheek.

She grabbed him and gave him a full-on, lengthy kiss on the mouth.

She let him go, giggling from being tickled by his facial hair. She felt her heart racing and an even more profound deep desire for him, which she worked hard to ignore.

"Sorry, Chris, I couldn't help it. I just wanted to. I never kissed a guy on the mouth before."

He took a breath. "Ah, that's okay. It was really nice. Thank you. Jenny, I like you."

"Like you too, Chris. Sleep well."

Chapter 28

Jenny lay there awake for a while. She heard Chris's breathing deepen into sleep. It felt good being close to him. It made her feel safe, secure, like when she was at her grandparents' condo. She liked his musky male smell, mixed with the desert smells of the piñon and sage. She felt an intense primal desire to share his body; she thought how strange this all was, how nice it all felt.

I meet this complete stranger, and I'm sleeping beside him. I feel so happy and comfortable with him, but what the fuck am I doing? What's going on? This is such a totally fucking weird place? I'm loving every bit of it.

She started to giggle, considering all this, then drifted off to sleep. She started to dream she was flying. She looked down and could see herself sleeping in the tent. There was a silver cord from her solar plexus connected to herself in the tent. It was strange. It was exhilarating. Then she noticed Chris flying along beside her. He also had a silver cord connected to his sleeping Chris. He reached out and took her hand, and they went higher. She could see the lights of Sedona. Then there was a huge place of lights to the south. Prescott? Phoenix? She was in awe, total bliss, and total trust in Chris.

He turned to her. "Time to go back now, Jenny. We have to return now."

She protested, "No. I don't want to! I want to keep going. Let's keep going."

He said again, only more forcefully, "We have to go back now, Jenny! We have to return. Now!"

Reluctantly, she obeyed, and he led her back to the sleeping Jenny and the sleeping Chris in the tent below. It was like she'd entered back into her own body. She awoke.

It was daylight. Chris stirred. "Good morning, Morning Glory. Sleep well?"

"Yeah," she said, yawning and stretching. "I did. How 'bout you?"

"Great, but I really gotta pee." He was out of his sleeping bag; he quickly slipped his boots on and left.

Jenny had to pee also; plus she felt a little strange. Too much wine? The pot?

They both stumbled back to the campsite, still a little groggy.

"Want to heat up some burritos? I think there might be still some left in the cooler."

"Sounds great. I'll get some coffee going."

"Sure, hey, wow, that marijuana was crazy. I dreamed we were flying together away above here last night."

"Yeah, that was fun, wasn't it?"

She thought for an instant. "What the hell are you saying? Yeah, I dreamed that you were there. But it was just a dream! My dream, right?!"

"Jenny, have you ever heard of an out-of-body experience? That's what we had last night. Do you remember the silver cords? They connected our ethereal bodies to our mortal bodies. Our physical bodies were sleeping. It's hard to explain. Amanda would do a way better job of explaining this than I can. It was like our souls or spirits were free of our bodies and, experiencing who we truly are, were able to experience the freedom. Oh, man, I am so screwing this up. I have done this before ... a number of times. This place seems to almost require OBEs as protocol, but I've never done it with anyone before. The first time I was so freaked out. I hiked for twelve straight hours to get back to town. It was late, but I went to Amanda's anyway and woke her up. I was so freaked. She explained it to me and got me calmed down. Damn, but it's really fun once you know what's happening."

"Quit shitting me, Chris! Seriously, just quit."

"Jenny, please trust me. I am not shitting you. Please talk to Amanda when we get back. Please, for my sake anyway. I'm sorry I can't do a better job of trying to explain this to you. All I can say is that it was amazing to be with you."

"Sure, okay, as long as you don't feed me any more tall tales about out-of-body stuff."

"Hey, let's change the subject here. Do you feel like a little drive today? We could head up to Jerome. It's a funky, old mining town hanging on the side of a mountain not too far from here. We could have lunch."

"Sounds fun. We can get some supplies and ice for the cooler to stay out a few days more. Maybe we should pack up and spend the night up there. Are there any hotels or anything?"

"There's the Miner's Hotel. I've stayed there. It's rustic but really nice, sort of pricey. We could check it out. We could always camp if that doesn't work."

"I want to do some more hiking and exploring, but yeah, sounds fun. Let's do it."

Chapter 29

They packed up their camp and headed out to Highway 89A. It was a wonderful day, sunny and mild. They headed through the desert toward a mountain range and then up a winding, steep road to the old mining town of Jerome. It truly was a funky, little town with narrow, windy streets, houses, stores hanging precariously on steep slopes, boutiques, antique shops, art galleries, a few restaurants, and the requisite T-shirt and souvenir shops.

Jenny and Chris spent the rest of the morning roaming various shops, coming to rest for lunch at an Italian restaurant. Some light food and iced tea later, they continued exploring shops and enjoying themselves, laughing, talking, and totally enjoying being with each other. They both did some shopping at an outdoors store, both buying some new clothes. At about three thirty, realizing they still hadn't found a place to stay and finding themselves right in front of the Miner's Hotel, they went in and found a room available, a double queen suite.

They looked at each other, smiled, and nodded approval.

"Okay, on me," she said. "My idea. I'll buy."

"Oh, come on. We can split. I have some money."

"Then get a haircut and a shave."

"What? You don't like the way I look? I'm not that bad after only three days. That's harsh."

Jenny cracked up. "Giving you crap. Sorry."

He laughed back. "Yeah, I'm a bit scraggy. I hear ya, but I still want to split the bill."

"Well, okay, if you insist."

They walked up to their room, which was a spacious suite with great views of the desert floor below, a luxurious bathroom with a huge spa-size tub, and a minibar.

"Wow, this is pretty amazing. The lap of luxury," she said.

"Not too tacky at all," remarked Chris. "Hey, can I shower first? I'll be quick. Then I'll head out and get a trim."

"Sure, go ahead. I'm planning on taking a long, hot bath."

Jenny threw her bag on the floor and fell onto the nearest bed. *Oh, this will be so nice.*

Chris showered and put on his new, clean clothes.

"Back in a few," he said and was out the door.

She went into the bathroom and started filling the tub. She threw in some bubble bath, got some of her new clothes from her shopping bag, took out a bottle of wine from the minibar, went in, locked the door, stripped off her clothes, and got into the steaming, hot bath. *Yum,* she thought as she soaked away the last few days. She soaked until the water started to cool, then got, toweled off and got dressed in her new, clean jeans and T-shirt. She was came out of the bathroom just as Chris came back, transformed with a haircut and a shave.

"For a desert rat, you clean up pretty good. You even smell good," she said.

"Yep, saw a barber shop about a block away. Got the full treatment."

They sat with a minibar wine each, enjoying the view of the desert, talking about how much fun they'd had together.

"Let's go out and look for someplace for dinner. I'm getting starved," he said.

"Me too. Let's go."

It was a week before Christmas, and the town was alive with lights and a festive crowd roaming the streets. They found an interesting restaurant that looked like it had come directly from the eighteen hundreds and went in. The interior carried the theme of the exterior, giving the feel as if they had stepped back into time when the town was indeed a mining town. But it was very upscale, with linen tablecloths and napkins, crystal glasses, and full settings of silverware. They ordered a bottle of Bordeaux, lamb chops and salad for Jenny, and steak and salad for Chris.

"This beats a tent and freeze-dried food any day," Chris said.

"Yeah, but it lacks the ambiance of the desert or the mountains, just being outside. I love the solitude, love being way from people. I feel safer, more secure."

"I like a balance of both really. I like being out for a few weeks, but then I'm ready to get back to civilization. I like my little cabin where I can write, where I can go into town for coffee, see a few folks I know, browse the bookstore, and eat some decent food. I like being warm and sleeping in a bed."

"Beds are overrated. I hardly ever slept in a bed over the last two years up until last October. It was just my tent, sleeping pad and bag. I miss it. I liked it that everything I owned fit into my backpack. It was total freedom. Now I seem to be accumulating stuff, furnishing my little house, new clothes, linens, blankets, towels, a Jeep. Where does it end? Our society seems to be so dependent on stuff. Everybody has too much stuff, way more than is necessary to live. Sometimes I still want to just shed everything and go back to living out of my backpack again."

They continued chatting and drinking their wine. Their food came, they ordered another bottle of Bordeaux and ate leisurely, enjoying what was wonderful food and an excellent choice of wine. Finished, their table cleared, each ordered a desert and an aperitif. They were both stuffed and a little drunk and giddy.

They left the restaurant and walked toward the hotel. He reached for her hand. She responded by taking his, looking up at him and smiling.

It was getting late, so they decided to call it a night and went to their room. Each fell into a bed, lay there, and giggled. Jenny was alight with happiness at that moment, happier than she could ever remember. She really liked this guy. He seemed to take her as she was, and he seemed to enjoy being with her. There was no judgment. He made her feel safe. It was nice.

Chris said in a quiet voice, "Jenny, I really, really like you. I think I might be falling in love with you."

She took a sharp breath, her mood changed in an instant. Her old demons flew out of the walls and circled around her like the merciless, black, awful creatures they were, laughing hysterically at her, taunting her. *You can't ever love anyone. Nobody will love you, ever. You are damaged goods. You are worthless; you are a shameful, pathetic little slut.*

She bolted upright and looked over at him. "You think you are falling in love with me! Falling in love … with me?! Hah!" she spat out, continuing in a sarcastic voice. "Oh Chris, thank you so very much. You are so incredibly sweet and wonderful and totally stupid!"

Then, in a more caring, serious voice, she apologized for her outburst. "I'm sorry. You didn't deserve that, you didn't. But please don't fall in love with me, Chris! I repeat, please do not fall in love with me. I haven't really told you the whole story about my crazy, fucked-up life; it's ugly, scary, and not pretty."

Chris sat for a minute and said, "Tell me, if you want to. I'm a good listener. I told you I'm not judgmental or critical. Give it a shot if you want. I'll just listen."

Surprising herself, Jenny started, and it all started flowing out of her, like a spring snowmelt torrent cascading out of the mountains. She told him the whole thing in more graphic detail than she might have intended. It was easy telling him, easier than it ever had been telling others before. Her voice was flat with no emotion, no fear, no sadness; it just was. Chris sat and listened intently, nodding every so often, raising eyebrows other times, but he never said a word. An hour later, she finished with the latest events in dealing with Michael and Peter, and fell silent.

"Wow! Jenny, I can—not—fucking—imagine! There's no way, no way, I could ever imagine what you went through, what you have been going through. But Jenny! This is your story! You have to write this! There are probably other women out there and so many more who need to know your story. Do it as a memoir or a novel. Do it third person. However you do it, you need to get this story out there."

She laughed at that remark. "You really think anyone would want to read this crazy shit about my crazy life? It's way too stupid and scary. Anyway, I just don't think I could ever do it."

"Yes, you could! Really. It would be a wonderful story. You can add characters or make it any way you want, as fiction. No one would ever know it's about you."

"Except for everyone who has ever known me," she said calmly.

"How long are you planning to stay in Sedona? You could come crash at my place. We can write. Do you have a laptop with you? I'll help if I can. Do whatever I can do to help you. What do ya think?"

"Whoa, slow down, Chris. What the hell! One thing I do not fucking need is any pressure. I do not need fucking pressure right now. Please!"

"Wait! Wait! I'm sorry. I tend to get excited and go overboard. I'm so sorry. I can act pretty nuts sometimes. I'll slow down and shut up, okay?"

"Chris, you're a good guy. I'm damaged goods! I just unloaded my sordid life. You know the shit I told you, the shit I carry with me every day. It's not a great story. The truth is, I'm unlovable. It's just the way it is. It is all fucking true! I can never love you back like you need to be loved. Never. Just don't. I don't know how to love anyone, so please don't. I don't think I'll ever be able to love anyone. I just cannot be your girlfriend!"

Chris thought about all he had heard. "Jenny," he said very gently and passionately, "please, just let go of your baggage shit. It doesn't do you any good. It doesn't make any damn difference to me. This is now. That was then. What don't you get about that? This is now, right now. This moment is all we have. The past is only memories. Neither of us can know what is in the future. There is only right now, this moment, this moment you and I are experiencing together. Right now! I have only known you for—what—three, four days? Already I cannot imagine ever being without you. You are amazing, wonderful. I love being with you. What don't you get about that? You're too hard on yourself. Please?"

"I ... I can't, Chris. I just can't," she said, choking back tears. "I'm sorry, Chris, I just don't know how or even if I can, for fuck's sake. I don't know if I can ever really truly love or truly trust you or anyone. My demons are right here. Right now. I see them. You can't understand. I have no idea what love even is! How can I know something I never had or ever experienced?"

He went over, sat down by her, took her, and held her in his arms. She put her head on his shoulder and broke into sobs.

She so wanted to love, to be loved, to know love, to understand love. She just wanted to curl up and sleep forever.

She awoke the next morning, fully clothed, still in his arms. He had held her all night long.

198

She turned to look at him with a drowsy smile. "Did you ever sleep?"

"Oh yeah, snuggled in right here with you all night long." She put her arms around him and kissed him, warm and long. "I don't know if I can do this, Chris."

"I know, but I'm not going to quit trying. Let's get straightened up and go get some breakfast, shall we?"

"Sounds good." She kissed him again and then just held him. "You're the best."

"Thanks. So are you," he said, choking back his own emotions.

Chapter 30

They checked out of the hotel and went for breakfast and lots of coffee. Afterward, they headed back down the switchbacks toward Sedona.

Chris said, "I'm not sure about you, but I'm ready to head back to Sedona."

"Yeah, I think I'm ready to head back as well. I want to stop and see Amanda. I have some questions for her."

"Hey, let's stop on the way back. We have time. I have a little hike that you might like. There's a place I want to show you. You might find it interesting. We'll need to take snacks and water."

"How long a hike?"

"About five miles from the road, round trip. But maybe we can get a little closer with the Jeep, if you want. There's an old dirt road."

"Let's check it out."

A few more miles up the road, Chris told her to slow down and then pointed to an almost invisible track running off into the desert. "Turn here."

She did and then drove down a rutted trail until it petered out.

"This is as far as we can drive. Hike from here. It's only about a mile now."

She went to her cargo carrier and got it out her day pack. She packed a few things and filled the hydration bladder. Chris had his stuff out; he also got some water, and they were ready to go. Chris led her through the ever-present, beautiful desert landscape. After about a mile, they came to what looked like a pile of very large, black, gray, and red-striated boulders that looked surreal and out of place in another wise, fairly flat landscape. The boulders varied in height from maybe ten feet to some about twice that size. They walked around the circumference. They appeared to be in a circle, about fifty feet in diameter, almost like some giant machine had located them precisely, with some purpose.

Jenny exclaimed with an expression of awe, "This is so strange. It's like they grew out of the desert floor."

"Yeah, it's very strange, but what's not strange out here?" He continued to lead her around to a space in the rocks, and he squeezed through. She followed and entered into another world ... and a deceptively large space enclosed by the boulders. There were strange writings on some of the rock surfaces, some crudely drawn pictures, and a circle of small stones in the center of the space. It felt very strange and disorienting to Jenny.

Chris said, "Let's sit and meditate for a little bit. We have time."

"Holy shit! What's happening here?! Where did you bring me? I'm feeling totally screwed up, like too much to drink. Wow!" She found a place to sit with her back to one of the rocks.

Jenny smiled. "Oh my God, it's beautiful, Chris." She closed her eyes and was gone into another place, into a deep meditation.

He did not meditate, but stayed alert and sat with her for almost an hour. She never moved; only her shallow breathing, interrupted intermittently by brief smiles and some giggling, indicated she was still even alive.

She finally stirred. She sat bolt upright. "What the fuck just happened? She opened her eyes, feeling disoriented. "Chris, are you there?" She said softly, "Chris? Chris?"

"I'm right here, Jenny. You okay?"

She answered, "Wow! What a trip! Really! Wow! So what the hell is this place? It was so amazing—just so amazing. I think I had a vision," she blurted out excitedly. "There were strange people, all in white, and they—were ... what—were glowing. They took me down a glowing white corridor, and there was this woman. She looked just like me, only older, and I realized it was my mother. It was my real mother. She held me, told me she loved me, that she was always with me. It was like the most beautiful thing ever, like I ... like, I don't know. I can't explain it. It was beautiful. I felt light and free. Then there were the dark, ghastly, scary entities that appeared. They were circling all around me. My mother extended her arms, and electricity or something shot out from her fingers and made the dark, horrible things evaporate, and then I was lead back here. I have no idea, but it was all so real, so very real. What the hell happened?" And she started to cry.

"It's okay, Jenny. It's really, really ... I don't know. I know it's really a weird, powerful place. I felt weird when I came in here the first time. It's like some sort of alternative reality. I saw stuff, like I was on some crazy sort of drugs. I had to lie down. I was weak. I was spinning. I was by myself. I thought I was going to die ... and I didn't even care. Then I relaxed, and my life fell before me. I saw everything. I was so freaking out, but I just went with it, and it was so wonderful. I was here, like, for hours."

"It was freaky, Chris." She sniffled. "I was given directions about my life, that I would be happy with one person that I already knew, that I would be a writer, that I would be successful, that my demons would die in the light. It was crazy but so real. I remember everything, like it truly was real. My mother was beautiful. Everyone was beautiful. I felt so good and so free. I love this place. I want to come back again and again. I want to see my mother again." And she cried in happiness and sadness at the same time.

"I know. My experience was similar to what you are saying. But I have been back here, like a dozen times since, and nothing, like it was a onetime shot. At least for me it was. Are you feeling okay? Want some water?"

She had finished crying and, realized she was holding onto him and let go. "Yeah, I need some water. Help me up, and we can leave. I need bright sky and water."

They got out from the rocks, and Jenny became reoriented. They each had a long drink of water. They got back into the Jeep, and Jenny reached over and gave him a long, lingering, loving kiss. She headed back out down the back road and hit the highway; then a short time later they were in Sedona.

Chapter 31

Chris said, "I remember inviting you to stay here for a while. The offer still stands. Why not hang out until after New Year's? We can write and talk and cook, just enjoy time together. I really don't want you to leave. Just being with you is really nice. How about it?"

Jenny thought for a few moments.

"Well, I really don't want to go back to Durango right now. I am still getting over being pissed at my so-called mentor, William. I accidently saw an outline he was writing. It was an outline for a story, a story about me, about my life! I trusted him, and he blindsided me. He was writing about my life ... my fucking life! He said it was a surprise for me to help me. But it really made me angry. I deep down know he meant well, but trust is hard for me to come by, and I trusted him. I guess I felt let down and just had to get away to think it all through. He's really a great guy, and I truly love him, like a father. I know I'll get over it. That's what scares me about getting involved with you. Everyone I meet seems to want something from me and then betrays me. I realize how on edge I always am. It's probably my own fears. I don't want to hurt you or get hurt." She stared off into space, then said, "I do find it interesting that both you and Will are trying to get me to write about myself."

Chris was silent for a while, thinking. "That's because we both apparently think you have a story to tell. And, you know, I can understand that you might feel this way from all you shared with me. But you speak so highly of him, of how much you care for him. My guess is, he truly wanted to help you get by whatever blocks you have, to get you writing. And from what you have said about how you want to write but have no stories, can't get started, I think you're blocked. He thought he might help by doing this outline.

"And I will again tell you that I am in this for as long as you will have me. I promise. I will not betray you. If things ever go sour, which I know they can in any relationship, I will talk with you about it. I will always be honest with you. I will not screw you over. I promise you that."

She thought on this for a few minutes. "I don't know. You talk about 'relationship.' I know nothing about being in a relationship. It's just that I have such a hard time trusting anyone. I want to, but maybe you're right. When I think about him, I have a hard time understanding why he would ever want to cheat me, to hurt me. I need to talk with him again. Maybe tomorrow I'll call and talk to him. He deserves that much from me.

"Anyway, he and our friend, Helen, have all these plans for Christmas: a big dinner and presents and stuff. I don't want to see Peter and have to deal with him. I don't have any presents for anyone. I really never celebrated Christmas before, not even as a little girl. There just was never Christmas. Are you sure you want me there? I don't want to interfere with anything you might have planned."

"I have no plans. You would be my plan. No pressure. We can go into town and get some groceries, some beer, some wine, and whatever else we might want to spend our time. It would be fun. So? Deal? I'd like you to stay as long as you want."

"Okay, then, let's see how it goes; maybe until after New Year's then."

"Yes!" Chris exclaimed, pumping his fist. "You can sleep in my bed. I'll take the couch."

"No, no, no! I appreciate your chivalry, but the couch is fine. I insist. No argument. Okay! You stay in your own bed."

"Okay, let me get you some sheets and blankets. No more sleeping bag. I'll help you bring in what you will need. We can freshen up and go into town. You wanted to see Amanda. I have a few errands to run. Then to the grocery store to get our supplies. I need a grocery list. What do you want?" He was excited and starting to ramble on.

"Okay, Chris," she said, laughing at his exuberance. "Slow down. Give me a few minutes, and I'll be ready. I can get what I need from the Jeep."

"Sure. Have to see what's in the fridge. Haven't been here for almost a week. Be thinking of what you might want for food and drink."

Jenny went out to the Jeep and brought in the bags she needed. Chris had made a place for her to put them. She unpacked her personal items, put them onto a bathroom shelf Chris had already cleared a for her.

She said, "When we go into town, let's get some lunch first. I'm starved."

"Yeah, me too. Sort of forgot about lunch. Let's go. You can tell me what food you want on the way."

They were off, planning the food list as they went the short distance to downtown. Jenny parked, and they went to the same café where she had eaten lunch on her first day five long days ago; it seemed like forever.

She was in a spin; so much was happening so fast. But she felt at ease with it all, very much at ease. She liked Chris. He made her feel good, almost like she was normal. And she did feel normal being around him. He accepted her; he liked her, even thought he might be in love with her. She felt protected and safe and happy.

They both ordered light salads with iced tea. They made light banter about a few tourists gawking around and talking loudly. They paid and left. Chris was off to the bank and bookstore to pick up a book he had ordered. Jenny went over to Amanda's store.

Chapter 32

"You're back," she said, upon seeing Jenny enter the store. "Have fun?"

"Yeah, it was fun, and I have a lot of questions for you," she started talking very fast, "a lot of questions. So much that happened is terribly confusing to me. Chris is great. I like him, but he thinks he's in love with me. And then there's ... what, OBEs? Then there were the rock circle thing and visions and, oh, I just feel so messed up. Am I, Amanda? Am I going nuts? Tell me I'm not. Just tell me I'm not losing it."

Amanda sat patiently, listening intently with undivided concern but smiling inwardly. Then they sat for a few moments after Jenny finished and started to calm down.

"Well, first off, you are certainly not losing it. Chris is one of my favorite people ever, and I'm happy you found each other. You are both very good for one another. My advice: take time, enjoy him, be with him, but don't hurt him. He appears hardened from the desert, but his shell is fragile. Please, please don't lead him on to somewhere you aren't prepared to go yourself."

"I promise, Amanda. He's become a very, very special person in my life."

"And an OBE?"

"Yeah, I guess." Jenny went on to explain what had happened that night.

Amanda confirmed what Chris had told her, that things like this were not uncommon, especially out in the desert, especially this big, red, mysterious desert. That they traveled together was indicative of what she had just said about them being good together.

Then Jenny went on to her vision at the boulder place.

"I know the place you are talking about. I have also been there and had a similar experience to yours. Chris told me about his after he was there. All I can say is that it's a very, very high-energy place, a vortex, if you will, where the thin curtain between our mortal reality and the spirit reality can be easily gone through or is maybe is even just nonexistent.

"Putting our mortal, perceived reality aside, I would say that indeed, your mother was there, as were all the entities you encountered: the light beings as well as the dark beings. I would also say that the dark beings or entities, as you called them, were some of your demons that you have been following you, primarily the demons of your abuse. Your mother did annihilate them with her energy, with her undying, never-ending love for you. As an aside, we might talk about souls sometime but not now. Have you felt any different since then?"

Jenny pondered this, pausing to wipe some tears. "Yes, in thinking about it, I feel lighter, more alive. Maybe more free? Really? You think that these demons might finally be truly gone? It seems too easy. My therapist would say that it was too easy, that I needed work to get beyond all my past crap."

"Yes, I do believe you might be free of those demons, but the dregs, the scars, the memories of it all will still be with you, probably all your life. It is how you deal with those memories that will make the difference now. You can choose to let them dominate you, or you can choose to work on accepting and releasing them.

"I have worked with all this metaphysical stuff for the last twenty years. I have seen lots of weird, crazy stuff firsthand and have heard many things from others. But I am also a realist. You will have to see how your life is or has changed or not. Please, please do not give up on your therapy. Keep with it. From what you told me, and what I saw when working on you, there is a lot of stuff you have been carrying and need to work on. I believe that the experience you told me about is a wonderful beginning. But—and a big 'but'—pay attention. Pay close attention to your feelings and your life. Be aware. Be mindful. Use your pendulum, like I showed you, to help you with answers when you need them. Trust yourself. Trust your intuition."

Jenny was trying to absorb all this and was silent for a long while. She thanked Amanda. Then Amanda asked what her plans were. Jenny told her about her time with Chris, that she'd had a little breakdown and told him everything and about how understanding he seemed to be. She went on to say she was staying with him until after New Year's Day.

"I promise I won't hurt him. I have warned him about me, but he's stubborn, won't take no for an answer. He still thinks he might be in love with me. I really like him, Amanda, but I don't know love. I can't remember ever feeling love. I guess my grandparents love me. I guess I love them. But it is a different feeling with him, different from what I feel for my grandparents. I like seeing them and all, but it isn't the same feeling when I'm with them. It's nice but not the same. With Chris, it's different. Am I making any sense?"

"Yes, total sense. There are different forms of love. There's parental, like what you feel for your grandparents. Then there is passionate love for someone whom you want to be with, to share everything with. The latter would be what you are most likely feeling for Chris, especially now in the throes of a new relationship. You can't get enough of each other. Everything seems new, alive, and magical."

"That sort of describes it. I do feel so full of energy and desires, feelings I never had before. Sometimes I feel out of control when I'm with him. I want to be with him every minute, right next to him, smelling him, hearing his breathing, feeling his heart beating, like our hearts are the same. Make any sense?"

"Absolutely," Amanda said with a nod and a big smile.

Jenny continued, "He wants me to write a book about my life, my struggles. He thinks there might be many of me out there who could benefit from hearing my story, knowing they are not alone." She remembered William and the outline he had written. Maybe he really had written it for her.

"I would agree with him about the book. Write it. There are tons of self-help books written by professionals who try to help. But you are 'first person.' You have the story, the real story. I encourage you to give it a go. I will look forward to reading it." She smiled.

"I will. I appreciate all your advice. Can I pay you?"

"No way! I enjoyed hearing your stories. Very powerful stuff. Pay attention and stay in touch."

"I absolutely will. Thank you. I so appreciate you and your help. I'm going to be around until after the New Year, so I'll see you before I leave."

"I look forward to it." And she turned to go into the back of her store.

Jenny went to her Jeep to find Chris waiting for her.

Chapter 33

"Sorry, hope you weren't waiting long."

"Naw, only a few minutes. Checking e-mails and phone messages. Seems like every time I'm gone for a few days, the world wants to call me, e-mail me, or text me. Is there some weird law governing that?"

"Maybe you will have to go back to the rock place and ask whoever is there for an answer to that rather cosmic question."

He laughed. "Yeah, good one."

They drove to the grocery store, making and checking the list on the way. Between them, they bought a large cart full of food and returned to the house. It was going on six o'clock; they were hungry, decided on a menu, broke out a bottle of wine, and prepared their food while laughing and talking.

Jenny, having never done any cooking other than making sandwiches, knew nothing. However, Chris seemed to know everything. Together they got the food ready, and he patiently guiding her through her first-ever meal preparation.

They had a long dinner filled with good food, wine, and conversation: sometimes fun, sometimes serious, sometimes sad. When they finally cleared the dishes, for washing in the morning, it was past ten o'clock. They were tired and said their good nights with a long kiss and hug. Chris went into the bedroom, and Jenny, who had borrowed one of Chris's T-shirts for a pajama top, got herself and her couch ready for sleep.

But sleep didn't come to her, tired as she was. She lay there thinking of the past few days, of all that had happened, of all the strange things that had happened, of how she was feeling ... about everything. There was so much to ponder.

She felt restless. Deep inside her, there was a primal urge for something. She considered this; it was new, something she wasn't familiar with. And it flashed into her mind: Chris. She had been close to him the last two nights, one night sleeping next to each other in the tent, and then in the same room, the same bed with him comforting her all night. She wanted to be with him now, be next to him, hearing his breathing, feeling his warmth, feeling his body, feeling his strength, feeling his calm reassurance.

She got up, quietly sneaked into his room, stealthily slipped into his bed, and curled herself up next to him. This was what she wanted, but she wanted more. The raw, primal urge finally erupted into desire; she desired him. She wanted to make love to him, to be naked with him, to have him touch her. But the thought of it almost made her sick to her stomach.

All she knew about sex, other than what Annie had told her, were all the painful, abusive experiences she had witnessed and experienced when she was a child. Sex seemed so horrible and ugly. She couldn't imagine how anyone could think sex was beautiful. But she liked being here with Chris. He made her feel safe and cared for. She fell into a dreamless, sound sleep.

She awoke the next morning to the wonderful aroma of coffee and a Bach violin concerto playing quietly. She stretched, curled up, hugged herself, and then stretched again, languishing in a wonderful contentment she wasn't used to. She felt so good. She so liked this guy. She liked being with him, sleeping with him; it occurred to her that he would be the first man she would have sex with. She seemed to know deep down that he would somehow make it beautiful for her. He respected her, and he liked her, even said he was falling in love with her. Maybe that was what she was feeling at this moment of bliss: love? She thought on this. Maybe it was love she was feeling. *Interesting.* She wished she could talk with Joan right now. It was new territory, and she wanted a map. She finally broke from her reflection, got up slowly, and went toward the bathroom.

"Good morning," a smiling Chris said. "Bacon, eggs, toast?"

"You sure know the way to a girl's heart. Back in a minute."

"I hope so. I would love to be there in your heart."

She appeared a few minutes later and went for the coffee, still in Chris's T-shirt and her panties, not the least concerned about her almost nakedness. She felt safe with him and happy and warm and—in love? She sat down at the table, facing his back as he was preparing their food.

"So, girl, was the couch too uncomfortable for you?"

"No, I was just lonesome. I just, it's ... I don't know, I ... Oh shit, Chris, please don't laugh at me, but I think I might be falling in love with you too, whatever love is. I don't think I really know. I just so like being with you, knowing you, learning more about you. You make me feel warm, secure, safe, cared for. I really need that TLC right now. I want to be with you. But ... shit, shit, shit ... this is so hard to say: I guess being in love means having sex, and I'm just petrified of ever having sex. I'm totally petrified. Everything dealing with sex has always been so terrible and awful, just disgusting, ugly. I'm scared of what might happen. Please understand. Please? You're the first guy I really have ever spent time with, slept in the same bed with, ever."

Chris was standing there, in the act of slicing bacon, stock still. He turned, came, and sat down, facing her.

"Okay, wow, I can understand how very hard that was for you to say, and I appreciate it. I can reiterate what you just said. I told you I was falling in love with you. I love being with you, sharing all we have shared, and I want to keep on sharing your life. I don't have a clue where this might be heading, but I'm more than willing to go along for the ride. I seriously want to be with you.

"Now, about the sex thing, I understand. I understand. I am totally willing to take all the time you might want, as hard as it is for me, he said, laughing nervously. "You are very sexy, and having you sleep with me every night is driving me crazy. But I'll live with it. You'll be ready whenever you're ready and not before. Okay? No pressure. Deal?"

"Thanks, Chris. You're a good guy. I don't have a clue how guys feel sexually. I just know how I feel, and it is two opposites running around inside me: I do want to have sex with you, but I just can't do it. I don't want to have something ugly happen between us, like what I experienced when I was a girl. I'm really sorry. I care for you too much to hurt you."

"It's okay. Nothing to be sorry about. I can wait. You're worth it. What I feel for you is something bigger than sex anyway, although sex would be a nice addition at some point. No rush. We'll take it slow. Promise. Okay?"

"Thanks." She got up, went to him, and kissed him. Feeling so much of what she thought might be love for him right then, she almost cried.

"Okay then," he said, "let's make some food—I'm starved."

Chapter 34

After they had some breakfast the next morning, she remembered she wanted to call Will. Deep down inside she knew he truly wanted to help and that she had reacted badly. When she thought about it, the only people who had ever helped her were her grandparents ... and Annie, to some degree. She wasn't used to it.

She went outside the cabin and called. He picked up. "Hi, Will, it's Jenny. How's things?"

"Doing well. How about you?"

"I'm great. I've been exploring the desert down here and loving every bit of it. I really wanted to call and tell you I am sorry for the way I over-reacted to that outline you did. I realize you were only trying to help, and I responded badly. I'm sorry," she said with a lump gathering in her throat and tears staring to form. *Dammit, I can't cry.*

"It is okay, Jenny. I understand. As I said, I should have talked to you about doing that. It was my fault."

"Let's just forget this ever happened. You're too important to me, Will. You know how I feel about you."

"I do, and thanks. I am sorry you won't be back for Christmas, though."

"I know, but to be honest, I met this guy. I want to spend a little more time with him before I come back. He's good to me and caring. Makes me feel secure and safe. We've been roaming this amazing desert together. He's smart and a writer also. Between your and his encouragement, I've set my mind to start on a project. I'm really excited."

"That is great about you starting to write. Good for you. For whatever it's worth, I'll e-mail the outline to you. Do you have Wi-Fi somewhere so I could send it?"

"That would be nice. I would appreciate that. Thanks. Hold on just a second for me to get it," she said.

She called Chris, who was inside the house, "Chris, what's your Wi-Fi address or, better yet, your e-mail?"

He grabbed a pencil and paper and quickly wrote down the address, giving it to her. She relayed it to Will. "I'll send it right after I hang up. But I thought you and Peter—"

"Will, all I can say is that Peter balked when I told him a little about me. I just couldn't handle that. I need someone who can accept me for who I am and not have to 'think about it.'"

"I understand. He is a lawyer. And he'll probably be a good one who ever relies only on solid evidence."

Jenny chuckled. "Thanks, Will. I love you. See you after New Year's."

"I love you too, Jenny. Be safe."

"I will." And she clicked off.

She then called her grandparents, letting them know what was going on and where she was. She asked about Michael, and the report wasn't good. The assault charges from the women in Colorado Springs were very solid and damaging. There was DNA evidence and a strong collaborative report from the victims of Michael's systematic patterns of abuse. Then there was his altercation with her at the restaurant. It wasn't looking good. Dean had contacted a good attorney, an ex-colleague in his old firm, to represent him. The best defense was going to have to be insanity. There was way too much condemning evidence against Michael.

"He is not doing himself any good either," Dean went on to say. "His bail hearing judge was a woman, who, probably rightfully so, denied any bail, saying he was both a danger to society and a flight risk. He went ballistic, calling the judge names I don't wish to mention, screaming how it was all your fault. Ever since you were kids together, you caused all his problems, how he would teach you and all women a lesson. He then threatened to kill you. The bailiffs had to forcibly remove him from the courtroom. His attorney wanted to quit right then and there, but I persuaded him to continue to represent him."

"It sounds like he has totally lost it. I have no idea why he would blame me for all this. This is really scary!"

"I am sure it is frightening for you. Understandable—but he is locked up and will be until trial, which most likely won't happen until sometime in the spring at the earliest."

They then went on to talk about other things in their lives. Dean asked about Peter, to which Jenny replied that things hadn't worked out without going into any detail. She didn't mention Chris. She again invited them to come to Durango in May or June to ride the train to Silverton, and Dean said they were planning on it.

"Thanks for calling, Jenny. It is so good to talk to you. Thank you again for being in touch, keeping us up to date. We appreciate it."

"You are welcome, Grandpa. I again apologize for being out of touch for those years. I had a lot to sort out in my life and needed that time of seclusion. I think I'm able to finally be a good granddaughter, especially after all you have done for me. Without your help"—she paused, choking back a sob—"I would probably be dead ... I love you both so much."

"We are so happy we could help. We love you too, Jenny. I have to go."

"Me too. Give Susan my love. Call you soon."

And they clicked off.

Jenny sat for a long while, pondering what Michael had said about everything being her fault. She had no idea, but a small niggle was now in her mind. There was something there, something hidden, like it was on the other side of a gauzy curtain, a thin barrier. But whatever it was, it existed just beyond realization. It was there; she could almost feel it, taste it, and smell it, but it remained elusive.

Chapter 35

Chris received a big package delivered from UPS. He opened it, and there were four gaily wrapped Christmas presents along with a card from his parents.

Jenny said, "You've never told me about your family. Do you have any brothers or sisters?"

"I have an older brother and sister, who lived close by my parents in the LA area. I was home last Christmas, and my mom and dad visited me here last summer. My brother and sister are almost ten years older, so we were never close as siblings. I told them I wanted to spend my off time from work here and in the desert and told them last month that I'd be staying here for this year's holidays. Of course, they were disappointed, but I told them I would get there to LA maybe next summer."

"Maybe I'll get to meet them all someday," she said, feeling a little jealous.

"I hope I can introduce you soon. They'll love you if they think you might get me to settle down and quit being a bum."

"You're far from a bum," she said, put her hand on his face, and kissed him.

* * *

Jenny and Chris spent the next days together, which included a very low-key Christmas. They had decided not to get any presents for each other, both not wanting anything. They went out into the desert for some day hikes. The weather was unseasonably warm, and their treks in the desert were filled with sunlight. They explored the local bookstore and stopped by to say hello to Amanda. All the time they laughed, held hands, and grew closer. At night they cooked food together, listened to music, and cuddled together on his couch. They read to each other while drinking wine and basking in each other's glow.

On one visit to Amanda's store, Jenny selected three nice crystal points—a smoky one for Will and two clear ones for Helen and Joan. She was about to go and pay, and she thought of Kelly. She found another smaller one for her. She was starting to miss everyone and was torn between staying longer but also wanting to be back in Durango.

* * *

Jenny looked at Will's outline, and it truly did give her inspiration. It was a good beginning. It laid out a rough time line of her life, with most events being fictitious, leaving room for her additions or subtractions, as she wanted. But it was a beginning.

She finally got the courage to sit down with her laptop the day after Christmas and began. She started the manuscript as a memoir but soon switched to a third-person narrative with different names, circumstances, and locations. Removing herself from first person helped free her up from being so personally attached. This technique worked better for her, and the story started to flow. She was really writing! She did a quick revision to William's outline and created each character's persona. Once started, she became almost obsessed.

After four days and over eight thousand words, she was quite proud of her accomplishment. So now she was writing, but she felt she was also neglecting other things, especially Chris. He was busy with his own writing. She began to take breaks and would sit with him, just wanting to be close to him. Finally, he insisted she keep up with her writing, that he was fine. Later in the afternoons, they would stop and share what they had written, usually over some wine. Sometimes they would critique each other but always give encouragement.

They slept together every night, being close and getting forever closer. Their souls were becoming as one. They both knew it and were happy.

New Year's Eve was in two days. Chris surprised her by telling her he had made dinner reservations at a restaurant in town for a seven o'clock dinner and then a party at a downtown hotel ballroom afterward. Jenny was excited and realized she had no dress-up clothes to wear. She grabbed him and took him to go shopping and help her select her party outfit. After two boutiques, she found a dress; she couldn't believe she was really buying a dress: a little black dress, cut above the knees with a scooped neck and back with wide shoulder straps. Next came shoes, with sensible heels, no spikes for her. And then there were some costume-jewelry bracelets and a faux pearl necklace. She was set.

She stopped by a beauty salon and made an appointment for the next morning and then took Chris to rent a tux, complete with a bow tie and patent leather shoes. They were going "stylin".

Morning came, and Jenny went off for a hair trim, style, and makeover, feeling like she wanted to be beautiful for Chris. She felt so much excitement she could hardly contain herself. As like Christmas, she had never celebrated New Year's before. Chris picked up his tux, and they were ready. They had a late-afternoon snack and got dressed in their duds. They were ready, and they observed each other. They burst out laughing, simply because they both looked so great, and it was so incongruous for them to be playing dress-up.

Chapter 36

"Oh my God ... Jenny, you look so radiant, absolutely beautiful. You are stunning. I can hardly stand it."

She was truly radiant.

"And you look so good I could eat you."

"Fine with me. Let's go and party."

She grabbed her down jacket. "Guess this jacket really doesn't work with the rest of me, but it's warm and will have to do."

Chris laughed. "You look fabulous. Not to worry."

They had a slow, relaxed dinner by candlelight with wine and quiet talk. The food was wonderful with nice portions and a wonderful chocolate mousse dessert they shared. They finished, paid their bill, and left around nine thirty, walking on down to the hotel. Chris had reserved a table for them with two of his friends and their dates, who were already there, seated, having drinks. Chris introduced Jenny and his friends to her: Carla and John, Amy and Bill.

The two other couples were excited to see Chris, wondering where he had been hiding out since they hadn't seen him for almost three weeks. He worked with John and Bill at the landscaping company. He held them off with tales of his desert adventures and of how he had met Jenny. They asked her about herself, and she replied that she was from Durango and had come here for a brief respite.

"So, where're you staying?" Carla asked.

"Oh, with Chris," she replied matter-of-factly to raised eyebrows. "We have been hanging out and hiking. We went to Jerome for a night. Chris has been showing me the desert and his haunts." She looked at Chris with big, loving eyes.

"Are you guys together or what?" Carla asked back.

Chris interrupted the exchange. "Yeah, I guess we are. At least we're heading in that direction, I hope." He looked back at Jenny like a moonstruck teenager with a big, silly grin.

Amy said, "Wow, this is awesome ... and fast."

Carla added with a chuckle, "So you snagged the illusive, never-dated-anyone Christopher Holdsworth. Never thought it would happen."

"Yeah, it's fast, we know, but it seems right, and we're going for it. We'll have to see what happens."

The music started, and people started to move to the dance floor.

The others got up to go, to the relief of Jenny, who didn't want to get into anything further on their relationship.

Chris took her hand. "Come on. Let's go dance."

She froze. "I have never danced. I guess I didn't know people danced at these things. I haven't a clue what to do. I don't want to embarrass you."

"Really, you've never, ever danced? It's not hard. This is a slow one. I'll show you. Just follow me. Come on. You won't embarrass me. Promise."

She reluctantly got up and followed him out to the floor. She was watching others move, noting how they held each other, and imitated what she saw.

"Now," said Chris, "just watch my feet for a second and then do the same, only backwards. I'll lead you. Just listen to the music and the rhythm. Just feel the music."

After a few minutes, she was actually dancing. Chris was a good dancer, and he led her gently around the floor. She felt almost part of him, and the dancing felt good and natural to her.

"This is fun, Chris."

"You're a quick learner."

"You're a good teacher." She moved in close, her face buried in his neck.

The night went on with them all joking, laughing, dancing, and chatting about local gossip. Everyone was having a great time. The women decided to go to the powder room, leaving the guys to chat.

Amy said, "So Jenny, how did you manage to lasso Chris? We have known him for the last few years, and he just never dated anyone. We all tried to line him up, but he always managed to duck away."

Jenny answered, "Well, as strange as it might seem, he appeared as a big, hairy guy at my campsite and scared the hell out of me, and I packed up and came back to town. I ran into him the next day in a shop I had been in and sort of knew the owner and got introduced. He felt bad and took me to lunch, and, well, you know, we've been hanging out ever since."

"So how's he in bed?" Carla asked, smiling, along with an eager-to-know Amy.

"What do you mean?" Jenny asked, feeling heat rush to her cheeks.

"You know. You're 'doing it,' aren't you?" Carla said.

"Doing what? You mean, having sex?" Jenny asked. "No, no! We're not! We haven't, just not."

Both women, seeing how uncomfortable she was, apologized and changed the conversation to other things

The women returned, and Jenny was very flushed. Chris wondered whether she had gotten grilled. She sat down and took his hand. She gave him a big kiss on the cheek and whispered in his ear, "I love you, big guy. I really do."

He squeezed her hand and winked at her, assuring her that the feeling was mutual.

Midnight was approaching, and champagne was being served to all the guests. A lot of folks were donning silly hats; there was an excitement building. Jenny felt herself being caught up in it all. She was having the time of her life.

Boom.

A loud report sounded outside somewhere, reverberating through the room. Everyone in unison hollered, "Happy New Year!" The band started playing "Auld Lang Syne," and people were singing. Chris pulled her into his arms and kissed her.

"Happy New Year, you wonderful, sweet girl. I love you."

"Me, too." She put both of her arms around his neck and returned his kiss, long and tender.

The party went on. After about another hour, Jenny asked Chris whether they could go home. He agreed, he too having had enough.

They went to the Jeep, and Jenny, who'd had only water and a glass of champagne since dinner, drove home. They were both silent, lost in their own thoughts about the night.

Jenny finally said, "I like your friends."

"They like you too." He reached over and put his hand on her neck.

She responded by rolling her head to his touch.

They got to the house and went in. Jenny grabbed Chris around the neck and kissed him.

"Thanks. This was a wonderful night."

"You are so very welcome. It was my pleasure, and you deserved it. Thank you for being with me. It was the best New Year's Eve ever. I'm ready for bed."

"So am I, in more ways than you can imagine." *Much more* than you can ever imagine. "Let's go."

Chapter 37

He went to the bathroom first and was only a minute. She went into the bedroom and got out of her dress and all her underwear; then she slipped into a T-shirt and went to the bathroom. Chris had gotten into bed and, already turned out the light, and was starting to doze. She took off her T-shirt and crawled into bed, snuggling up next to him. Chris rolled over to kiss her good night. He put his arm around her.

"Jenny, holy shit! You're naked!"

"I know. I want to have sex with you tonight, Chris. I so love you. I want to be part of you."

He sucked in a breath. "Jenny! Are you sure about this? I want you so terribly bad . You know that, but please don't rush yourself."

"Don't argue ... I'm ready." She took his hand and brought it to her breast. She shuddered with his touch, with anticipation.

She was trembling with passion. She so wanted him, trying to keep her fears in check and focus on the intense desire filling her body. Her thoughts went to Lady Chatterley, thinking about what she had read about her passion, wondering whether this was what she'd felt: this intense need, a need to have her fulfilled as a woman. At that moment, there was nothing else in the world that mattered other than having Chris inside her.

He fumbled with his pajama bottoms and T-shirt. She moved an exploring hand to him and felt his erection. He moaned. He reached for the side table drawer, fishing for a condom, found one, unwrapped it, and slipped it on. He moved a hand between her legs and felt her wetness.

"Oh God, Chris. Now, right now. Please, right now."

And he rolled onto her and entered her. She could hardly breathe. She felt a sharp pain and then an intensity of pleasure, like every nerve ending in her body was on fire with pleasure, with joy. It was alive with something so intense she thought she might die. Momentarily, her body convulsed uncontrollably in sheer ecstasy. Chris's body stiffened, and he drove so deep into her she thought all of him was inside her. They both were breathing like they had run a marathon. Their bodies went limp, still together, more together than Jenny could ever imagine. She buried her head in his shoulder and cried.

"Jenny, are you okay? Did I hurt you? I'm sorry."

"Oh God, no ... I'm crying out of such sheer joy. This was so beautiful, more beautiful than I could ever imagine. God, I love you so much. Thank you, thank you. I love you."

"I love you too, Jenny, now and always."

He backed out of her and rolled to her side, holding her close. There were no more words. He started to doze off and was soon asleep, still holding her. She lay awake, considering what had just happened, trying to sort out her feelings. All she knew was, this was the most wonderful thing she could remember happening to her, and how much she never wanted to ever lose this guy..

Jenny awoke first in the morning. Still both naked, she moved her hand to him, awakening him and stroking him to an erection, to which he responded by making love to her again, more slowly and deliberately. She never wanted to let him go, ever. She was in absolute bliss and never wanted this moment to end.

Chris was the first to break their reverie. "Jenny, I really have to pee."

"Me too, so make it speedy." She laughed.

"You go first. I can wait a minute."

She jumped out and ran to the bathroom. Chris followed her. She finished and went back to the bed and crawled in.

Chris came back. "Still can't get up? I'll make us some coffee and bring it in." She lay there in her bliss, but that niggling memory rose again in the back of her mind, now stronger than before. The sex was wonderful. She knew it was her first time. But something about it seemed familiar. She considered Dory. No. Her father. No. He was usually too stoned to do much of anything. She thought about the other attacks. No. She just couldn't place any such event.

Chris returned with two coffees, gave her one, and slipped in beside her. They both sat up; Jenny snuggled in beside Chris. They sipped their coffee.

"So, Jenny, are you okay? This has all been pretty intense. Are you feeling okay?"

"Yeah, I feel great. Chris, you were amazing. I just can't describe how it felt to me, how I feel now. I have never felt more alive than right now. I'm still tingling all over." She didn't mention her little niggle to him.

They spent most of the day in bed, making love four more times. They caressed and explored every nook, cranny, and crevice of each other's bodies—tasting, touching, loving.

The rest of the time they spent eating snacks, exploring each other's innermost thoughts.

It was now a quarter to three. They were both sexually and emotionally spent. They got up and took showers, got dressed, stripped the bed, put on clean sheets, and put the others in the laundry. They broke out of their cocoon to enjoy the rest of the afternoon sun with a walk in town. The day was sunny and slow. The streets and sidewalks were almost deserted; most folks were probably recovering from parties, having post parties, or were watching football. The fresh air and sun revived them from their sexual exhaustion. They both woke up and regained some energy.

They fooled around outside until darkness began to settle down. Back at the house, they cracked a bottle of wine and made some salad and cooked some burgers on the grill. They cleaned up the kitchen and crashed down together on the couch, each with a book. They were exhausted and went to bed early; they kissed good night and were sound asleep.

* * *

The next morning, they woke together and made love, got up, and had coffee. Each had a bowl of cereal with a sliced banana. They went for a hike in the desert, came home, took a shower together, made love, and had a nice dinner.

"Chris, I really need to head back to Durango tomorrow. I have an appointment with Joan the day after. I need to see her. I have a lot to talk about. And I want to get back to the group sessions. I have missed two and need to be there. Will you come with me? Please? You can stay with me. You could move there, and we could be together."

"Oh, man, Jenny. I have to start work again in a few days. My boss landed this huge contract at some mansion on the edge of town. Some wealthy guy from San Diego just bought it and wants the whole area around the house xeriscaped. The previous owners had lawn all around like a freaking golf course. Took a zillion gallons of water to keep it green. This guy wants it to be like the desert. There's a lot of money involved. Probably going to be two to three months of work and good pay. I'm getting to a point that I need the money. Then maybe? I've been to Durango, liked it. I don't want to be away from you either. Can you get back here sometime? Sometime soon?"

"Damn! I don't want a long-distance relationship. I want us to be together. You could find work in Durango."

"Jenny, this job will set me up with money for a while. My boss pays me really well ... really, really well. To be honest, I'm about broke. Our last job was over back in early November. We can be apart for a little while. Just knowing we'll be together soon will be enough to keep me going."

"Not what I really want to hear. I can maybe get back in a few weeks. But there's my brother. I haven't had time to process a lot of what my Grandpa Dean told me was going on with him. I am really worried about him. Please understand. It's really hard for me to go, but ... but I really need to head back."

They went to bed, made long, slow love, and went to sleep. Jenny clung to him, not ever wanting to let go.

During their time together for the last weeks, neither had thought of living together or being apart. The reality of it hit both of them hard.

They made love again in the morning and had a quiet breakfast, both already missing each other, neither wanting it to end. Jenny helped clean up the dishes. She got her stuff together and threw it in the Jeep. It was about a six-hour drive so she would be back in Durango in the late afternoon. With their separation anxiety having already taken hold, their good-bye was brief and much more painful than they could express. Jenny got into her car and headed out. She felt empty, emotionally drained; there were quiet tears running down her cheek.

Chapter 38

The day was again sunny and pleasant. She could see clouds gathering to the far north, but they didn't concern her. She drove, feeling empty like there was no more blood left in her heart, like it was pumping only air. She stopped in Tuba City for gas, then again in Kayenta for a potty stop. She pulled into her house at four thirty.

Her little bunkhouse, once her comfy hideaway, now seemed empty, cold, and lonely. She turned up the heat and unpacked her stuff. She held up her new dress to her breast, remembering every detail of the last few weeks, and cried again silently. She found her crystal and set it by her bed.

She called him; he answered immediately.

"Chris, I made it home safe and sound. I miss you already. I wish you here with me."

"Yeah, me too. My cabin feels so empty, so hollow without you being here."

"That's the way I feel too: empty and hollow. I love you. Please, let's talk every day, just so I can hear your voice."

"We will. Promise! I love you too. You have totally changed my life ... for the better."

"Yeah, me too. We'll talk tomorrow night?"

"Absolutely. Be well."

"You too."

And they clicked off.

There was a knock on her door. She answered it to find William.

"Hi, stranger. Welcome back. How are you? Missed having you around, as did Helen and Cat." The cat ran over and rubbed against her legs, happily meowing. "Happy New Year." He gave her a hug, which she at first was reluctant to respond to. She returned it, hanging on longer than she expected.

Will said, "Are you okay? Did you get the outline I sent?" After a pause: "Are we okay?"

She looked at him for long moment. "I'm good, really better than good. I did get your outline and it is being a big help. Thanks. And we are absolutely good. I apologize again. I overreacted, Will. I'm sorry."

"No need to apologize. I was wrong for doing it without talking with you first. Both Helen and Joan chastised me royally."

"No, Will. What you did was to get me off my ass. I started and have written over eight thousand words so far. Once I got going, it just seems to flow."

He smiled and hugged her again. "Congratulations, author."

"Thanks, Dad. Thanks for everything. I love you."

"I love you too, Jenny. Thanks for coming into my life."

After she wiped her tears, she said, "I missed you and all my friends here, but my trip was good. No, better than good, actually fantastic. I told you I met a guy. I really like him. We spent my time there together. I had some great adventures and experiences being in the desert. It was—what—mystical? Magical? That's as best as I can describe it."

"You met a guy? Interesting. I think Peter was liking you a bit."

She looked away. "Yeah, I know. I like Peter too. I'm sorry. I really like him, but you know what I said earlier. I told him about me straight up, and he balked. He hesitated, Will, and I just couldn't deal with hesitation; either accept me and my baggage or don't. I'm not easy, Will, I know. I carry a huge bunch of bullshit with me. I can't be with someone who is scared of me for who I am. He was scared. If you want to be with me, you have to accept all the bullshit, but he hesitated. I'm sorry, Will. He is a good guy, but he needs someone who isn't me."

"I understand, Jenny. I do." He smiled. "As I said, he's a lawyer."

And she turned and threw her arms around him. "Just hold me for a minute."

She broke away. "I have a present for you." She went to her bags and rummaged, finding the crystal and presenting it. "Hope you like it." She went on and told him all about Amanda and her store.

He looked at it for a long while, wiping his eyes with his sleeve. "Sorry. It's the best present ever. Thank you. I will treasure it always."

"It makes me happy you like it. Wasn't real sure." She went on and eagerly explained all about crystals to him. "Will, please hold me for a minute. Please. For some reason, I'm feeling something is wrong, seriously wrong. I'm really scared right now, and I don't know why."

Chapter 39

After a fitful, dreamless sleep, Jenny got up, did some yoga, and a short meditation. Then she went for a short run.

She went to her appointment with Joan, who greeted her with a warm hug and a "Happy New Year." "I missed you, stranger."

They sat, and Jenny unloaded everything in vivid detail. Joan sat there with her eyes wide, doing everything she could to keep her mouth from dropping open. Jenny finished by talking about her "niggle," that there was something very familiar and weird about having sex, even before her sexual encounter with Chris. But she knew she never had.

Joan called her receptionist to tell her she would be going over her hour and to please hold all calls.

"Jenny, you have me speechless, and that is hard to do for me. First, I am happy for you, I truly am. But are you sure about this Chris? It's only been like—what—three weeks? How are you feeling deep down? I understand the newness and the excitement of falling in love. It is a very wonderful high that comes with all the newness of discovering someone.

"And let me add that to love someone, you have to totally trust them. Do you trust Chris?"

"I think I know what you are saying, and strange as it may seem, yeah, I really do totally trust him like ... like I have never trusted anyone before. Wow! I never thought of it. I do trust this guy. I really do.

"I love being with him. He's so considerate, so supportive. He makes me feel secure, protected, and he has gotten me to sit down and write. I'm excited to be actually getting words out."

"That's good, Jenny. It is. I just want you to be very careful. You are treading in new waters here; you are still very vulnerable. And what if you never saw him again? Would you feel so energized about writing?"

"Hmm, yeah, I think so. I wasn't going anywhere much with my writing until he got me going, along with Will's assistance. Also, he accepts me, reassures me, and makes me feel safe and cared for. That's something I'm not used to, except from the few friends I've made here. But this is different, I know. It's a different feeling from how I feel about everyone else, even my grandparents, even William.

"Apparently I have some things to think about. But what about my memory of sex I never had? It's so there! I can't access it in my brain. It keeps haunting me, driving me nuts. I just can't understand where it's coming from or what it is."

"That is interesting. There are such things as blocked memories, especially if there was any trauma involved. Have you ever tried hypnotism?"

"Hypnotism? No, I always thought that was some sort of magic trick or something."

"Not at all. Sometimes you can uncover blocked, hidden, or repressed memories, like possibly what you are experiencing. I believe from what you are telling me that there might be something there you have repressed for whatever reason. If you want to try, I have a psychologist friend I have referred clients to before. I can go with you if you would like. Want to give it a shot?"

"Sure, why not? This is truly driving me crazy. It's always there, like right now. I want to find out what's there, to be rid of it."

"Understandably so. Let me give her a call, see when she might have time."

Joan picked up her phone and tapped in some numbers. After a brief conversation about what she wanted, she agreed, thanked the person on the other end, and clicked off.

"She had a cancellation, so how about tomorrow at nine?"

"Great. Where should I go?"

"Come by here at about a quarter till, and we'll go together. Meg's office is a short walk from here."

"I'll be here at eighty forty-five. Thanks. Appreciate you hearing me out."

Jenny gave Joan her crystal, which she loved, then continued talking more about her Sedona experience until Joan's next appointment. They got up and had a good-bye hug; then Jenny left.

Jenny stopped by to see whether Helen was in her studio, but she was gone for the day. She picked up some groceries, went home, and wrote for the rest of the day.

* * *

That night she used her pendulum to ask about the hypnosis. The answer was a strong yes. Then she asked again about Chris; another strong yes.

She went into a deep sleep with dreams of unlocking doors and being very frightened by what she found. She awoke with a start, happy to be awake with the dream gone. It was another beautiful, sunny January morning. Cat was snuggled in with her reassuring purr.

She was at Joan's office at 8:45, nervous and apprehensive about what was going to happen, what she might uncover from possible repressed memories. They walked to Meg's office on the third floor of a bank building, where Meg Palmer met them in the reception room. Joan introduced them. The office was nice with windows looking out to the west. There was abundant natural light. Walls were a pleasant off-white with photographs of the Animas River and posters of Durango events from previous years. The space had a nice feeling. Meg was in her fifties, Jenny guessed. She was attractive, wearing jeans and a nice white blouse. Jenny noticed a big diamond on her left hand. She seemed pleasant enough but all business. She took Jenny into a quiet room adjacent to her main office.

Meg explained what she was going to do, that Jenny would be alert and awake, but she would be in a place to access what she was looking for. Meg asked her to sit in a straight-backed chair. Then she told her to take a few deep breaths and relax. Pulling up a chair, she sat facing Jenny.

Meg held a pendulum in front of Jenny, asking her to follow it with her eyes as it went gently back and forth, back and forth, back and forth. Meg softly, gently coaxed her to relax and focus, and soon Jenny felt herself relaxing as she entered into an altered state. Her mind for an instant flashed on her time in the boulder place in Sedona, except this time she was awake and alert. Through questions and direction, Meg led Jenny deep into her memory bank to see what might be buried deep within her psyche.

Meg asked her numerous questions to establish some sort of trust and get a basis.

"So, tell me, Jenny. Have you ever had sex before?"

After a long pause: "Yes, I have."

"Was it consensual?"

"No, it wasn't consensual. I didn't want it. I was forced."

"When?"

"I was sixteen."

"Who?"

Another long pause, then she screamed, "It is Michael! My god, Michael's raping me!"

Jenny began screaming for him to stop—screaming, crying, screaming. "No! No! Michael! Don't! Stop! Please! Stop!"

Meg snapped her finger. "Jenny! Jenny! Wake up! It's time. We are here, and you are okay. It's all right. Michael is not here. You are just remembering something really bad."

Jenny's wild eyes regained focus. She looked around for a few moments and took some deep breaths, remembering. She screamed, "That fucking son of a bitch! My own fucking brother! That bastard. He fucking raped me, his own sister. I hope he fucking rots in hell."

And she started sobbing uncontrollably, almost falling off her chair. Joan had heard and rushed in, grabbing her and holding her as she cried and screamed all at once, body wrenching with convulsing sobs. She beat on Joan with her fists. After maybe ten minutes, she started to calm down and relaxed into shuddering sobs. Finally she collapsed onto Joan, holding on to her like she was a life raft and her only salvation.

Joan motioned to Meg that she should leave them alone. They sat there, not saying a word for almost thirty minutes.

Finally, Jenny loosened her grip and looked up. "I'm so tired ... I need to lay down now ... I need to sleep. I'm really tired ... so tired." She started to fall asleep in Joan's arms.

She was lead to a couch, and there she lay down. She was covered with a throw and left to rest. Joan went out to talk to Meg.

Joan called Helen, who came in to stay with Jenny. Joan went to her office for some appointments. Jenny slept soundly and quietly until late morning, and then she woke with a start.

Helen said quietly, "Hi, sweetheart. I am here with you."

"Where am I?"

"You are in Meg Palmer's office. Do you remember anything about what happened?"

Jenny wiped her eyes. "What time is it? I remember being hypnotized ... I think. Oh shit! Oh shit! What did I say? I think it was about Michael?"

Helen said, "Just a minute. I need to get Meg."

She stuck her head out and called Meg, who was at her desk. She called for her receptionist to call Joan. Meg was in the room an instant later with a bottle of water.

"Hey, Jenny, how are you feeling? Here's some water. That was quite a bit that you got out. Do you remember any of it?"

Helen excused herself and left, going back to her studio, knowing Joan would be there in a few minutes.

Jenny thanked her for the water, opened it, and drank most of the bottle. She realized how parched she was. The cold water was good and helped her recover some more. "It was about Michael, right? It was him, right? He raped me, right? My brother raped me!" Her voice was hollow, as if from deep in cave, but hard and mean with anger. "I'm remembering it all. It was him who walked with me into the forest that day. I didn't escape from him like I thought I did. He hit me really hard, and I remember that I wasn't unconscious but dazed from his fist. He ripped off my shirt and bit my breasts ... ripped off my shorts and rammed himself into me. God, it hurt so bad. I was crying, screaming, asking him to stop, to please stop. Please stop doing this to me! I'm your sister!"

She stopped for a moment; she was crying and talking at the same time. Meg handed her some tissues. She settled herself down for a moment and continued. "All he said was that I was a 'a fucking bitch slut' and deserved it. You should want to be fucked. You are just getting what you know you want. It's all bitches want ... all any of you are good for ...

you stinkin whore. All girls stink. I remember it all now so vividly. It hurt so terrible bad. He just kept ramming himself into me.

"'How do you like this, you bitch? You are just a stupid bitch.' He just kept saying that over and over and over. I think I passed out for a few minutes. I vaguely remember him jerking and having spasms ... laying on me for a minute, then getting off and hitting me again with his fist. He told me that if I told anyone, he would kill me. He got up and walked away, just leaving me there. God, Meg, I hurt so bad. I hardly could walk back. My face was bruised. My nose was bleeding. I hate him! I always knew I was uncomfortable being around him. Maybe this is why he blames me for all his problems and hates me.

"He's totally crazy, Meg. He's nuts and should be locked away. I'd testify against that son of a bitch at any trial in a heartbeat. Thanks for listening to all that, Meg. Pretty crazy, huh?"

"Not crazy, Jenny, just very hard. It was so very, very wrong what happened to you. And it is certainly not surprising that you put that away in your memory for so long. Victims tend to block out such severe trauma sometimes, and what happened to you was very, very severe. You will need to rehash all this again with Joan. She is here now and will take you back to her office. Do you think you are able to walk?" Meg asked, smiling.

"Yeah, no problem ... I'm good. It'll probably get easier, won't it? I guess I have a lot more to work on now. So much seems to be coming back, like the proverbial floodgate has opened. Thanks, Meg, thanks for everything. I hope to see you around, hopefully under better circumstances next time."

"You are most welcome, Jenny. I hope to see you too. I'm sure we will."

Jenny and Joan left. The day was bright and wonderful, but Jenny felt heavy inside. She just wanted to float away, with the south breeze blowing gently up the street, and never come back. She took Joan's hand and squeezed it, continuing to hold it until they reached her office.

"I have time, Jenny, if you want to talk. Or we can wait. There is no rush now. Apparently you have gotten through the hard part with Meg. It's up to you. I know this has to be a serious shock to you."

"Let's do it now. I want you to know every shameful, ugly detail."

She sat with Joan for two solid hours, repeating what she had told Meg. Then she went on, telling more about the verbal abuse and bullying, about Michael apparently telling everyone how she'd wanted to fuck him and that he'd felt obliged. What a cheap little whore she was. She was nothing but a fucking bitch slut, fucking her own brother. From then on, she had no friends; all the kids there at the Farm laughed at her, taunted her, bullied her, even moreso. She had considered suicide, but she was afraid. She just wanted to run away, to leave. She found some solace in the books she scrounged. She was able to hide in the stories and fantasied her life into the stories. She also hid herself in her own story writing. Then her grandparents found her and saved her. She was crying softly by the time she finished.

They both sat quietly for a while, Joan evaluating all she had heard. Jenny, whose mind had just stopped thinking, said she was thirsty and hungry, actually very hungry. Joan finally broke the silence. "Jenny, I want to start seeing you twice a week, Tuesday and Thursday as before. And I want you back at group. There is a lot we need to work on after all this. No more trips for a while."

"I know. I promise. Do you think I'll ever get over this?"

"You will over time, but there is a lot we have to do."

"Yeah, apparently so. Hey, I'm starving. Do you want to have dinner with me? I'll treat. We could call Helen."

Joan agreed, called Helen who would meet them in ten minutes. They headed toward one of Jenny's favorite places, got seated, and ordered drinks. Helen joined them in a few minutes, and they had a great time of talking, eating, and imbibing, which Jenny did a bit too much of. Helen took her home with her. They sat up, and Jenny unloaded everything on her. Helen listened, and they both ended up crying.

Jenny slept soundly and happily in Helen's guest room, dreaming of how happy and grateful she was to have the good friends she had found. She thanked Helen for all their help and care in her healing, for all the love she'd felt, love she had really never known before. *God, I so want Chris to be here with me. I miss him so much.*

Chapter 40

January was over. Life was settling down and getting into a routine for Jenny. She was meeting regularly twice every week with Joan and going to group on Tuesday night. As hard as it was, she had shared her story of her rape with the group. She found out that night that several of the women in group had also been raped or sexually abused, not by siblings but by their fathers or other family members, such as uncles. Her therapy was going well; she was beginning to feel better about what she had uncovered about Michael.

She started to teach three beginning yoga classes at the studio under Helen's tutelage. She was having more students come to her class as weeks went on. Jenny enjoyed teaching. She continued going to Helen's intermediate classes three days a week, still managing to get in some running. She gave Kelly her crystal, which made her cry. The two started going running together every Saturday. Kelly got her up to the high country for some snowshoeing, which was total happiness for Jenny, being in her beloved mountains.

Jenny told Kelly all about Chris and her time in Sedona together. Kelly was excited for her. She couldn't wait to meet him. Jenny didn't share her discovery about Michael.

She was writing every day. William was reviewing her work and helping her, encouraging her.

She enrolled in the Mindfulness Meditation class, which met once a week for six weeks. She was a busy girl. She liked her newfound stability.

Then there was Chris. She hadn't heard from him since they talked after she got home over three weeks ago. She called him a number of times, but her calls kept going to voice mail. She left messages, but he never called back. *Guess I was just a good roll in the sack for him, and now he's probably got some other girl on the leash. Stupid me. Should have known better. I am such a stupid sucker! Screw him!*

She went out for a run on a Tuesday after her session with Joan. Jenny had gone a few miles in and was feeling great. Running always cleared her head. Her phone buzzed, and she looked; it was Chris. She stopped and answered, her heart pounding.

"Chris, where have you been? I thought you wrote me off."

"Awe, I'm so sorry. I dropped my phone into John's hot tub right after we talked that day you got back. Fried it. Started to work on this project the next day, sunup to sundown. I just got to the phone store.

"My boss is under a strict deadline for completion and wouldn't give me two fucking hours off. Finally this morning, I went to work and faked being sick after lunch so I could leave for an afternoon. My boss wasn't happy, but I couldn't stand not talking to you. I am so sorry, really! I miss you so much and want to see you so bad. I got the new phone and saw all your calls. I'm so sorry."

"Wow, Chris. I was worried. Then I thought you wrote me off as just a good fuck," she said with a nasty tone in her voice.

"No! No! No! Wait! That is so not true, not true at all. Everything I told you is true. Please don't think that you were a one-time deal. I've never been as serious about anyone as I am about you." And he trailed off.

"Yeah, I'm sorry. You didn't deserve that. I was just so damned frustrated and angry, not hearing from you after everything and our time together. So much has happened. I love you and everything you are. But, hey, I'm out running, and I'm cooling down, getting chilled, and need to get my butt going. I'll call ya tonight?"

"Yeah, for sure. Love you." They clicked off.

She returned to the house twenty minutes later, sweating and smiling with elation after hearing from him.

She and Chris talked again that night for over an hour. Jenny didn't tell him about the hypnotism or what she'd found out about her and Michael. She needed to do that face-to-face. They talked or texted almost every night from then on; their commitment to each other, despite the long distance, was deepening every day.

It was into February. The weather had changed from a bright balmy January to almost constant snowy weather, especially in the mountains. Skiers and snowmobilers were happy, but it was seriously hindering Jenny's running schedule. She was focusing hard on doing yoga, teaching, and learning.

Michael's attorney had been in close contact with Dean. Michael's trial date was set for the first week in April.

The day before Valentine's Day, she received a big box of chocolates and a beautiful card from Chris. *Damn, I didn't realize.* She never celebrated Valentine's Day before. She called him, apologizing for being such a slacker. She was forgiven. They talked for two hours.

Two nights after Valentine's Day, she stayed at Helen's after she taught her yoga class because it was snowing and the roads were bad. She dreamed she was naked, tied down with rope, spread-eagled on a table. There were thousands of Michaels lined up, taking their turns raping and beating her, calling her "slut bitch" and worse. It was as if she were above herself, watching. Then it all ended. Still in her dream, Michael came back, covered her with a blanket, cut the ropes binding her, and tenderly massaged her wrists and ankles with salve and lotion. "I am the final one and will be the last. I am so sorry, sis. This is all over. I am so sorry. I am gone forever. Now you can heal."

She awoke in a cold sweat, trembling, nauseous. She looked around, not knowing where she was: Helen's. *Where was Helen? 8:15. Helen would be at the studio. That dream had been so real. It all seemed so very real.* She checked her wrists. They were fine. She felt a knot in her gut. She felt that something was wrong. Very wrong. She shook off the feeling and got out of bed, went to the bathroom, and washed her face.

Going back to the bedroom to get dressed, she checked her muted cellphone and saw she had several voice messages. They were all from her grandparents. "Jenny, please call us. You need to call immediately." She thought one of them had gotten sick or worse. She called back.

Dean answered, "Jenny, thank God you called. Are you okay? Is there anyone there with you?"

"I'm alone. I just got up. Why? What's going on? Are you okay? Is Grandma okay?" Her voice shook with apprehension.

"We are fine. Please sit down, Jenny. It's Michael. It's not good. I am sorry. It is not good at all, Jenny. They found him this morning. Oh God, Jenny, Michael committed suicide last night." His voice shook. "He somehow was able to cut his wrists. I am so sorry. We don't have any more information right now."

She crumbled to the floor in a heap, unable to breathe. Her phone fell from her grip. Her nausea grew. She crawled back into the bathroom and retched into the toilet, but there was nothing but bile. She retched and retched until she collapsed on the floor. She lay there, whimpering, all her strength gone. All the joy, the lightness, and the power she had been feeling were gone.

I think my soul has left. I feel like everything inside me has been scrubbed out with a stiff brush and lye soap. I feel so raw. Maybe I'm dying. Maybe this is what dying feels like. It's really not so bad. I think I want to die. All my life is really all a sham anyway. Who am I kidding? My brother raped me and told me I wasn't worth anything: soiled, spoiled. Who could ever love the empty shell of something this pathetic, nothing-but-a-bitch slut whore? All his problems were my fault. Maybe I really did kill him. Maybe I was there and cut his wrists. I just want to die like poor Michael did.

She lay there as if in a coma. She couldn't move, as if all her bones were gone. *No wonder I can't get up. When my soul left, it took all my bones with it.*

Helen came home a little after ten and called for her. No answer. Her Jeep was still outside. She looked into her guest room and was starting to go back to the living room when she heard the whimper from the bathroom.

"Oh my God, Jenny!"

"Get away from me. Don't touch me. I am a filthy, filthy whore. Don't touch me; just let me lie here and die. That's what I deserve. I killed my twin. It's my fault. I killed him—" She trailed off and was silent, her breathing ragged and shallow.

Helen ran out for her cell and called 911. She got a cold washcloth and went back to Jenny, rubbing her forehead. She speed-dialed Joan, telling her about Jenny. Helen kept wiping her face and forehead with a cool washcloth, trying to console for what, she had no idea.

"Oh, Jenny! Oh, Jenny!" was all she could say as tears ran down her face. Jenny had passed out and was unresponsive.

Chapter 41

Around two thirty, Jenny came around. Joan was there with her and buzzed for the nurse.

"Hi, sweetheart. It's Joan. I am here with you. You are in the hospital. You are going to be fine. Can you hear me? Can you understand me?"

Jenny nodded and looked over at her with sad eyes. "I remember everything. Oh, God, Joan. He killed himself. My twin brother fucking killed himself. How could he just fucking do that? I think he took part of me with him. I feel so empty, just so empty of everything. I think I am dying. Please hold me and keep me here with you. Please hold me. I don't want to die."

"You are not going to die; I'm right here with you, sweetheart."

The nurse came in and took vitals; she said the doctor would be around shortly. Joan asked whether the others could come in. The nurse nodded. "Yes, they could but only for a few minutes." Then she turned and left.

Joan reached down and did a bed hug, holding her for a long time. Helen and William were there; they came in and did the same, telling her how much they loved her and wanted her to be okay, saying that they would be there for her and help her and support however they could. Jenny felt their warmth and love, holding onto them like she was drowning in an angry, dark bottomless sea.

Helen had called Dean and Susan, who caught an early afternoon flight to Durango that morning and were arriving shortly. William left to pick them up at the airport. They were back at the hospital an hour later.

They all left the room so she could be alone with her grandparents. Susan and Dean, each to one side, sat and held a hand, not able to say anything.

Jenny would stay the night in the hospital. Visiting hours were over, so everyone left except Joan.

"I'll be here with you tonight, Jenny. Since I am your therapist, I'm allowed to stay. You should be released in the morning. Helen's getting things you might need tomorrow."

All Jenny could do was give a weak smile and nod. She turned away and fell asleep.

On the way out of the hospital, Dean asked William whether he would take them to a hotel, but he insisted Dean and Susan would stay at his house. The four of them left. William dropped Helen off at her place and headed for the north valley.

Chapter 42

Jenny was to be released at ten o'clock in the morning. William, Dean, and Susan arrived to bring her home. Jenny was wheeled out in a wheelchair a few minutes later. They noticed how tired, haggard, and pale she looked. She said with a weak smile and weak voice, "Hi, please take me home, right home. I want to be home. I just want to sleep. I feel so tired."

They arrived at William's compound. Jenny went toward her bunkhouse, announcing that she was going to take a shower and go to bed; Susan went with her. They disappeared inside. Dean went back to William's place. He was in his living room, having coffee; William invited Dean to sit. He got Dean a cup of coffee as well and asked how Jenny was.

Joan went out to Jenny's around three thirty. She went in and chatted with Susan a few minutes, then woke Jenny.

"Hi, I see you are getting some rest. Do you have any questions for me? Do you want to talk?"

"Yeah, what are the drugs I'm taking? I hate drugs!"

"Just a mild antidepressant. Please take your dose as prescribed. It will help. Please. You will need to take it until we see how you recover."

"Recover from what? From all the shit that my fucking family has given me. I hate all of them. I actually feel glad that Michael is fucking dead. He deserves it. I hope my father rots his ass off in prison. And I hope fucking Dora dies of syphilis. I fucking hate them all." She stared blankly straight ahead, without facial expressions.

"Okay, Jenny. It's okay to feel angry—"

"Angry doesn't even fucking begin to say what I feel. I have been so fucked over by all of them. They were supposed to love me and care for me, and all they fucking did was treat me like shit and rape me. I hate all of them!" She broke down in tears. "I just want to go hide from everyone. How can anybody ever love a bitch slut like me?" She sobbed, rolling away from Joan, hiding her face in her pillow.

Joan placed her hand on Jenny's shoulder and just sat, not saying anything, just letting her cry it out. Jenny's sobs finally subsided into intermittent gurgles. Joan grabbed some tissues and handed them to her.

"Oh, Joan, I feel so horribly empty, so lost … like my life is done … like there's just nothing left in me. I so want to go back into solitude. Things were easier when I was away from everyone and everything. I hate the way I feel. I hate it! Hate it! Hate it!"

"I cannot begin to understand how you feel. I have heard so many women who were in the same place you are, and they have all recovered. It will take a lot of hard work on your part. I will do everything in my power to help you, but it's going to be up to you; you are going to have to want to. I know it sucks right now, but it will get better. I promise. I know I keep saying that, but trust me, it will get better. I want you in my office tomorrow at nine for our session. Are you up for it?"

"What choice do I have? I'll get over this, or I won't. If I don't, I'll be destined to live in the mountains and desert by myself for the rest of my life."

"You will heal. I promise. I will get you through this. Please hang with me. You have a lot of people who really love you. Remember that. Okay? Promise?"

"Okay then. We'll give it a go ... I'll see you tomorrow morning. Let all the fucking fun begin," she responded with sarcasm in her voice.

Joan squeezed her shoulder, got up, and left. She met Susan on the way out and said, "Take good care of her. She has a lot of people out here who really love her. Will you stay with her at night?"

"You can count on it."

Joan went out and drove away. Susan went in to check on Jenny. She was already back asleep.

* * *

The next morning Susan took Jenny to town to her appointment with Joan. Susan left and went for coffee and did some shopping. She returned and still waited for over an hour. Finally, Joan and Jenny appeared. Joan looked concerned. Jenny looked very drained and pale with dark circles around her red eyes.

She walked straight out to the front door. "Let's go, Grandma. Get me out of here!"

"I will be there in a minute. Just wait for me in the car."

Susan went in to talk with Joan and asked what she thought about Jenny. Joan explained that Jenny had had a very abusive childhood, emotionally and sexually with no other specifics, and that her brother's suicide had exacerbated her otherwise tenuous condition, which they had been dealing with since October. While they had been making some headway up until now, this was a severe setback for her. Essentially, she couldn't handle any more and had simply had a nervous breakdown.

"She is borderline serious depression and is extremely fragile at the moment. She will need help and would need to have someone monitor her to make sure she keeps to a schedule and is taking her meds as she should; plus, she needs someone who will be a loving person to her. She will need a lot of tender love and care, no fawning or pity, but just wholesome genuine direction and caring."

Susan replied, "I'm planning on staying with her for as long as she needs support. Dean is flying back to Denver and returning in week. He's driving back and going to bring what I need for an extended stay. Jenny is now my only grandchild, and I'm going to do everything I can to make sure she will someday be healed and have a happy, normal life."

She left and went to the car. She found Jenny sitting and staring straight out the windshield, seemingly in a trance.

"Are you okay?" Susan asked, getting into the car.

"Just thinking, Grandma, just thinking."

"Anything you want to share?"

"Yeah, maybe. Let's go and get some coffee, maybe sit and talk."

"Okay, where to?"

Jenny gave directions to Raven's. They got their drinks and sat down at a table.

"Want to talk about anything in particular?" Susan asked.

"I want to share everything with you, Grandma, if you want to hear all the crap that has been my life."

"Whatever you want to share, Jenny, I will listen."

Kelly appeared. "Hey, Jenny, where've you been? Missed you at yoga." She started toward their table. "Are you up for our run on Saturday? There's a trail I've been wanting to do for a while. I have a couple of other people who want to go, too. Hey, I just bought some new running tights. You have to see them. They're really cool."

"Not now, Kelly! Not now! Please. Please just leave me alone. Just go away. Please just get the hell away! And stay away!"

Kelly held up both palms. "Well, okay then. Screw you! Please just excuse the hell out of me. Sorry. So sorry to intrude on your private space. What the hell! I thought you were my friend. Screw you!" she retorted bitterly, turned, and walked away.

"Who was that?" Susan asked.

"Nobody ... just nobody. Sorry, Grandma. Let me continue."

Jenny began telling her grandmother the whole story, her voice shaking, from her earliest recollections, including the sexual abuse, Old George, Michael, everything. By the time she finished, she felt in control of herself and stronger with a sense of some of the power she'd once felt. It felt good to tell her grandmother her story and why she was in the state she was in.

Her grandmother had sat stone silent, absorbing every word and pulling tissues from her purse to wipe her eyes. Jenny had talked for over an hour, capturing the essence of her living hell in California.

"That's about it, Grandma. That's my story. Nice, isn't it? What a fucking happy life I've had!" she said with a hard, sarcastic note.

Susan took a few deep breaths and sat for a long while. "I can't believe this, Jenny. This all cannot be true. It just can't be."

"Believe me, Grandma, it is, way truer than I want to believe myself. I've gone over this so many times in my mind with Joan. And yeah, it's true ... very, very true. I'm sorry to tell you all this. I'm really sorry; you were surely not prepared for all this. But I wanted you to know."

"But Dory, Michael, those other people. They were your family. They should have protected and nurtured you. I just cannot believe that Michael ... that Michael ..." Her voice trailed off.

"Yeah ... Michael, dear, sweet Michael. I couldn't believe it either, Grandma. I guess that is why I buried it so deep, so deep that I couldn't remember it myself. I'm so sorry. I'm really so sorry about him, so sorry that he was so messed up, so sorry to drop this bomb on you, so sorry for everything. I'm trying to be a good person, Grandma. I really want to be a good person. I just want to be free of all this. I'm tired ... really tired. We need to go. I just don't have anything left."

"I don't think I can ever understand all of this, but rest assured, we will do everything in our power to help you, to help you heal from all this. I just can't imagine. Let's go."

They got up and left, and Susan drove them home. Jenny went in to her bed and fell asleep, dreaming of being with Chris in the desert. Amanda was there. She did some sort of ceremony. A raven came and landed on Jenny's shoulder, whispering in her ear that she would find peace.

Chapter 43

Susan took Jenny to her next appointment with Joan on Thursday. Afterward, Joan pulled Susan aside and told her Jenny needed to get back on some sort of schedule with her yoga classes, running, and writing. And she told her to make sure Jenny made it to group next Tuesday.

When they got home, Jenny was restless, pacing around the little house. She knew she was making her grandmother nervous but just couldn't help the restlessness she felt, as if there were snakes inside her, trying to get free.

"Jenny, why don't you get out? Go for a run, get some fresh air, do something."

"Maybe a little run would do me good. Yeah, I need to get out. It's a beautiful day. It might help me clear my head."

She changed her clothes and went out for a four-mile run.

"I'm home, Grandma. That really felt great to move. Running always seems to help me clear my head. Thanks for getting me going. I'm heading to the shower."

"Good to hear. We can plan dinner when you get out."

After dinner, she went to her bedroom and called Chris.

"Jenny, are you okay? I haven't heard from you. I've tried calling you, but I just went to voice mail. What's going on?"

"I'm sorry, Chris, but to make a long story short, my brother committed suicide in prison. Then there's the other shit I found out a while back too. I haven't shared any of it with you. I can't talk about it right now. I need to do it face-to-face; let's just leave it for now. I don't want to talk about it on the phone. I ended up in the hospital. I had a nervous breakdown, I guess."

"My God. My God, Jenny, this sounds like serious business. I'm coming up tomorrow."

"But, Chris ... your job!"

"Fuck my job! You're way more important! I'll quit. I'll find something in Durango. I'm packing up and will leave in the morning."

As much as she wanted him to, she replied, "Wait, Chris. There's really nothing you can do. I have so many people right now fawning over me, taking care of me, and worrying about me. It's almost a little much, really."

"But Jen, I'm concerned about you."

Jen? Jen? Nobody's ever called me that before. I think I like it.

"Oh, Chris, please don't be. Stay with your work till it's done. I'll try to get down there in the next few weeks. Promise!"

"Promise? Yeah, okay, but I'm really concerned."

"I know you are, and thanks. You mean so much to me, especially right now. Just talking to you makes me happy. I love you, Chris. I miss you so much."

"Yeah, me too. Let's talk tomorrow night?"

"Promise. Later." She clicked off.

She went to bed, feeling happy, and slept with dreams again of being in Sedona with Chris and Amanda.

Susan got her up early for her yoga class. She was anxious to get back to teaching.

"Why don't you join me this morning, Grandma? I can lend you some clothes. It would be fun to have my grandmother in my class."

"I would like to, but I am not up for any advanced class. My classes in Denver are geared for people my age."

"Oh, it's a beginner's class, and I'll be easy on you. There're several other women around your age that come all the time. I never expect more than anybody's able to do. It'll be fun. Promise."

"Okay, I'll give it a try, but you might have to haul me home."

"Naaaah, you'll do fine."

Susan smiled at her exuberance. There seemed to be a little change for the better.

And so off they went. The class was full. Jenny was gracious to Susan, helping her with some of the poses she wasn't familiar with. Susan liked the class, meeting several other women afterward, one whose husband was there with her. They all wanted her to join them for coffee. Susan declined, wanting to get Jenny home, but Jenny insisted that they go. She wanted to go as well. They spent the next hour having coffee and talking about themselves and getting to know one another. The group finally got up and said their good-byes with Susan committing to be at class again on Monday. She and Jenny left for home.

Susan said on the way, "That was really nice, Jenny. You are a good teacher. And everyone there liked you. I am so proud of you."

Jenny's heart swelled like it would burst. "Thank you, Grandma. That means a lot to me for you to say that."

They got to the house and made lunch. Afterward, Jenny excused herself, wanting to sit and do some writing in her journal, something she had neglected ever since she heard about Michael's suicide. She spent most of the afternoon writing and processing everything about her brother and their mixed-up relationship.

Friday and the weekend passed with Jenny working on her book, running, and enjoying Susan's companionship and care. Jenny, Susan, and William enjoyed Friday night dinner together. Helen joined them on Saturday and Sunday nights.

Susan went with Jenny to yoga again on Monday. On Tuesday night, they went into town for Jenny's group session. Susan said she was going to the bookstore and then for some coffee or tea and would be back at eight thirty. Jenny went in to the group room and took a seat. There were several women already there. The rest followed shortly, including Joan. And they began.

Jenny said she wanted to go first and started with "Well, I found out that that my twin brother, whom I told you about raping me when I was sixteen, committed suicide about a week ago … and it really sucks."

Everyone sat stone silent until Joan finally asked, "So, anyone want to comment?"

They all started talking at once, all wanting to express their concern for Jenny as well as relating to her some their own stories of loss. Joan finally got them under control. The night went on with stories of lesser abuse: violent abuse, emotional abuse, shame, alcohol, drugs, and on and on. Jenny's story encouraged everyone to try to relate and comfort. Everyone tried to make sense out of what she had experienced. There were tears of anger, fear, and sadness. Finally at eight thirty, Joan called for an end to the discussion.

Joan said, "Well, this turned out to be an interesting and very lively night. Thank you, everyone, for sharing and showing support. Any final words?"

Jenny, who hadn't spoken since she dropped the bomb that started it all, said, "Thank you, all. You're all my sisters and …" She paused, choking down her tears. "You have all helped me realize I'm not alone. Thank you."

They all got up and had a huge, long group hug.

"Anyone want to go out for a drink and some munchies?" Juanita asked.

Shelly and Ann were game, but Mary and Barb needed to get home. Jenny and the drinks and munchies group left, found Susan, and went and had some beers, wine, coffee, and two plates of appetizers. They chatted about everything except what had gone on that night in group.

On the way home, Susan said, "I really enjoyed meeting those young women. It was fun. I'm loving being in Durango; it's such a beautiful place, and everyone is so nice and inviting. Makes me feel at home."

Jenny just smiled and said, "That's exactly why I love living here. This is a place where the energy from the desert and the mountains joins together. And it is good."

Chapter 44

Dean returned on Wednesday, driving his big, black Mercedes. He brought all of what Susan had requested as well as what he needed for an extended stay. Jenny was writing, and Susan was reading as he came into the bunkhouse, looking for them. They were happy to see him, and each gave him a long hug, then asked about his trip.

"I have news about Michael. The coroner completed the autopsy, and it was ruled a suicide as we suspected. I had the body sent to a mortuary for cremation and the ashes to be kept there until we can pick them up. I suppose we maybe should do a memorial service."

Jenny responded, "Why should we? It would just be us. Dad's in prison, Dory's who knows where, and personally, I wouldn't want to participate. I would have nothing good to say. And the idea of sending him off with anything but disgust doesn't appeal to me at all."

"I can understand," Dean said, "but shouldn't we do something?"

"I would simply scatter his ashes somewhere and be done with it," Susan added.

"We don't have to make a decision right now," Dean said. "Let's all just think about it for the time being and figure it out when we get his ashes."

And the matter was dropped.

Dean camped out in William's guest room, and Susan continued to stay with Jenny. A routine developed for Jenny and Susan. Three mornings a week they went together to yoga. Jenny met with Joan twice a week as well as group. She was happy teaching her beginner's classes along with going to Helen's advanced class and running three days a week, weather permitting. March had brought more welcome snow, mostly in the high country.

Jenny was writing in her journal, working on her book every day, and meeting regularly with William, who was going over her work with her. He liked what she was doing, editing and encouraging her along the way.

It was already the second week in March. There were still snowstorms in the mountains, and chain laws were in effect on the high passes, but the weather at lower altitude had starting warming enough that Durango and the north valley were getting rain. There were daffodils, crocuses, and other cold weather plants emerging from the winter.

Jenny was beginning to feel happier and more stable. Susan had moved over to William's. She, Dean, William, and Helen were becoming close friends. They were sharing a lot of time together as couples, with movies, concerts, and dinners together.

Chris called her almost every night. She had put off getting down to see him; as good as she thought she felt, she knew she was still very unstable emotionally. But he wasn't going to be done with his job until April sometime. She really wanted to see him as well as pay a visit to Amanda. She decided it was time. It was Monday night, and she made her almost nightly call to Chris. She mentioned joining him for the next weekend. He was excited that he would see her.

The next day Jenny announced, "I'm planning on going to Sedona this coming weekend."

Susan said, "Jenny, I am not sure that would be a good idea right now. You have settled into a good routine, and maybe you should just stick with it for a while without bringing an added distraction. A trip to Sedona? I don't think it would be a good idea at all. Have you talked with Joan about this?"

Jenny argued back, "Thanks for your concern, Grandma, and no, I haven't talked with Joan about this, but I'm a grown woman and I want my to see my friend Chris who I haven't seen since right after New Year's. I need to see him, and that's it. Period."

"Well, why can't he just come here instead?" Susan asked.

"Because of his work. We want to see each other. It's really important to me." She told Susan about her adventures with him, excluding the magical experiences in the desert and her sexual experience. Some things were better left unsaid.

"Maybe I could go with you," Susan said.

"I'd love to have you, but it would be awkward since I'll be staying with Chris. His place is really small, smaller than the bunkhouse even. You would be left to your own devices."

"Maybe Dean would come, and all of us could go. Dean and I could stay at a hotel and leave you two to do as you wish."

Jenny stifled a groan and said she would consider it.

She called Chris that night with the proposed plan, explaining her "grandparent dilemma," saying that both of them wanted to come with her. Chris thought that it would be great if her grandparents came. He would love to meet them. They could have dinner together Saturday night and maybe do something together on Sunday. Jenny responded that she selfishly wanted him all to herself. Maybe dinner, but that would be it. She reluctantly agreed.

The rest of the week dragged on slowly for her. She told Joan of her plans at her counseling session. Joan thought it would be good for her to go and also thought it was a very good idea for Susan and Dean to be with her.

They all left together on Friday morning in Dean's Mercedes. It was pleasant for Jenny to just ride along, watching the stark emptiness of the Navajo Nation, and then to go up into the tall pines south of Tuba City, to Flagstaff, and down I-17 to Sedona. She was filled with anticipation and dread. What if it would be different? What if her time with him earlier had really not been as great as she thought? What if he really wasn't what she wanted to remember? What if she really couldn't stand to be around him?

They went into town. Dean checked into their hotel, where he had made reservations. They went to a coffee shop where Dean had coffee, and Susan and Jenny had tea. They had time to walk Main Street. Jenny stopped by Amanda's shop and took them in, introducing everyone. Jenny asked whether she might have time tomorrow for a session. Amanda had an eleven o'clock time slot that would work. They left, and Susan asked all sorts of questions about Amanda, including what the session was about, all of which Jenny answered vaguely. Susan finally dropped the inquiry.

Dean suggested that they should get rooms at the hotel so they could all be together. Jenny replied that maybe tomorrow night she would ask Chris, and if they did, they would want only one room, raising the eyebrows of both grandparents.

"Might as well know. We slept together the whole time I was here last winter. He is a very special guy, and I plan on being together with him as much and as long as we can stand each other."

"But Jennifer," Susan responded, "don't you think this is too sudden, too quick? You hardly know this young man."

"So, what is too quick, Grandma? He and I are both unconventional people living somewhat unconventional lives. And truth is, I know him far better than you can ever imagine. I really feel as if I have known him forever," she finished, smiling inwardly.

"Jennifer, it's just that you have been through so much. You are dealing with so much right now."

Jenny responded, "He knows everything, Grandma, and I need to talk to him about everything that has just happened with Michael. He is very understanding and caring. Hell, I think I'm in love with him. I just want to be with him. Please understand."

"Does Joan know?"

"Yep, told her everything—how I feel, that we had sex, that it was beautiful—and she was happy for me. So—?"

"I cannot wait to meet this young man. Apparently, you are quite smitten."

"Totally, and it's time that I head to his house. Will you take me?"

"Of course," said Dean, who had been listening quietly to the interchange with a big smile. "Sure, let's go."

They got to Chris's house. He wasn't home yet. Jenny got out, grabbed her bag, found the key under the rock, and bid them a good-bye.

"Chris works tomorrow, so we can go shopping and exploring in the morning. I want to see my friend Amanda at eleven, and then we can have lunch afterward and go from there. Can you pick me up here around ten? I'd like to go for a short run first."

"We'll see you then," Dean said.

Jenny went in and felt at home; everything was so familiar: the books, the bedroom, the smells. She took it all in, savoring it all; she was both excited and nervous to see him. She curled up with her journal until Chris got home around five thirty.

"Oh my God, you're here; you made it," he said as he walked in.

"Yup." She ran and threw her arms around him, giving him a lingering kiss.

"Dinner? Want to go out for a bite?"

"Sure, whatever's easiest."

He cleaned up from work and was ready in ten minutes. They went out and took his old Toyota pickup into town to a Mexican place, had a quiet dinner, and caught up on the last few weeks, except for the hard stuff in Jenny's court.

Back at Chris's, he opened a bottle of wine, and they both sat on the couch, one on each end, facing each other to talk.

Jenny said, "Okay, ready for some more of the really bad shit?"

"Yeah ... sure, go ahead."

She told him everything that had happened: the hypnotism that brought up her rape, her brother's suicide, her trip to the hospital, her therapy, her grandparents, everything.

Chris listened, not saying a word.

Jenny finished with a weak smile. "So, there you have it! Wonder why I'm messed up?"

He sat for a few long minutes and finally was able to speak. "God, Jen ... I don't know what to say. I'm so terribly sorry about all this. It's hard to try to wrap my brain around all of it, all this stuff. I can't imagine how hard it must have been, how hard it must be for you right now. It makes me feel, I don't know, numb, angry, really sad."

"That's why I didn't want to tell you all this on the phone. I've a hard time imagining it as well, that all this stuff keeps coming down on me. I do think that I might actually be done with having any more surprises like all this recent shit that happened since I left in January. I'm feeling a little better and more in control of my life; Grandma is like a mother hen, and I am afraid she'll never leave me alone again. She was reluctant to leave me here with you," she finished with a chuckle.

"It must be so hard. I ... I don't know what to say."

"Don't say anything." She changed positions to lie back against Chris and snuggled in with him.

Chris said, "I do want to say, however, that this does not make any difference in how I feel about you. It doesn't change anything about the way I feel for you. You are really just so very special."

"Just as long as you don't feel sympathy. I don't want sympathy. Okay?"

"Nope. No sympathy from me. No way! I promise," he said with a little laugh.

They moved away from that topic, and Jenny talked to him about tomorrow, about her grandparents' desire to have dinner with them, and about getting a room tomorrow night. Chris liked the idea as long as they would be allowed to share a room. Jenny explained that she had already set them straight as to sleeping arrangements. Chris said he would be off work at three o'clock and would meet them at the hotel at four.

They drank their wine slowly, not speaking, just enjoying their closeness. They went to bed early and made love slowly, naturally, and easily. They fell asleep in each other's arms.

Chris was up at six and off to work. Jenny languished in bed, got up, did a short run, showered, and had some cereal and a banana for breakfast. Chris had left her coffee. She called her grandparents at about 9:15. They would be right out to get her and were looking forward to the day ahead.

They picked up Jenny and went into town, checking out interesting shops. It was just before eleven, and Jenny excused herself after deciding where they would meet for lunch. She ducked into Amanda's for her appointment.

Chapter 45

They greeted each other with a hug. Amanda put out her "Closed, Be Back Soon" sign, and they proceeded to the room at the rear. Jenny told her all about Michael. Amanda told Jenny she would like to clear all that negativity from her. Jenny anxiously agreed.

She lay down on Amanda's massage table and relaxed. Amanda did her thing, and Jenny felt a tingling in her body and then it was like something releasing from her, something very heavy, like a plug had been pulled and old bathwater was draining out: old, filthy, and dirty. She suddenly felt very light, like she could float off the table.

Amanda told her she was done and to take her time getting up. Jenny lay there for a few minutes, getting her bearings.

"Whoa, that was interesting. What did you do? That was like I felt when I was in that 'boulder place' before Christmas."

"I cleared away a lot of the negative energy you were carrying from Michael, and there was a lot, more than you probably thought. How do you feel?"

"Lighter, much lighter, like a weight I didn't know I was carrying was suddenly removed."

"You should feel better, but again, I want you to promise to stay working with your therapist. I think you'll need to keep talking all of this stuff through with her. While I cleared that negative energy, you'll still have the memories and the scars. She can help you deal with them better than I can."

"Totally. No problem doing that. I'm guessing it might be a little easier now."

"I think it will be. I have this little stone I want to give you to wear around your neck. It will help protect you from any recurring bad energies that might still be hanging around. It is different from the first one I gave you; wear this one now."

"I should pay you for it."

"No, it's on the house."

It was almost lunchtime. Jenny paid Amanda for the session along with a big tip. They hugged good-bye. Amanda held her for what seemed longer than necessary. When she let go, she looked deep into Jenny's eyes, "Please be well and stay in touch".

"I promise, Amanda. I totally promise."

They said their good-byes and was off to meet Susan and Dean for lunch. They chatted about this and that, but there were no questions about Chris or last night. Jenny wanted questions but went on with the conversation. She told them she and Chris would stay at the hotel, and Dean called for and got a single room. They spent the rest of the afternoon browsing shops, with Susan and Jenny trying on various clothes and Dean being, patient and supportive. Both women bought several new clothing treasures they would wear for dinner.

Chris met them at four at the hotel, dressed nicely in chinos, a nice blue shirt and a dark-gray sports coat, a far cry from his normal jeans and untucked shirts. They did their introductions and necessary small talk. Jenny and Chris checked into their room. Then they walked a block to a very nice and expensive restaurant of Dean's choosing.

After being seated at a table with a view of the sun setting on the red, rocky desert, they ordered drinks, and the questions started for Chris, which he fielded with total confidence in himself and his life. Jenny listened quietly to the grilling, ready to jump in if he might need saving, but that never happened. He got on extremely well through the interrogation, and Jenny could see that Susan and Dean were impressed with her man. She felt very proud and loved him even more.

The rest of their two-and-half-hour, five-course, and three-wine dinner was wonderful for Jenny. She felt more alive than she had in months and so totally in love with Chris that she just wanted to have him for dessert, which she had later that night several times.

Chris suggested renting a jeep for the next day; and he would take them to some of his favorite places in the desert. Everyone thought it would be fun and that it was an excellent idea. He excused himself to make a few calls. When he returned, he had everything arranged to get the vehicle at ten the next morning.

They were up, had breakfast together, and went to get the jeep. It was ready to go along with a picnic lunch with wine and iced tea. Susan was very impressed with Chris's arrangements. She voiced her approval, almost gushing, but was able to restrain herself.

Chris drove with Dean as copilot, the two women in the back. They toured back roads to some haunts Chris thought only he knew about, including what he knew were some vortex areas. Susan reported feeling quite alive and even a bit buzzy at two stops of some energy places. Jenny smiled to herself. *If she only knew.*

After roaming in the desert and having their lunch, they returned to town by midafternoon, and Susan and Dean went to the hotel to clean up and have a quick nap before dinner. Jenny and Chris went to his house to do the same.

They met for dinner at six, which was a much shorter and a less extravagant repeat of the night before.

Dinner finished, and Chris and Jenny excused themselves. Chris had to go to work bright and early in the morning, and he and Jenny wanted some time for themselves. Susan and Dean would be by to pick her up around nine for the trip back.

Jenny and Chris got to his place and both sat, tired and content.

"Jen, thanks for coming down this weekend. I really like your grandparents. They are really nice folks. I had a great time hanging out with them."

"Me too. By the way, I like it when you call me 'Jen.' Nobody ever called me that before. When will I see you again?"

He smiled. "I like saying it too. This job should wrap up about mid-April, and I intend on loading up my truck and moving to Durango the next day. I have to be close to you, to be together. We'll never know how well we will get on together until we are together."

"It makes me so happy and excited thinking that you'll be there. You can stay with me. Yay!"

"Are you sure you want me to move in with you? We really, truly hardly know one another after being together— what—maybe only three weeks all told?"

"Yeah, know what you're saying. I sort of feel the same. So why not stay with me until you can find some place of your own ... maybe a week, two weeks. It's not like we haven't stayed together before."

"Sounds like a plan."

"Again, be warned about what you are getting yourself into with me. I'll have all my baggage for the rest of my life. I'm hoping I can learn to get a grip and hopefully someday be normal, whatever normal is. I really have no idea what normal might be."

"Well, I think normal is being where you are at any given time. After all, every moment is all we really have at any given time."

"Yeah, know what you mean. You've said that before. We'll just have to see."

"Let's go to bed."

And they retired to a wonderful hour of slow, sweet lovemaking, both falling asleep within minutes afterward.

Chris was up at six and slipped out of bed. Jenny awoke a bit later to the smell of coffee, gabbed one of his shirts, and shuffled out to the kitchen, still drowsy.

"I love your coffee. I love you."

"Me too," he replied. "I have to get going in about a half hour. I wish we could spend another day and night, the next week, the next month ... years together."

"I know. It'll happen when it happens."

They each sat quietly and ate some breakfast. There was nothing more to be said that would make good-byes any easier. Chris got up and took their dishes to the sink. Jenny said, feeling lonesome already, that she would wash them, that he should get going. They hugged and gave each other a lingering kiss. He turned and was gone. She watched him go, waved good-bye, and immediately felt empty and lost. Her grandparents picked her up at nine sharp. They headed back to Durango.

Chapter 46

After their "Good morning. Sleep well?" exchanges, they rode in silence. Jenny was lost in her thoughts. Dean and Susan listened to classical music. Dean wanted to go on I-40 from Flagstaff to Gallup and then head north as an alternative route that would take them through western New Mexico. About an hour later, Susan asked Jenny how she was doing.

"I miss him already, Grandma. I know this all seems very quick, but I really think I'm in love with this guy. He makes me happy, happier than I ever remember being. But it's really confusing to me. I don't know how to trust my feelings with something like this."

"We understand more than you realize. We like him as well. He seems to be genuine, and he looks at you in a way I remember Dean looking at me back then, and well, he still does, sometimes." She gave him a poke and laughed. Jenny was again lost in thought and tired from little sleep last night. She wondered how Chris's day was going, and she dozed off, sleeping until they were almost to the south end of Durango, when Dean broke the silence. "I am really loving this country. I love the openness," he announced when arriving at William's place. "I think I might like to move here. We've talked about getting out of Denver. We've lived there long enough. What do you think, Susan?"

"I like it here also. It is so much quieter and easier than the city. And Jennifer is here, and we have met some wonderful people," Susan added.

Jenny, now waking up and a little groggy, said, "It would be really nice to have you here. Do you think you would really consider doing it? You've, like, been in Denver forever."

"Been there long enough. I am really done with the firm at this point. Most of the partners would most likely be happy if I were farther away and not hanging around the office all the time, looking over their shoulders. There is really nothing for me to do there anymore."

"We should look at property then," Susan said.

"It would be so great if you were here. Like, I could have a real family for once."

They arrived at William's compound. That night William invited them all to enjoy burgers and talk about their trip. The night ended at about eight. Jenny was exhausted and called it a day. She slept deeply with dreams of her and Chris camping in the San Juans at one of her favorite places. There was a meadow covered with wildflowers: reds, yellows, whites, purples, magentas.

Chapter 47

The next day, Tuesday, Jenny met with Joan for her session, telling her all about her weekend with Chris and her grandparents, including her session with Amanda. It had all been so perfect, except having to come home and how empty she felt inside. She missed Chris.

Joan was sympathetic and moved on to her feelings about sharing all the drama surrounding Michael with Chris. Jenny responded that Chris had understood and was supportive. Nothing seemed to faze him.

"When I am with him, I feel like the 'Michael cloud' disappears. I feel light, free, happy, alive. And then sometimes, when I am alone and look into a mirror, all I see is hurt, sadness, fear."

"What about anger, Jenny? You didn't mention anger. You were very angry early on. Do you feel any anger now?"

"No, I don't know. Maybe my anger is gone. I just still feel so much pain, betrayal. Oh, Joan, this is all so confusing. I don't know what I feel anymore. Sometimes I am just so tired. Sometimes I just don't think I care anymore."

"I know I have said this before, and I will say it again. You are not responsible for what your father, Dory, or Michael did to you. They made their choices, and you are the victim, trying to resurrect herself.

"Now you have to make your choice: to unload all the hurt, sadness, and fear you feel you are carrying. I know it is easier said than done, but trust me when I say you can do it.

"Amanda's right. She may well have lifted the heaviness, but the memories and scars are all still there, and you will have to reconcile yourself to dealing with them. It may take a long time, maybe forever. It takes work sorting through all the crap, to deal with it, but you can. I know you can. The objective will be to feel like you do when you are with Chris, to feel that all the time."

Jenny hung her head and reached for a tissue to wipe some tears and said, "I know what you're saying is true. I trust what you say. I'd really like to be in that 'Chris place' all the time like you say. Please help me get there."

"I am doing what I can do. You have to do the rest."

"Yeah, I know, I know, I know."

Their time was up. Jenny went home to rest up for group at six thirty. Everyone was gone, doing errands. She spent two hours writing in her journal about what she wanted, about where she wanted to go with her life, about her new friends, her grandparents, and trying to understand her feelings for Chris.

* * *

Weeks went by. It was early April, and spring wanted to arrive, but the continuing cold coming off the mountain snowpack still pushed it back.

Jenny saw Kelly at yoga frequently, but Kelly always avoided her. Jenny didn't blame her after the way Jenny had told her to leave her alone. After Friday's intermediate class, Jenny made it a point to corral Kelly and apologize, begged her to join her for a cup of coffee. Kelly accepted somewhat frostily. They walked in silence to Raven's and got some coffee, found a table, and sat.

"Kelly, I'm really sorry, so very sorry, for the way I treated you. I feel like such a drama queen, but I have had so much shit dump on me, and the time I dissed you, I thought I was losing any remaining grip I might still have had on my life, seriously. I was in really bad shape, still am for that matter. Sadly, you happened on me at a very bad time. I'm so sorry about what I said. You are the best friend I ever had. Please believe me."

Kelly said, coldly, "Okay."

"I told you about being attacked by my brother in Denver and that he was arrested and was in jail. What I was never able to tell you is that I found out through hypnosis that he actually raped me when I was sixteen. That was bad enough, but then he committed suicide about three weeks ago. All this shit in just over eight weeks.

"I ended up in the hospital in shock. I had just gotten out when you saw me, and I was so awful to you. My grandmother stayed with me for weeks and just recently moved out of my house. I've been on antidepressants and under close observation ever since. I am so sorry if—"

"Holy shit, girl. Holy, holy fucking shit! This is so awful! Oh my God, I can't believe this. I had no idea about all this. This is all so fucking nuts. How're you doing? Are you able to cope? How are you able to cope? I cannot believe all this. I wish I'd known."

Kelly dug into her pack for some tissues. She had tears running down her face.

Jenny, for once, wasn't crying. She reached across the table and took Kelly's hand, she now being the consoler. "It's okay, Kelly. I'm doing a lot better over the initial shock of it all, at least. I went to Sedona a few weeks ago and connected with Chris. He is such a great stabilizer for me. I'm totally in love, Kelly. I really am. I had no idea I could ever feel this way about a guy, any guy ... ever."

"Wow, so what's gonna happen? Are you moving down there?"

"No, he wants to move up here when this landscaping project he is working on is done, probably in around maybe two or three weeks. Sort of makes me nervous, wondering how it will be with him around all the time."

"Where's he going to live?"

"With me for a while, I guess. I asked him to, until he finds his own place."

Kelly said, "I'm sorry, Jenny, for the way I acted as well. Sometimes I'm too overbearing and too wrapped up in myself to pay attention to what's really happening around me. I shouldn't have barged in on you that day like I did. But I was so happy to see you. I'm sorry I didn't respect your space."

"It's okay, Kelly. You didn't know. How could you? Still friends?"

"Forever!" Kelly replied.

The two of them chatted on for another thirty minutes. Then Kelly had to leave for her work and a client. They parted with a long, hug, and Jenny committed to go trail running with Kelly on Saturday, if the weather held with no rain.

Chapter 48

It was mid-April, and the days were warming, but the nights continued to be cool from the snowpack in the mountains. There was still the occasional snowstorm in the mountains, which was rain in the lower valleys.

Jenny's therapy was going well. She was down to seeing Joan from twice a week to once, hopefully moving soon to once every other week. Group also was going well for her. She was feeling better and stonger. Dean and Susan had committed to moving to Durango and had made an offer on a nice Victorian on the pricey boulevard two blocks east of downtown. They had called a realtor in Denver and had put their penthouse on the market and already had two offers.

Dean and Susan had also told Jenny that since Michael had died, she would be the recipient of his part of the trust. She was a little shocked; suddenly she was an even wealthier woman than before and wasn't too sure how she felt about it. Susan urged her to buy a house of her own in town to be close to them, but she was reluctant to leave her bunkhouse. She liked it there, enjoying the solitude and quiet. She liked being close to William for his coaching and help in her writing. But she also realized the convenience of being in town, where she went every day for errands, yoga, or maybe just coffee. Still, she didn't want to move, not right now.

William had been helping her with her writing. One day she was at his house, going over some ideas with him. "Will, have you thought about writing another book yourself?"

"Well, Jenny, yes I have. Any ideas I have generally go back to the template I have made my living at, nothing very new or inspiring, same old stuff and same old formula. Did you ever bother to read any of my books? You have never said."

Jenny reluctantly responded, "Yes, I have, part of one anyway."

"So, what did you think? Honest opinion."

"I'm sorry, Will, but to be honest, I wasn't much impressed. I'm far from any sort of literary critic, but what I read, well, it was well written, but the story—it was just all fluff. Pretty inane, to say the least. I'm sorry."

William sat there for minute, thinking, finally saying, "Thank you for being honest. I know exactly what you are saying. It's just, I don't know, I was able to help you get over your block, but I can't do it for myself."

"So maybe I should write a 'secret' outline for you?" she said with a coy smile.

"Touché. I know, I deserved that dig."

Jenny laughed. "Sorry, but I couldn't resist. It was too easy. But seriously, is there anything I can do to help? Maybe you should write another romance, but take it in a different, more serious direction. Maybe incorporate some sort of self-discovery along the way. Maybe a road trip. Did you ever read *Zen and the Art of Motorcycle Maintenance* by some guy, let me think … Yeah, it was Robert Pirsig, I think. I can look it up. But it was about a road trip with his son and another couple from Minnesota to California. There were a number of intertwining plots along the way plus a discourse on quality versus quantity, as I recall, anyway."

"I have not read it. Do you have a copy?"

"You're in luck, because I still have mine from when I was in college. It wasn't assigned reading. Just one I happened to come across; it took me three readings to get it. But I thought it was brilliant. I'll find it and lend it to you."

He thanked her, and they moved back to her reviewing her writing.

Life was rapidly changing for her. Chris indicated in their nightly phone calls that his job was wrapping up, and he would be heading to Durango in about two weeks. This news started to make her both excited and nervous, knowing she might be committing to something really big, like this relationship, and she counseled with Joan about it.

Joan was concerned that Jenny was still fragile and wanted her to be cautious about a serious relationship. Jenny said she and Chris agreed to try it, and if they decided that things weren't going to work, they would move on. She would keep Joan abreast of everything involving Chris in their sessions.

Jenny went on her first trail run on Saturday with Kelly, and she loved it. There were miles and miles of single track and hiking trails all around Durango, more than she could ever imagine.

After their second Saturday run, they were having a beer at one of the brewpubs. Jenny said, "God, Kelly, I love this. Thanks for getting me out on these trails. I can't believe how free it makes me feel, like the two summers when I was living out of a backpack."

"Yeah, I know just how you feel. That's why I do it. I'm just happy we're running buddies and friends. I love sharing that time with you. Thanks."

"And I thank you. You're really a very special friend and a confidante, I might add. My first-ever girlfriend."

Chapter 49

Chris called on the Wednesday night of the second week in April. They had finished the project that afternoon; he was loading his stuff, heading out tomorrow, and would see her probably mid to late afternoon.

She was excited yet increasingly apprehensive, and she didn't sleep well that night. She met Kelly the next morning for an early-morning run, which helped clear her head. They went for coffee afterward.

Jenny said, "This is happening. Chris is arriving this afternoon, and I'm really nervous. Do you think I'm making the right decision, Kelly?"

"Well, I have absolutely no experience in this sort of thing. All I've ever really done is go out on a few dates with guys. None of them ever clicked with me. All most of them ever wanted to do was party and get me drunk and into bed. I'm afraid, girl, you're on your own on this one. But you know by now I'll always be there for you and for sure try to help you sort out anything you might want to talk about."

The day seemed to drag on forever. Jenny tried to write but couldn't focus. She went over to William's, but he wasn't home. Then around three thirty, an old Toyota pickup pulled up to her bunkhouse, and he was there.

She saw him. *Wow, so here we go.*

When she went out to greet him, all the fear she had been feeling melted away into the warmth of her love for this guy as she threw her arms around him with long, deep kiss and embrace.

Finally she broke away and asked excitedly, "Want a beer?"

"Yeah ... wow! This is a beautiful place."

She led him inside her bunkhouse, cracked two longnecks, and invited him to sit. They both took long pulls on their beers.

"Chris, I have to admit, I've been a bit nervous and scared about this, but now I'm so happy you are here. Really. I have so much to show you and so many friends for you to meet."

"Well, I'm just a bit nervous myself, to tell the truth, but I'm so happy to be here with you. It does feel a bit weird. We really can see each other every day, all the time. It's like we are committing to something, something big, wonderful, and scary."

"Yeah, I know what you're saying. I feel the same. But, good news, I'm feeling so much better, but I still have a long way to go. I still can have difficulty with decisions sometimes. I still need structure and predictability in my life right now. I know I've said this before, but I don't want to get hurt or to hurt you. I can't ask you to be my caretaker or babysitter. I've got to learn to be good with myself before I can be a decent partner.

"I have a small circle of friends. Some know my circumstances, but some don't. I feel good with them. I just let myself get as close enough as I want to be with them. I can't wait for you to meet them."

"I'm really looking forward to getting myself reorganized into a new place and a new life. I was just biding time in Sedona, but now I feel like I'm maybe settling into a place— who knows, maybe forever. I guess it's something I had never really thought about. I just know I want to be with you, close to you right now."

"Yeah, I'm really excited that you are finally here. It'll be good—I know it will. I love you," she said, looking at him with happy eyes. "Hey, let's go over to William's. I think I just heard him pull up. I want you to meet him. He's the greatest. Bring your beer." She got up and took his hand to lead him next door.

William answered her knock, and she introduced the two men. William invited them in and had them sit. He and Chris started talking like old friends. William got some more beers, and they chatted for over an hour. Susan and Dean came back from doing their errands, greeting Chris warmly. Susan gave him a big hug. William suggested that they all have dinner together; he had some steaks in the freezer and what was needed for a big salad and some potatoes. He called Helen to join them. Dean had brought a dozen bottles of wine to replenish William's supply, and he opened a bottle of red and found a bottle of white that was already chilled. They all moved to the kitchen to help, chatting and laughing.

Helen arrived. "I hear there is a party."

Jenny said, "I guess so. Helen, this is Chris."

"Great to finally meet the mystery man." She leaned in for a big hug and whispered in his ear, "I love Jenny like she is my daughter. Do not ever hurt her, or I will kill you. Understood?"

He backed away, eyes wide, smiled, and said quietly to her, "No worries, Helen. Totally understood, my solemn vow."

She smiled back and winked at him.

The dinner was finished, and the group broke up around nine o'clock.

Jenny helped Chris carry in the bags he needed for the night; the rest he might need could wait until tomorrow.

"That was a fun night," Chris said. "Everyone really made me feel so welcome; they're some great people."

"They're the best. Hey, Susan and I are going to go to yoga in the morning. Why not join us?"

"Never did yoga in my life."

"No time like the present to start. You could come to my eight thirty beginners' class."

"Probably not tomorrow for sure; I really need to start looking for a place to rent. Any suggestions?"

"Don't have a clue. I'd have to check the paper or call a rental agency, I guess.

"Let me show you where everything's at. There's not too much to show. The place is about the same as your Sedona place."

She showed him the bathroom, where she had made space for his things and then took him to the bedroom; she had made space for him in there as well.

"Make yourself at home," she said. "There's food in the fridge. I'll be leaving at about seven thirty, and I'll see you when I get back around one. Will you be okay?"

"Yeah, no problem. I might go into town and explore while you're out."

"Why don't you ride in with Susan and me? You can take the Jeep while we're in class if you want or just walk around. We can meet after my class, around eleven, for coffee or an early lunch."

"Yeah, that sounds good. I'll go in with you then. This is a very cool, little house. I'd love to find something like it," he said as he opened his bag, took what he needed, and headed toward the bathroom.

They both got ready for bed and crawled in. Jenny snuggled in close to him, kissed him, and said, "I'm really so happy you're here. It feels good, really good. Thanks for being here."

"I'm happy to be here and together. It'll be great to be close, to see each other, and not to have a six-hour drive every time."

After they made love, they fell into a deep sleep.

Jenny dreamed that she was on top of a mountain, looking out over yet more mountains. *How many more mountains do I have to cross?*

They were both awake early. They made love again and would have liked to just spend the day languishing in bed, but Jenny needed to get Susan and head to class. She missed Cat's presence. *Guess she knew I had a guest.*

Chris was excited to do some residence hunting. They had a quick breakfast of cereal and fruit; then he got Susan, and they all headed to town. They parked about a block from the studio.

"Here's the keys. Let's meet at Raven's. It's a coffee shop about two blocks that way, right on Main Street. Say about eleven."

"I'll see ya then."

After class, Jenny and Susan walked down to Raven's. Chris wasn't there, so they each got something to drink and sat, chatting about the class.

About fifteen minutes later, Chris found them and sat down. "Hi, sorry I'm late, but I've had a stroke of luck."

"Oh, guess you are a little late. No problem. We're just talking. So what's up? Luck?"

"Yeah, I found a place to live already, right up on Third Avenue, a guest house, great guy, great rent. I can't believe it. He needs a part-time caretaker for when he and his wife are gone during the winter. Three hundred dollars a month. From what I've heard, this is a bargain for here in Durango. It's furnished. There's a place for my writing desk and bookcase. It's quiet. I love it."

Jenny and Susan wanted to go see. They finished their coffee and walked up to Chris's new abode. Both Jenny and Susan were impressed. The landlord, Douglas, appeared at the door with his wife, Elly, in tow. They introduced themselves. All three women started talking like they were old friends.

Elly said, "I was concerned when Douglas told me he had rented our apartment to some man he had just met in the coffee shop ... without my approval, but I think he did well. Happy to have you, Chris, and so nice to meet you, Susan and Jenny. Hope to see more of you both."

Susan said they would be neighbors; they had bought a house a block away. They agreed that it would be fun to all get together after Susan and Dean were settled in.

Douglas and Elly left, and the three of them looked around, remarking on Chris's good fortune.

The three of them decided to go home for lunch and left for the Jeep. They ran into Mark and Gary on the street. and Mark said with a big smile, "My God, Jenny, great to see you. Haven't seen you since the Thanksgiving soiree. We wondered if we would ever run into you sometime. How've you been? How'd you survive the winter?"

Jenny gave each of them a hug and introduced everybody. They all stood there talking and catching up, deciding to finally move on because they were blocking the sidewalk.

"So how do you know those two?" Chris asked.

"Oh, they were at Thanksgiving at William's. I have met a lot of people there. Seems like it's only a matter of time until you know everyone. It seems like every time I go to the grocery store, it takes an hour longer because I always run into somebody I know, and they all want to talk. Pretty crazy."

The next day Chris and Jenny took his things to his new place and carried everything in and got it all arranged and put away. Then they went to Walmart and got linens, a new blanket and bedspread, towels, and a few other necessities. Then after grocery shopping, they headed back to his place and got everything put away, with the bed made and towels hung. Chris liked it; he felt at home.

"Want to spend the night?" he asked.

"Hmmmm ... I'll consider your offer," she replied with a coquettish flirtation in her voice, then added, "Tomorrow is Saturday, and I'm scheduled to go for a run with my best friend, Kelly. It's our girl time together, with breakfast after. Sorry, but no boys allowed."

"Guess I'll have to live with it then." He grabbed her and kissed her, a gesture she returned. She went back to her place and got what she needed for the night and morning, and returned to town. Chris had a bottle of wine chilling and plans for making a nice dinner to inaugurate his new home.

After dinner, they snuggled together on the couch; Chris read to her from a Hemingway book he was reading. They went to bed early. Jenny dreamed of a mountain trail, where she was running open and free with unbounded energy.

On Saturday morning, she was up and off and met Kelly for their run at the trailhead they had decided-on. They did a ninety-minute trail run, then went for breakfast.

Dean and Susan had gone to Denver to close on the sale of their penthouse condo, packing clothes and getting everything ready for their move to Durango. They had sold the place furnished, so they had only personal things to get together. They were coming back in two days, along with the moving van, for good, moving into the restored Victorian they had bought on Third Avenue.

Chris drove by a nursery and went in to ask about work. "Can I speak with the owner or whoever is in charge?"

"Yeah, I'm Frank, the owner. What can I do for you?"

"Hi, my name is Chris, Chris Holdsworth. I'm looking for work and was wondering if you might have anything. I just moved here from Sedona and worked for a landscaper down there. I can run pretty much any equipment and have my CDL license for anything but semis."

"Can you start now? I'm shorthanded, and the season is forging ahead. I'm already way behind. I'll have to start you at minimum, but if you can do what you say you can, wages will be commensurate."

"Okay, wow, thanks. Thanks a lot. That's great. But I really can't start until tomorrow. I'm still getting my place organized."

"Tomorrow it is then. Be here at eight o'clock sharp. Sarah, our office manager, will get you through all the paper work. We're going to be going six days a week, eight to five most days, maybe later on some days. Time and a half for Saturdays and overtime. You up for it?"

"I am for sure. Hey, thanks again. I appreciate you hiring me off the street like this. Thanks. I promise I won't let you down."

They shook hands and Frank said, "Good to meet ya, Chris. Look forward to working with you."

Chris drove back to his apartment, wondering how everything had fallen into place so easily. All this must be meant to happen. He just started laughing with excitement.

* * *

May arrived. Jenny and Chris were amazed at all the flowering trees in Durango: white, pink, purple. Then there were the bushes and flowers. It was like the city had come alive with beautiful color and new life. The Animas was running high, with spring runoff from the mountain snowmelt. The rafters and kayakers were out in numbers. There were all sorts of fun and interesting events to go to: the spring art walk, the Taste of Durango, and the farmers' market, just to name a few. Tourists were starting to flow in. The town was buzzing.

They enjoyed their time together more and more every day. They were apart only when they were working, now spending every night together at one or the other's place. Chris was working five and a half days a week, but he always made time so they could be together.

Jenny met with Judy on every other Tuesday, with group on the same night. She did her yoga classes on her three-day schedule, and she had her Saturday-morning runs with Kelly. She and Chris enjoyed nights out with her friends. She had her chats with Helen and lengthy literary discussions with William. She and Chris were settling into a steady, growing relationship and routine.

Her book was growing word by word, page by page, chapter by chapter. She was now over sixty thousand words. William continued to help her craft it and kept on encouraging her. He wanted to contact a few agents he knew about the possibility of getting it published. He needed the first chapters to send to them. She excitedly agreed.

William had started his own project after reading *Zen and the Art of Motorcycle Maintenance*. It was a romance, but it also included a road trip, self-discovery, and a discussion about metaphysics and science. He was doing a lot of research into subjects he wasn't familiar with, but he loved what he was creating. He never stopped telling Jenny how much he appreciated her advice.

Chapter 50

June arrived with warm sunny days, moving into July with its afternoon thunder showers the locals called 'The Monsoons." There was live music on open patios every night; Jenny and Chris spent several nights a week enjoying the downtown ambiance, the food, and the music. Hardly a weekend went by that they didn't try to do a day hike or go camping together, at least for a night, in the mountains by themselves or with friends.

Peter had graduated from law school in May and moved to Durango, interning at a small law firm. He and Kelly struck up a friendship that was rapidly escalating into something else. They all spent time together as couples.

Jenny often thought, *Funny how things turn out.*

It was the first of August; Jenny felt better, more balanced but still unsure about her life as a whole. Michael still haunted her as well as memories of her young life while growing up at the Farm. Where was her father? Was he really in prison? Was he even still alive?

One night she dreamed about a man she recognized, but she didn't know him. She knew she knew him. He radiated an aura of love she knew was directed toward her. He smiled at her. "Jenny, oh Jenny, I'm sorry." His words made her feel warm and cared for, like she did with Chris and Will. From deep inside, she felt a deep love for this man. He faded away into a white mist. Who was he?

She awoke with a start to the morning dawn. Jenny lay in her bed, remembering the dream, trying to understand.

Then it hit her. *Holy shit! It was Julian. My father, Julian. Where were we? Is he alive or dead? Holy shit! I need to find him. I have to. Oh, yeah. He's alive. I know he's alive. I have to find him.*

At her session that same morning, she excitedly told Joan about her dream and what she'd figured out. She boldly announced, "I'm going to find him and go see him. I want to see my father. I know I can find him. I just have to. I feel this newfound warmth and love for him. Why, I have no idea. I just know."

Joan looked at her for a moment and finally said, "Your father? What do you think seeing him might accomplish?" She wanted to see where Jenny might be going with this.

"Yeah, my father. It was him in my dream—I know it. More than anything, I know this. I think he's in prison in California for drug trafficking, according to my brother's letter from some years ago. I've asked Dean and Susan, but they either don't know or don't care."

"If you do find him and see him, what do you think you will gain?"

"Closure. Final closure to all this. Don't you see?"

Joan smiled. "Yes, I do. I'm just concerned that what you might find might not be helpful. What if he's crazy or mean, or doesn't want to see you? He might not even remember you. Then what?"

"I don't care, Joan. Then at least I'll know one way or the other."

"You are certainly determined."

"Yes, I am. I don't think I ever realized how much I need to at least let him know I'm still even alive."

"Do you think he knows about Michael?"

"I have no idea, no idea how he would know. But Joan, it's just, I don't know. I just want to see if he's okay. I want to see if I can forgive him. He's my father, and I feel like I need to try to, what, hopefully reconcile maybe."

Joan sat considering all this for a few moments. "I really do think that could be one of the last pieces you need to finally get on with your life. It might be a good thing for you to do. But it might be hard for you. It could be really hard. And I am a little concerned about your well-being, but I'm also thinking you are now strong enough to be up for it. I'm just worried about any setbacks you might encounter in seeing him."

"I think I really can handle it. I think I need to do this. I really do. I could use a road trip. There are several stops I want to make on a journey to my past. Want to go with me? I might need a therapist."

"I don't think so, but thanks for the invite. It would be nice to have someone to travel with, though. Any idea where he might be incarcerated?"

"Not a clue. California's all I know for sure, so I'll start there. I don't think either Susan or Dean has any idea. I'll go home and see what I might find on the Internet."

With that, they ended the session, and Jenny left for home on a new mission.

Once there, she made herself a cup of tea and went online. After about two hours of researching prison registries and making a few phone calls, she located her father, Julian Morse. He was at the California Men's Colony in San Luis Obispo, serving ten years for drug trafficking. It was apparently a prison that accommodated minimum- and medium-security inmates and provided a mental health system as well as a mental health crisis unit. The facility provided inmates with programs for self-improvement, such as academic and vocational education, prison industry work skills, and inmate self-help group activities. She called and found out visiting hours and the protocol for visitation.

She consulted her pendulum; it gave her a definite yes to make the journey, that she needed to see him.

She knew how busy Chris was with work but decided to call anyway and ask whether he could go with her to California. They could go see his family maybe. She wanted to meet them.

"I'd love to go see my family," he said. "I've been trying to get a week off all summer, but I'm just swamped. I just can't get any time off right now. Probably won't until later in the fall when things start to slow down a bit. Why do you ask?"

"Well, okay, this might sound weird." And she told him her plans.

"Wow, I so want to go with you, but I just can't right now. Can you hold off until we can go together? We could fly out. You thinking about flying?"

"Flying would make sense, but I had planned on driving. I want to stop to see Amanda on the way. There is another stop I want to make as well. I want to go back to the Farm."

Since her plan started to evolve on seeing her father, she had also started thinking about the Farm and seeing it again, if it still existed, to see who might still be around. It was a visit she dreaded, but she felt strongly she needed to go. She wanted some closure to that part of her life as well.

"I really want to drive; it'll give me time to think, prepare myself."

"So, driving? It's like two full days, you know. Why not wait until I can go with you? It would make sense. Then we could see my parents. I don't think it's wise for you to go by yourself anyway."

"What? Not wise. I'm not sure what you mean by that, Chris. I can take care of myself, thank you very much. I don't need a chaperone!"

"Hey, I'm sorry. I just don't want anything to happen to you."

"God, Chris, get over it. I survived on my own many years before you came along. I don't need you to be my guardian."

"I'm not trying to be your guardian. Can't I be concerned?"

"Oh, just forget it! I've already plotted my route. I know where I want to go, what and who I want to see, and I'll be going solo," she finished, angry and disappointed that he couldn't go.

"I'm sorry, Jenny. It seems like I just got here, and now you're leaving."

"Dammit, Chris, what don't you understand? I fucking need to do this! I fucking want to see my father who is in fucking prison. If you can't handle my life, maybe you should go back to Sedona. Then you wouldn't have to try to run my life for me. I'm sorry, Chris. I'm just a little on edge about this, but I have to do it. I just have to. Please understand."

"I know. I'm being selfish. I'm sorry for the way I reacted."

"Yeah, me, too." She gave a little laugh. "Guess we just had our first argument."

"I guess we just did. Sorry."

"Thanks. I'm sorry, too."

* * *

The next day Jenny packed for her trip and included camping gear if the possibility might arise. She went into town and loaded up on travel food, mainly trail mix and PowerBars. She went to see her grandparents to tell them about her plans, but they were hesitant to give their blessing. Then she talked to Helen, Kelly, and Joan, whose only concern was that she would be okay and not get into something she couldn't handle emotionally. She said she'd keep in touch.

She went home, found William, and told him she would be gone for at least a week, if not two. Then she went to her computer and wrote. Chris came out. They had a light dinner, read until nine, and then went to bed.

Jenny had a restless night, filled with dreams of trying to get to an unreachable destination. Always in slow motion, she was never able to focus, always finding herself on unfamiliar roads leading nowhere.

Chapter 51

Up at dawn, she said good-bye to Chris and was on the road across the Navajo Nation to Flagstaff; then she headed down to Sedona to see Amanda. She called her on the way to make an appointment, but Amanda was busy all day. However, she invited Jenny to her house to have dinner and spend the night. She reached Sedona early, walked Main Street, and looked into some familiar shops. It became time to head to Amanda's.

Her house was on the same road and beyond where Chris used to live. Jenny drove by his place and stopped. It was empty—everyone, everything, was gone ... but the memories still remained of those heady days last Christmas. There was an empty ache in her chest, and tears came. She sat for a few minutes, dried her eyes, and drove off.

She pulled into Amanda's, grabbed what she needed for the night, and started up the walk to the house. The yard was like an entrance to a shrine, with carefully placed stones, a few very large crystals, and statues of Buddha, Ganesha, and other entities. Amanda greeted her and lead Jenny into a warm, inviting house filled with tapestries and artwork on the walls, soft furniture, colorful pillows, wonderful aromas of food cooking, and a huge, long, warm embrace. The house seemed filled with magical energy; Jenny felt like she had entered another dimension.

Amanda had some wine ready to pour, and they sat. She asked how things were. Jenny gave a short version of what had transpired with her therapy, of Chris, and of where she was headed and why.

"Jenny, are you wearing that protective talisman I gave you?"

"Of course," she answered, pulling it out from under her top and showing it. "I've been wearing it ever since you gave it to me. If nothing else, it reminds me of you."

"Thanks for the thought, but I think it does more than that."

After more conversation and another glass of wine, dinner was ready. They sat and ate.

Jenny felt happy being there. "Amanda, I somehow feel I have known you forever. Thanks for your kindness."

"Maybe we have in other lifetimes. I'll have to check on that," Amanda said, smiling.

They cleaned up after dinner and sat to finish their wine. Amanda asked, "So you are on your way to see your father? How are you feeling about that?"

Jenny laughed. "What do you see in my aura?" She turned serious. "But to answer your question, I've really no idea. Maybe I should have just written him a letter. But I really need to see him and let him see me; confront him, I guess. I just want to try to come to terms with him and everything that happened to me. What do you think?"

"Well, I think you may find out things that will surprise you, anger you, and shock you, but I think this definitely will be beneficial in the long run. I can't elaborate, but things will unveil themselves and maybe will give you a better perspective."

Jenny asked, "So Amanda, do you always show such concern and hospitality to your other clients?"

Amanda hesitated for several moments, had several sips of wine, took a deep breath, and responded, "No, I don't. The truth is, Jenny, I have a special empathy for you." She took a few more deep breaths and continued. "I was also abused as a young girl. Only you and one other person are the only people who know this, so please—"

"Oh my god, Amanda. I'm so sorry! I promise I'll never tell anyone. I'm so sorry. How many abused women must there be?"

"I don't know, but I'm guessing there are many of us."

Jenny asked gently, "Do you want to talk about it?"

"If you don't mind."

"Of course I don't mind. I've learned from my therapy how healing sharing can be. Please tell me whatever you want."

Amanda said, "It was my father. It started when I was around twelve or thirteen. He came into my room one night." She stopped, choking back a sob and taking a deep breath. "I told my mother, but she said I was lying. She ignored my pleas for help. She just ignored me ... but I know she knew. She just didn't care.

"Finally, I couldn't stand it anymore. I was systematically stealing money from my parents in small amounts, trying not to cause any suspicion. It took a long time, but when I had what I thought I might need, I sneaked out and ran away one night. I was sixteen. I hitchhiked out of Columbia, Missouri, where I grew up, and headed west. A woman picked me up. I lied and said I was nineteen. She believed me. I said I was going to California.

"I wanted to get as far away as I could from my parents. This woman, Rachel—God, I so love her—she became my mentor and rescued me from my life. She believed in me. She was coming here to Sedona. I rode with her all the way, using what money I had to share gas and buy a little food. I had my driver's license, and I helped her drive.

"I was broke when I got here. She gave me a job at her shop, now *my* shop. I bought it from her ten years ago when she retired. She taught me everything I know or do." She stopped to get some tissues and wipe her eyes.

"She became my surrogate mother. She still lives nearby with her husband. I see her often. I would like you to meet her sometime. You would like her. I love her dearly."

Jenny nodded. "I would love to meet her sometime, Amanda. That's some story. Wow, did you do any counseling?"

"Regretfully no. I should have. Rachel was my only counselor. She helped me so much. She did work much like I do, only more so. She has the real gift. I am still working on getting to her level. But I regret not having worked with a counselor. I know it would have helped. I am forty-nine years old and have never had a relationship with a man. I have had ample opportunity but sadly could never trust men.

"So, that's my story. That is why I care for you so much. I went through similar abuse."

They were silent for a long time, each thinking about what had been said. Amanda poured each of them more wine.

Jenny finally said, "Maybe it's not too late, Amanda ... for counseling, I mean. It has helped me so much. You should truly do it."

"I know you're right. I just never had the courage."

"It's hard. Trust me on that. But once I got through sharing the really ugly parts with my counselor, Joan, the rest sort of started to fall into place. Can't say any of it has been easy, but I'm not sure where I would be right now without her help and yours as well."

Amanda said, "Okay then, enough about my past. Let's come back up to the present. Tell me more about what is going on with you."

Jenny told her about Chris's move. Amanda asked how it was going. Jenny replied that their passion had settled a bit but that they enjoyed being together more and more each day.

Amanda then told her what she saw for them: that they were destined to be together, that they were soul mates.

Jenny smiled. "Pardon my ignorance, but what is a soul mate?"

Amanda explained that Jenny and Chris were both separate parts of the same soul, separated sometime in some other lifetime; they had both incarnated in this life to become one again.

Jenny said, "I'm going to have to try to wrap my brain around this concept. Wow, really?"

"As strange as it may sound, the answer is yes," she answered, getting up to find Jenny a book that would explain souls more in depth.

"Here, read this. Keep it, and you can return it the next time we see each other. We can talk more about it then if you want."

It was getting late, and they both said good night. Jenny's room was comfy and small, also decorated with tapestries and artwork as well as stones and crystals. It felt so warm, and she felt very safe and protected there. She slept soundly with dreams of flying, her body being simply pure energy and light. She awoke early, her first thought being how much she liked being here with this woman.

Amanda was already up; they exchanged morning pleasantries. Amanda made coffee and toast. Jenny ate quickly, anxious to be on the road. She grabbed her things and hugged Amanda long and hard, thanking her for her kindness and hospitality.

Jenny said, "I wish we lived closer so I could have you for a friend."

"We *are* friends, my dear young woman, very close friends, even with the distance factor."

"Love you, Amanda."

"Love you, too. Be careful out there."

"For sure. See you soon. Promise." She left.

Chapter 52

Jenny went back up I-15 to I-40 at Flagstaff and headed west, pushing hard to get to Bakersfield for the night. She called the prison at a gas stop and asked about visitation for the day after tomorrow, which was Tuesday; there were no visitation hours on Monday. The person at the prison told her she would be the first person to visit her father since he had been incarcerated there eight years ago. Jenny asked her not to tell Julian she was his daughter.

She made it to San Luis Obispo on midday Sunday, found nice lodging in the town proper, and spent the rest of the day walking around the little city. Then she went out by the seashore to roam and think. She was very nervous, just short of being terrified of what she was going to do tomorrow.

After a nice dinner, she went to her room and called Susan and Dean, Chris, William, and Joan to tell them she had arrived and was all right. Joan wanted to talk and find out everything about her trip so far, including how she was feeling, essentially a phone therapy session. Jenny just wanted to be left alone at this point and was gracefully able to cut her off and bid her a good night. The next day, Monday, she drove up the coast, taking her time stopping, enjoying the different beauty of the place and her solitude. Jenny stopped at some of the little towns along the way, visiting various shops that caught her interest, returning late afternoon to her little hotel. She went out for the early evening, enjoying a glass of wine in a little bistro.

A young man came by her table and tried to strike up a conversation. She ignored him; she didn't want company. He got the hint and walked away. She had a light dinner and went back to her room. She called Chris and talked for thirty minutes, then curled up in bed with Virginia Woolf's *To the Lighthouse.*

After a dreamless but restless night, she awoke early, did her meditation, went for a run, and had breakfast at the hotel. Then she waited, with nervous anticipation, to go to the prison and see her father.

Chapter 53

Jenny arrived at the main gate and was let in. She was checked over and had to leave everything she carried on her body, except the clothes she was wearing, at the guard station. They didn't take any chances. A guard led her into a banal green waiting area, where there were a number of people already sitting on cheap plastic chairs. There was no conversation, and everyone was singular and subdued in his or her thoughts and maybe in anticipation. Jenny's heart pounded like a jackhammer, and she consciously struggled to do some deep yogic breathing exercises to avoid passing out.

She was soon called and directed to a booth with a phone handset, and there she waited. Shortly a man appeared on the other side of the heavy window, wearing an orange jumpsuit. She hardly recognized him. He was thinner than she remembered, almost gaunt. His face was lined, and gray streaked his hair, but he was definitely her father, Julian.

He sat without looking up and got situated. He looked bewildered, and shock filled his face. They both sat there for what seemed like a long time, but in reality it was only a few seconds. Finally, Jenny reached for her handset; Julian followed suit.

"Hi, Daddy, it's Jenny ... your daughter," she said, with a quivering voice, tears running down her face.

He sat there, just looking, and was finally able to reply, "Jenny, oh my God, I can't believe it. Jenny! Jenny? My beautiful daughter?" He dropped the handset, dropping his face to his hands and breaking into convulsive sobs.

"Daddy, it's okay, it's okay. Please don't cry," she said as she also sobbed uncontrollably.

The guards turned and respectfully looked away.

Finally able to talk, Julian said, "Jenny, my beautiful, beautiful daughter, it's been so long. How have you been? Where have you been? Tell me everything. I'd given up all hope that anyone even knew I still existed, that I'd ever see you, or anyone, ever again."

"It's been a while, hasn't it? I've so much to tell you. There's just so much ... so much—"

"Have you seen Mom and Dad? Are they okay?"

"They're great. I see them a lot. We're all living in Colorado, in Durango, down close to Arizona. They send their love," she lied.

"What about Michael? Do you see him?"

"Saw him before last Christmas. Let's talk about him later, if that's okay?"

A sense of foreboding clouded his face. Jenny was afraid to tell him about Michael, dreading the moment she would eventually have to.

Julian replied, "Sure, Jenny, sure. Later then. I'm so happy to see you. You're ... you're like a vision. You look just like your mother. God, Jenny, I loved her so much, and then ... and then she died. It broke me, broke my heart, broke my spirit, literally killed me inside. I just wanted to die too.

"I was lost. I had you two babies, and I didn't know what to do. Then Dory. I met Dory. She was wild, fun, and crazy. She knew about this commune in California where everything was paradise, so I took you two and went with her to that damned place.

"I was already drinking too much, and there at the commune, drugs were plentiful. I let her be in charge of you two kids while I stayed drunk or stoned almost every day. I needed money. I started hanging out with a couple of guys;

we'd go to San Diego and pick up a 'shipment.' We'd take and distribute it to people in San Francisco, Sacramento, even as far as Vegas sometimes; and of course we had a good trade going on out of that fucking commune ... there was so much money involved.

"I'm so sorry. You can't imagine the guilt, the regret, and self-hate I have about your childhood, about everything that happened. I was such a rotten father.

"Finally got busted shortly after you disappeared. Me and seven others. Thankfully I ended up here rather than one of the harder places. I got cleaned up and went through a lot of rehab, AA, and such. There's good support here, and I was once again able to face life. I had no contacts for anyone; there's no way to reach anybody to let them know where I was. I didn't think anyone would care anyway. And now you appear; an empty hole just got filled. I never thought I would ever see you or any family again. And I couldn't blame you. I can't believe you're here ... I really can't understand why you would, after the way I neglected you and Michael ... what Dory did to you. Why did you ever bother?"

Jenny sat for a few moments, digesting what she had heard, knowing there was a lot more, but she was satisfied with this for the time being.

"I came, Daddy, because I needed closure. Now I see maybe you do too. It's good. It's okay, Daddy. We've both had it tough."

She started to tell him about her life. But how quickly their time was up. She had to leave. The guard had come to escort Julian away.

"I'll be back tomorrow, Daddy. Is that okay?"

"I already can't wait. I want to hear everything about you and Michael. I love you so much! I'm so happy you came. I'm sorry to have rambled on so. I just needed to unload. It's been so long. I've so many regrets. Can you ever forgive me for being such a waste?"

"I think I probably already have ... and I love you too, Daddy." She got up and left, tears running down her face.

After she returned to her hotel room, she sat for a long while, simply thinking about her father after seeing him after all these years and digesting their hour-long visit. She was happy she had made the effort to come and see him. She realized they would never have those twenty some years back, but they could have this time to reconnect, to be a father and daughter.

She went back on Wednesday and Thursday. On Friday, Julian pressed her about Michael. She knew she couldn't avoid the truth any longer; she braced herself, took a deep breath. "Daddy, he was really messed up. When I saw him in Denver and we were going to have dinner together, he just went off on me ... started screaming at me in this restaurant, threatened to knock me around, said I was just another stupid woman who needed to have some sense slapped into."

And she related the rest of the incident to him, and finally, they came to something she was dreading. She started feeling sick to her stomach, and she wailed, "And then he killed himself!"

When she finished, she had tears streaming down her face.

"I'm so sorry to have to tell you all this, Daddy. I'm so sorry."

Julian, the color drained from his face, was silent for a long time. He finally said in a hollow, monotone voice, "If I would have just been a father to you kids. I wasn't! I'm so sorry, Jenny, so damned sorry. I can't ever forgive myself ... never!" And he just sat quietly with tears running down his face.

"It'll be all right, Daddy. You still have me. We can be together when you are released. I'll get you to Durango. You'll be fine. I have some great friends there."

"Jenny, I can't ask you to do anything for me. I haven't earned anything from you. You don't owe me anything. You owe me nothing."

"You aren't asking. I'm offering. I want to have my father back. I need him back. I'm just being selfish. I want you close, to be together."

"It might be strange. After all, we don't really know each other, do we?

"But you're my father, and I want to know you. Please believe that!"

He was about to speak when the guard came. "Sorry, Julian, but we really have to head back. I've let you go overtime as it is."

"Yeah, I understand and thanks." He got up to leave.

"See you tomorrow, Daddy," she said with a smile and blew him a kiss.

She went back on Saturday and Sunday. They continued to talk about Dean and Susan and Michael. He wanted to know every detail of her life. They had so much to catch up on. Jenny asked about Dory. He had neither seen nor heard from her since right before his arrest.

Jenny left him on Sunday, promising to be back later next week. She had another place she needed to visit and would see him before heading back to Colorado.

While she and Chris talked most very night, she realized she hadn't called Joan all week. She went out by the ocean and called her at home. She picked up right away. Jenny apologized for not calling sooner and then for calling her on Sunday. But she wanted her to know she was fine and that seeing her father and reconnecting were very hard and bittersweet, but also very good. She kept it brief, said a good-bye, and clicked off.

Jenny went back to her hotel. She got her maps out and plotted a route to Sacramento. She wondered whether she could find the Farm and whether there would be anyone there she still knew, if it still even existed. She hoped so; there were more answers she needed for closure.

Early Monday morning, she went to see the warden and discuss Julian. She found out he was a model prisoner and would be up for parole shortly. With his good record, he would certainly get released. Jenny asked what the process of being on parole entailed. She found out he would need to go to a halfway house, have a guardian or overseer, stay in state, and meet with his parole officer regularly. That he would need to join a local AA group and that hopefully he would find work.

Jenny asked, "Do you think I could be his guardian?"

She responded, "This might well be a possibility if you lived in California. Parolees generally aren't allowed to leave the state."

"Okay, thanks for your time. I'll be back in a few days for another visit." They shook hands, and Jenny turned and left. As she walked to her Jeep, she considered what the warden had said about Julian leaving the state.

She got in and called William, telling him what was going on and what she wanted to do. Could he recommend an attorney who might help? William gave her two names and the numbers to call. After she clicked off with William, she called the numbers. The first one said he wasn't interested; the second was busy with a client but would call back. She got her call back about forty-five minutes later. She pulled to the side of the highway and answered it. Jenny explained her the circumstances. The woman, Cynthia, sounded interested in the case; they discussed fees, which Jenny agreed to. Cynthia would look into the possibilities and be in touch. Jenny thanked her and continued on to Sacramento.

Chapter 54

Jenny got to Sacramento and was trying to remember how to get to the Farm, how to backtrack her escape route from almost eight years ago. She found the train station and was able then to locate the street and road she had come in on all those years ago. She headed out, starting to recognize some landmarks along the way.

Getting close to where she remembered the commune to be, she stopped at a convenience store at an intersection and asked the older man behind the counter whether he knew of a hippie commune anywhere nearby. He said he knew of a bunch of folks living together up north, about ten miles away. He thought for a moment and gave her directions.

It was getting late, and Jenny asked whether he knew of anyplace to stay nearby. He gave her directions to Interstate 5 and said there was a motel at the interchange. She thought about camping and, deciding against it, drove another fifteen miles and found a Quality Inn, a gas station, and a restaurant by the intestate. She got a room, became situated, and went for some food. She went back to her room to think about what she was going to say to whoever might be left at the Farm she might remember. She slept a dreamless sleep.

She got up early the next morning, meditated, had some breakfast, and headed back the way she had come and then followed the directions the fellow had given her. She came to the little village she used to walk to as a little girl. Suddenly, everything came back to her.

After driving two miles up the old lane, there it was, still the same, only things looked better, cleaned up. There was a large garden area and a new grow dome. People were busily going about their day. She recognized everything like it was only yesterday, but it all seemed so much smaller now.

She parked, got out, and started walking around; the old yurt was still there, only it looked so much better. Buddhist prayer flags fluttered over the door as well as everywhere else. A young man she didn't recognize came up to her and asked whether she needed help. Jenny told him who she was and said she had grown up here; she wondered whether any original residents might be left. He asked whether she remembered Annie and said she had been there forever.

Jenny's face lit up. "Of course, she was one of my few favorite people. Oh my god, she's still here. Do you know where I could find her?"

"Should be around her cabin. Remember where that is?"

"Sure do. Thanks so much. Appreciate your help." She turned and quickly walked down a familiar path to a cabin, where she knocked on the door.

A woman opened it and looked out; a smile of recognition beamed across her face, "Oh my God, Jenny. Is that you? Oh my God, Jenny, it *is* you, all growed up. Come in! Come in! I'm making tea. Want some tea? Please sit ... but first, give ol' Annie some love. Then I want ta know everything about you. Oh, come here, you sweet girl."

She grabbed Jenny and hugged her so hard, Jenny could hardly breathe.

"I'd love some tea, Annie. Thank you. Great to see you."

Annie proceeded to pour their tea, offered some cookies, and sat, facing Jenny. "Jenny, dear sweet girl, you look great, absolutely wonderful. Where have you been for—what—ten years?"

"Almost eight, Annie, and you look wonderful yourself. Has life been good to you?"

"Actually it has ... after the big bust, that is, but I'll get to that. Please tell me, are you still in California? You just up and disappeared, and no one knowed where you went or what happened. We all wondered and worried about you. We searched 'round everywhere for you, didn't know if you was dead or alive. Then the ol' bitch Dory told us all your stuff was gone, so we suspected you just run off. No one really blamed you."

Jenny responded, "Yeah, I'm truly sorry about that. It's a long story. I'll try to give you a quick version."

She covered the highlights of her escape. Then she proceeded to tell her about the abuse she and Michael had suffered from Dory and Old George. She finished by telling her about how she had found out about Michael's raping her. She discussed her grandparents, college, the mountains, Durango, and the real reason why she was back in California, to see her father.

Annie sat, listening, without a word. Jenny finished her saga. They both just sat for a moment. Jenny's tea had gone cold.

Finally, Annie spoke. "That's just so horrible, Jenny. There's all sorts of shit going on with that Dory. I remember your father beating her a few times, once severely. Two guys stopped him one time, or he might'a kilt her. He caught her fucking Michael when he was only, like, fourteen, as I recall."

"Holy shit! I remember that. I was there. I saw it all, what she and Michael were doing, and Daddy coming in and finding them. I guess I thought Daddy probably beat her all the time."

"Naw, it's just a few times and that one bad one, really bad one, as I recall. Anyways, he woulda like kilt her if he weren't stopped."

313

"So, what sort of stuff was it with Dory, other than that she was a total bitch and was sexually abusing me and my brother?"

"You never knew? Dory and the four or five bitches she brought with her was all whores, plus this's a place to buy drugs back then. There're always men around ... and women coming by to buy drugs or spend the night with a woman or a man, for that matter. They weren't exclusive. There's sex and drug parties all the time. You didn't know?"

Jenny remembered those nights and what went on in the yurt when she and Michael were supposed to be sleeping.

"Yeah, I guess I do ... I just thought it was people from here all getting together."

"Oh no! They's all outsiders: Sacramento, Frisco, other places. They paid money, lots of it, for a good ol' time of gettin' laid, stoned, or other stuff. Dory, that bitch! I hated her and those other bastards. A lot of us wanted them gone, but there's threats made. We's all scared, so's we just looked the other way. There's a lot of outside money involved, big money from Sacramento and Frisco; more'n we could mess with. We figured that the mob was involved, maybe Vegas types."

Then something clicked in Jenny's brain. "Holy shit, Annie. I bet that bitch was training Michael and me to be whores, just like she was. She stopped her abuse toward me after I threatened to kill her one day."

Annie said, "She mighta been. Wouldn't a put anything past that whore. I's going to leave a number of times but never did; had some good friends here, and we's just wanted to stay the hell out'a the way, below the radar. That's until the feds rolled in one day. Came in with a vengeance. Got all 'em bastards. Searched every one of our places, mine too. Most everyone was cleared 'cept for Dory's crowd. Somehow that bitch Dory had conveniently disappeared right 'fore it happened. All the others 're busted."

"Is that when my father was arrested?"

"No, he's arrested 'bout two weeks before. We's all figured he and the other guys spilt the beans about the operation. Where's he now?"

"Prison, San Luis Obispo. He's doing good and should be out pretty soon, from what I was told. Looks older but looks good, clean, sober, healthy."

"That's good. Always thought he's a good man. Sure got in with the wrong crowd when he came here with that bitch, Dory. She's a real piece of work. Just a real skank!

"And Michael, poor guy, hung around for two years after. Some of the guys finally took him to Sacramento, kicked him out, and told him to never come back. He'd gotten real mean and nasty to all the women; figured he's miss'n Dory. Guess he somehow thought she was in love with him or somethin'. Maybe he just liked bangin' her, and hell, none of the girls here'd ever gave him the time a day. Just got hateful, nasty mean to everyone. It was good riddance."

"Ever hear what happened to Dory?"

"Heard a few years ago that she's runnin' a call girl ring outta Oakland. She's found in an alley with two bullets in the back a her head. Somebody saw it in a newspaper. Guess the cops thought it was an execution. I could give a shit. Well fuckin' deserved."

Annie got up and made them some more tea. Jenny wished she could have a had a glass of wine or a beer after all that had been said, but the tea was wonderful.

"Oh yeah, you'll probably be happy to hear that Old George died three years ago. Nobody much liked him either. Buried him on the other side of the hill. Nobody misses him much. You weren't the only one he showed his pecker to. He's a sad old man."

"So, the place looks really nice. You're actually growing food?"

"Yeah, after the 'big bust,' we's able to get more serious. Had to. No money coming in after them bastards was gone. So we went to growin' veggies, became a real farm." She chuckled at her little joke. "Got some bigger fields the other side a the creek. Lot's a work, but we're part of the community-sponsored agriculture movement, where we sells shares up front for a year's worth of veggies. That does real well for us. Deliver big loads a veggies inta Sacramento every week most a the year. Now's we gots a grow dome. Didja see it when ya come in? We's also got booths at the Sacramento Farmers' Market. All 'n' all, we make enough to keep ourselves fed and clothed. It's a good life, really. Main reason I come here all those years ago. It's like that until Dory and her crew showed up. Do ya think ya wanta come back?" she asked with a grin. "Love to have ya."

Jenny noticed for the first that several teeth were missing. She felt sorry for her but didn't say anything. Jenny suddenly felt sick to her stomach and couldn't breathe; she needed to leave. She had heard enough, more than enough. She looked at her watch and said she had to get back to San Luis tonight; she wrote down her contact information for Annie and told her to stay in touch, knowing she never would.

"Thanks for everything, Annie—for being my only friend when I was a little girl and for all you told me today. It fills in a lot of blanks for me. It was wonderful to see you and how well everything looks here. You take care of yourself."

"Thank ya, yourself, for comin' by an' seeing' ol' Annie. Come back anytime. Love ta see ya anytime yer around these parts."

Jenny got up, gave her a hug, and left. She didn't look back, leaving behind the sad memories of her childhood.

She arrived back at the little hotel late in the afternoon and went to her room.

After dinner, she spent the rest of the night writing in her journal, processing the bittersweet experience of seeing her father and visiting Annie at the Farm.

She went to see Julian early the next morning and told him where she had gone and about her conversation with Annie.

"So now you know it all," he said, "all the crap I was involved in and the other stuff. I'm sorry you had to find out. I didn't know about Michael being thrown out. God, Jenny, it's all such a mess, and I'm to blame for everything that happened to you kids. I can never forgive myself ... never." He hung his head and wiped his eyes.

"Daddy, I can forgive you ... and I do. We've the rest of our lives to live. I want to live mine and want you to live yours, to be father and daughter. I have a lawyer working on getting you to be able to serve your parole in Durango. Nothing certain, no promises, but we're working on it.

"It'd be really nice to have you close by. It's been so great to see you. I want to have my father around."

"Thanks, Jenny. It is so wonderful that you came. Thank you, thank you. I take it you're heading back?"

"Yeah, it's time. I need to see some people. It was so great, Daddy. I do love you, and I forgive you for ... for ... everything. Please ... please find it in your heart to forgive yourself. I have all your contact information, and I promise I'll keep in touch."

"When will I see you again?" he asked.

"Soon, I hope. We'll talk soon." As she blew him a kiss, she turned and left, her head bowed down, tears running down her face. What she wanted more than anything was to hold him close and never let him go.

* * *

She got as far as Kingman that night, listening to some new age music as she drove. It added to the peace she was now feeling in her life. The stark emptiness of the Mojave Desert added to her sense of peace. She thought of being back at her little house, feeling an overwhelming warmth and love for her adopted community. She had found people she could trust, people she could love, whom she called friends, who loved her back. She felt she finally, really, had a home.

As soon as she reached her motel, she called Chris and told him she would be back tomorrow. She wanted him to come to her place as soon as he could after work.

That night she dreamed she was on her favorite ridge at eleven thousand feet, looking out over the vast, shimmering mountain landscape, arms wrapped around herself, trying to stay warm, under a cold, bright sunrise unfolding over the San Juan Mountains.

She had quietly sneaked out, careful not to wake Chris who was still sleeping in their tent a few hundred feet below. She wanted to be alone to experience what she had enjoyed many times over the past years. She never tired of this view, which seemed to let her soul sail in freedom over this place she loved. She loved that Chris was there with her. She loved that she had all her friends and family in Durango. She looked wistfully at the wedding band on her left hand and felt so blessed that her father had been there to give her away. Her right hand dropped to her belly to feel the new life growing there.

She awoke from her dream and felt a warmth flowing from deep within her heart. *Interesting. Something to look forward to.* She hugged a pillow to her body and fell back to sleep.

She was home in Durango late afternoon the next day.

About the Author

Ed Lehner is a retired professor of graphic design/visual communication from Iowa State University, Ames, Iowa. He has journaled and written poetry for over 40 years. He started to write prose a few years ago starting with writing short stories. Ed began his first novel in December 2015. He is a luthier, a musician, a Reiki Master, and lives with his wife, Julie and his cat, Emma Lu in Durango, Colorado.

Printed in the United States
By Bookmasters